PENGUIN BOOKS

Shame On You

...ara Salaman is best known for playing DS Claire Stanton in the long-
...ning ITV drama *The Bill*. She has written for Granada Television, and
...me *On You* is her first novel.

C153498421

Shame On You

CLARA SALAMAN

PENGUIN BOOKS

PENGUIN BOOKS

Published by the Penguin Group
Penguin Books Ltd, 80 Strand, London WC2R ORL, England
Penguin Group (USA) Inc., 375 Hudson Street, New York, New York 10014, USA
Penguin Group (Canada), 90 Eglinton Avenue East, Suite 700, Toronto, Ontario, Canada M4P 2Y3
(a division of Pearson Penguin Canada Inc.)
Penguin Ireland, 25 St Stephen's Green, Dublin 2, Ireland (a division of Penguin Books Ltd)
Penguin Group (Australia), 250 Camberwell Road, Camberwell, Victoria 3124, Australia
(a division of Pearson Australia Group Pty Ltd)
Penguin Books India Pvt Ltd, 11 Community Centre, Panchsheel Park, New Delhi – 110 017, India
Penguin Group (NZ), 67 Apollo Drive, Rosedale, North Shore 0632, New Zealand
(a division of Pearson New Zealand Ltd)
Penguin Books (South Africa) (Pty) Ltd, 24 Sturdee Avenue,
Rosebank, Johannesburg 2196, South Africa

Penguin Books Ltd, Registered Offices: 80 Strand, London WC2R ORL, England

www.penguin.com

First published 2009
1

Copyright © Clara Salaman, 2009
All rights reserved

The moral right of the author has been asserted

Set in Monotype Garamond
Typeset by Rowland Phototypesetting Ltd, Bury St Edmunds, Suffolk
Printed in England by Clays Ltd, St Ives plc

ISBN: 978-0-141-04126-1

To Clement and Juliet Salaman,
with love

I

Mr Steinberg was young and fresh and beautiful, and we were all dumbfounded by him. On his first day at school, he had stood before us at the front of Room 8, holding his black briefcase up in front of him with both hands, like a shield.

'Hi,' he said. And with that one word, we knew that he was different. We could almost smell the outside world on his breath.

Everything about him didn't belong: his perfect teeth, his modern round glasses, his smile, the biro sticking out of his pocket, the ring on his middle finger, the word 'Hi'. He clearly didn't know that biros, jewellery and slang were not permitted here. Someone asked him how old he was and he had blushed and run his hands through his thick, dark, wavy hair and said, 'Twenty-two.' Only he hadn't said that, he'd said, '*Twenny-two*,' because the best thing about Mr Steinberg was that he was an American. I had never met an American before, but I knew that most things that Americans did were forbidden.

I wondered how on earth he had ended up here with us, all the way across the ocean. They had probably told him he was saving the world or something; us children, this new school, we were the future. One day, they'd have told him, it would be down to these children to spread the word. (Which was 'Om', by the way. And personally,

I wouldn't be spreading it; I'd be keeping quiet about the whole thing. We attracted enough unwanted attention as it was.)

Mr Steinberg had come to teach Ancient Greek, which was a modern language to us. We only learnt Sanskrit, the oldest language in the history of the world. I imagined it was what the cavemen spoke, 'bahbah dahdah gahgah' sort of thing. That's what it sounded like; all breathy and primitive. Thousands of years ago, the Sanskrit people had written the first ever book of rules called the Vedas, and Miss Fowler told us that the mysteries of the universe were held in just the Sanskrit alphabet alone. Which was why we had to chant it endlessly, hoping they'd slip in by osmosis, I suppose. We were sick to death of the mysteries of the universe. Greek would make a pleasant change.

We could listen to Mr Steinberg's beautiful voice all day long, and sometimes we did. He taught us to chant the first three chapters of the *Odyssey* from memory, and boy, oh boy, did we chant. We'd mimic his accent as we did so, and at first he wouldn't notice but, when he did, he would laugh so hard that he would have to take his glasses off and wipe his eyes. Watching him do that would make the whole day worthwhile.

Everyone wanted to get betrothed to Mr Steinberg. Everyone was in love with him, so, naturally, everyone was good at Greek. Even the thickos were excelling themselves. But for me, Greek was more than a subject; I wasn't just *good* at it, I was the *best* at it. I didn't even have to try; it all just stayed in my head as if I already knew it.

It was, therefore, most upsetting to be stuck in the cupboard at the back of the classroom when Mr Steinberg was out there taking the Greek class. I had been hiding from Fowler but had mistimed my exit and when I'd attempted to reappear, it was too late; they had already started 'pausing'. Eyes tightly shut, chins up, palms facing upwards like curling leaves on their laps, clearing their minds, making space for something new.

I carefully closed the door and resigned myself to the fact that I would have to stay in the cupboard until the end of the lesson.

'Om paramatmanaynama attah.' As one, they mumbled the beginning-of-anything prayer.

For a while, I listened in the darkness as Mr Steinberg handed out the homework, blindly picking the paint off the back of the door, still annoyed with myself for getting stuck.

'Where's Caroline?' I heard him ask and I stopped picking; it felt good to hear him say my name and notice my absence.

'She's ill,' said Megan.

It was cramped in the cupboard. There was only room enough for two people standing up, although we did once go for a record and squeezed six of us in, piled on top of each other like Smarties in a tube.

I felt around for some jumpers and decided to make myself a little bed. I sank to my bottom and leant against the pegs. I must have been leaning against Kate's blazer, I could smell her. She'd smelt the same since we were tiny, musty with a hint of mothball. I leant to my other side and inhaled an aertex shirt, doughy and milky. Easy peasy japoneesy, that was Megan. I moved my nose along the row. Pears soap, that'd be Jane. I tugged at a jumper above me and pressed it to my face; grassy with a touch of pee, Anna's without a doubt.

Whenever my parents were away on retreat, I always made a point of staying the week with as many people in the class as possible, just to compare notes. I'd pretty much stayed with everyone, but our houses were all much of a muchness; functional, minimal and holy. However, one thing I had noticed was that whole families smelt the same, even houses. The moment you entered Anna's house there was a whiff of wee. I wondered what smell my family gave off. I sniffed my knee – chlorine from the swimming pool. I licked it then sniffed it again. It was rather nice.

Years ago, when I was about five, before Miss Fowler and I hated each other, I would ask her every lunchtime if she could butter my bread for me. She would get up from the head of the trestle table and come round and put her arms over mine, and I'd sit there as she buttered the bread, inches from my face. I could actually butter my own bread, but I did so love the smell of her hands; they smelt of Dettol. Now, of course, I can't bear the stink of disinfectant.

When I got bored of sniffing clothes, I lay on my back and stuck my legs up against the boiler and waited whilst the rest of them did a vocabulary test. I marked myself with hardly any cheating. Nineteen out of twenty.

Every now and then at the end of a Greek lesson, if we'd been especially good, Steinberg would make his way around the table, rubbing his hands, a crafty smile on his face, and he'd perch on the edge of the table, right at the front of the classroom and say, 'Well, Form Two, would you like to hear the story of Medea?' or 'Who knows the story of Theseus and the Minotaur?' or 'Did I ever tell you about Oedipus?' Immediately, we would all shut our books and sit on the edge of our seats in anticipation, hanging on to his every word. He'd tell us stories full of gore, murder, incest, sex and death, and our tongues would hang out. None of us would breathe a word about these stories out of class, at home. They were our secret. Mr Steinberg never quite got the hang of the Organization, and we weren't going to enlighten him.

When I heard the class hush excitedly, I knew exactly what was happening. This just wasn't fair, to be stuck in the cupboard on a storytelling day! Oh, how I wished to be out there! I sat up as quickly as I could and pushed the door a little so that I might catch a glimpse of him. You had to watch him telling his stories.

There he was in all his easy elegance. He was wearing his grey suit with a blue shirt. He pushed his glasses up his nose, the way he always did when he was excited.

'Who knows the story of Orestes?'

'Not me, not me!' I heard everyone say, shutting their books and sitting to attention.

'Not me!' I said in the cupboard, shuffling forward, pushing the door a little more so that I could see all of him. I turned my ear towards the gap. His voice was almost a whisper as he began. I had to really strain to hear him.

'Orestes, which by the way means "mountaineer" or "he who can conquer mountains", was the son of Clytemnestra and Agamemnon. He had one brother and two sisters, Iphigenia and Electra.'

I could see Kate's knees jiggling on the edge of her seat.

'Now, when Orestes was about your age, twelve, thirteen or so, Agamemnon went off to fight the Trojans. And in order to secure victory, he sacrificed his daughter Iphigenia. Which I guess his wife was none too pleased about. Now, beautiful women by their very definition attract a lot of attention . . .'

God I hoped I was a beautiful woman.

'. . . And I suspect Clytemnestra was a beautiful woman because Agamemnon entrusted his finest voiced singer to take care of her in his absence, chiefly to distract her from any suitors.'

What's a suitor? Someone ask!

'What's a suitor?' It was Amy.

'An admirer,' he continued. 'Sure enough, when Agamemnon was away, Clytemnestra took a lover.'

He said the words 'took a lover' so lightly and sweetly in his lilting American voice that he made it sound like the most delightful thing in the world.

I pushed the door a little wider; I didn't want to miss a thing. I needed to see Steinberg's whole body.

'What *sort* of a singer?' asked Deborah. She was always quite particular about things.

'Well,' he said. 'I guess it'd be the equivalent of having a radio. Instead of turning on the radio, you'd say, "Hey singer! Sing!"' Then Steinberg clicked his fingers and let his glossy, American hair fall in his eyes and he sang, 'I love rock and roll, put another record on the jukebox, baby . . .'

The class broke out into laughter. We loved it when

6

Steinberg did things like that and you really knew he was an outsider, that he'd come from the normal world. We weren't allowed radios. Pop music created chaos in the mind. It was strictly banned, and we were banned from any places that played it.

'Oh! Sing us some more!' I wanted to say and I would have said it if I'd been in the classroom, and, guess what, he might have done it. He liked me.

But then Steinberg remembered who he was talking to and that he must put his past behind him. You could almost see the shadow cross his face, the corners of his mouth dropped slightly.

'Anyway, girls,' he said, gently, and it sounded like pity in his voice. 'Agamemnon gets back from war . . .'

Steinberg pretended to look all exhausted, nursing a broken arm. 'With, might I add, a new mistress, Cassandra. You remember Cassandra?'

Yes, of course I remembered Cassandra. She had the gift of prophecy but the curse that no one would ever believe her.

'Anyone?' he said, looking round the room with mock disbelief. 'Anyone remember Cassandra?'

'Prophecy!' I whispered loudly in the cupboard.

'Hey, you guys! Cassandra? The gift of prophecy?'

I sighed. Damn it. I wanted to be out there. I wanted him to know that I knew. I wanted him to be impressed by me, his eyes unable to hide his delight. I shuffled in the cupboard, making a paper bag scrunch, and missed the next bit. I pressed my face into the small gap between door and cupboard.

'Well . . . Agamemnon's lying in the bath!' Steinberg

whistled and mimed washing his back with a back-scratcher. Everyone laughed. I laughed in the cupboard.

'In comes Clytemnestra and Aegisthus and they throw a net over him and kill him with an axe!' He said it crisply, murderously, his eyes glinting behind his glasses. He was totally fantastic. Steinberg moved out of my sight line, so I had to stand up.

'So when Orestes returns, ten years later, he's a man now, he's like my age now.'

And Steinberg swaggered, and everyone laughed again. I laughed in the cupboard. He was a man, he was a real man.

'And Orestes first kills his mother's lover and then murders his own mother! Now, there is no crime greater than matricide. And murder cannot go unpunished! So here come the Furies! Now get this, girls. The Furies, although acting within the law, are three mad, terrifying women . . .'

Ah! Furies? Furious. Infuriated. They must be connected. Someone ask him, please, someone ask him about the word. I bite my tongue.

'. . . They are the most scary, demonic beings with claws for nails and serpents for hair. They have blood dripping from their eyeballs.'

'What do they want?' That was Amy.

'They want to drive you insane! They'll scratch you and claw you until they do so. Then you'll kill yourself!'

Wow!

Steinberg looked at his watch, and the whole class gave a groan of disappointment as he did so.

'No!' I said to the cupboard. He mustn't stop now!

8

Did the Furies drive Orestes insane? What happened?

'We've run over, guys! Got to stop!' he said, jumping off the table, clapping his hands.

I knew that, in a moment, he would take his seat at the chair and shut his eyes, and everyone would fall silent as they paused, then he would chant the end-of-the-lesson Sanskrit prayer, and we wouldn't hear the end of the story.

'Okay, let's pause, everyone,' he said, sitting in his chair, straight back, all pleasure gone from his face. He was just like all the others when he did that.

I couldn't help myself. I pushed open the door, 'No! You can't stop, Mr Steinberg! You haven't finished! What happened to Orestes? Why was he called a mountaineer?'

Everyone turned around. Mr Steinberg looked most surprised.

'What are you doing in the cupboard, Caroline?'

'I . . .' I floundered. 'I was hiding . . . earlier . . . and then you arrived, um, sorry . . . please don't send me to Miss Fowler.'

I couldn't tell whether he was going to send me to Fowler or whether I was going to get away with it. He stared at me, and I stared back, trying to beseech him with my eyes.

'You've been listening in the cupboard?'

I nodded.

'The whole class?'

I nodded again.

'Did you do the vocabulary test?'

I nodded. 'Nineteen out of twenty.'

'Which word didn't you know?'

'Threshold.'

He carried on staring at me, undecided which path to take. Please, God, please don't send me to her. Then I could see the half smile appear. Slowly, he began to shake his head, looking at me all the time, trying hard to get rid of that smile on his lovely lips.

'Shame on you, Caroline Stern!' he said. 'Shame on you!'

Those were the most thrilling words in the entire English language, and whenever he said them, it never felt like shame. It felt like the best feeling in the whole wide world.

It was Amy's thirteenth birthday, and Mr Baker, for a treat, had sent us out into the streets of South Kensington to observe trees. We weren't allowed paper or pens, we just had to find a tree and look at it for forty minutes. But *really* look at it until we felt ourselves merging with it. Then later, we'd have to return to number 50 to paint it.

Mr Baker, who was normally very strict about the Organization rules, must have forgotten that Megan and I weren't allowed to be partners, that we were always meant to be separated. He had let Amy chose two people to be in a group with, and, of course, she had chosen Megan and me, and we were sent out into the early spring sunshine.

Once we got over the initial and familiar horror of being stared at by normal people as they passed us at the end of Onslow Gardens, 'pausing' en masse in our stupid bright purple uniforms, we began to enjoy ourselves.

The three of us wandered up and down the streets, feeling quite free and merry until we came across a nice tree. It was on the sunny side of the road outside a big, white house with a basement flat behind black railings.

We sat on the little wall, our legs swinging, Amy and I on one side of the trunk and Megan on the other, and we looked up at it. None of us had any idea what sort of a tree it was, but it had just started blossoming, maybe eighty per cent there; pale pink flowers had either stretched themselves awake or were tightly folded and just about to. You felt that, if you kept staring at the little closed pink buds, they might suddenly burst open like a firework. The leaves around them were auburn red, exactly the same colour as Megan's hair; her face was just the same pale pink as the petals and the way sun shone on them both, Megan was almost invisible except for the stupid purple uniform, of course. She was on the other side, looking up. She caught my eye and smiled at me.

'Isn't it lovely?'

It was, especially so, because it was framed by the pale blue sky beyond. The colours would be fabulous to paint. High, high up, the tracks of an aeroplane were disappearing behind the pink petals. On street level, over Megan's shoulder I could see Mr Baker striding towards us.

'We're here!' Amy waved. She loved Mr Baker, even though he was hairy like a monkey. He even had hairy fingers. She hoped that one day, when she was much older, maybe when she was sixteen like the other girls, she would get betrothed to him. Amy had loved him for years; even when we were about six I remember her always wanting to sit next to him at lunch.

'Ah!' he said, as he looked up at the tree. 'Yes! Girls! What a beauty!'

He stopped at my side and he gazed up at it, his grey

eyes flicking through the foliage, taking it all in. He rested one foot on the little wall beside me. His shoes were a shiny black with lots of little holes in them and his sock had slipped down so that I could see his calf. Long, black, thin hairs sprouted out of his shin like spiders' legs.

'That is truly a glorious specimen!' he said, almost tearfully. I checked that no normal people were watching his embarrassing display of wonder.

'Now, you have to get to know this tree properly, girls. Every little detail. Appreciate the gifts of the Absolute. Look how the branches grow! Where do they spring from? What happens at the ends? Where does the blossom come from? How many petals? What happens in the middle? Look into its nooks and crannies. What are the proportions? Remember it all! Mark it in your heads! Merge with it! Share its secrets! And remember it!'

He tapped his nose and smiled. 'Now where did Kate and Joanna go?'

'They're round the corner!' I said, and he got up to go. I watched him, as did Amy. He moved a little bit like a monkey too, all long-armed and lolloping.

'I'll be back!' he shouted.

We looked at the tree. Megan pulled down a branch and picked off a clump and was pinning it in her hair. Amy had her eyes shut. She must have been fixing the tree in her head. I stood up and pulled a low branch towards me to get a better look at the blossom; the five symmetrical petals, the darker pink centres. It was all so precise, so delicate. The Absolute had thought of every little detail. Nothing, no matter how small, had been left out.

We sat in silence for a while, just staring at the tree.

'If you were the Absolute,' I said, turning to Amy. 'What do you think you might have forgotten?'

'If? If?' said Megan. 'She is the Absolute!'

'All right! All right!' I said. 'I mean God, how normal people believe in God. As in something that's on the outside, not something on the inside ...'

Megan had lowered a branch and had her nose buried in the blossom.

I continued, '... If you were God right at the beginning, what do you think you might have forgotten to create?'

Amy looked up to the sky in thought. I liked watching her think, the way she appeared to be catching her thoughts with a blink of her big, blue eyes. She twisted the end of her long, fine plait around her fingers. Her hair was white blonde and squeaky like the nylon hair of a doll. Amy was brainy. I was always quick and clever, but I'd never be brainy like her, super-brainy. Sometimes she worked things out quicker than teachers.

'I think I would have forgotten Free Will.'

I had wanted her to say blossoms and flowers. I wasn't quite sure what Free Will was. I knew 'wilful' was a bad thing, Fowler called me wilful all the time, but I'd never associated it with something good.

'What's Free Will?' Megan asked.

'It's the best bit,' Amy said. 'It's the bit that means you can think whatever you want. You don't even have to believe in God, if you don't want to.'

'Really? Do some people not believe in God?' Megan asked with great surprise. Amy not only had a twin brother, Marcus, with whom to share all sorts of bodily bits of information but she also had an uncle who said 'fuck' and wasn't in the Organization. She knew about all sorts of forbidden things. Her uncle played the guitar and sang Beatles' songs. She knew all their names and everything. His girlfriend had given Amy a beautiful hair clip that sparkled in the light, but Miss Fowler had taken one look and confiscated it. She didn't like shiny things.

'Does your uncle believe in God?' I asked, eager to get outside information. We all were.

'No.'

'How come you're allowed to see him?'

'We hardly do. He and my dad always end up arguing.'

'If he doesn't believe in God, what does he believe in then?' I asked, truly curious.

'Nothing.'

'Nothing? You can't believe in nothing.'

Megan and I laughed.

'You can!'

'How can you not believe in God?' Megan asked, brushing a petal on her upper lip. I was glad she asked it because I was thinking the same thing but I didn't want to sound too babyish.

'Do you think some people don't believe in re-incarnation?' I wondered out loud. The idea had never occurred to me.

The Organization was very clear about reincarnation, as was I, up until this point. Every living being had one aim and that was to return to the Absolute, the Self, to become self-realized. This might take many lifetimes (especially if you weren't in the Organization). Each life-time you chose to learn different lessons, but ultimately you had to get rid of your ego and not care about material things. Miss Fowler had once told us that we were like garments that had to be washed and washed and washed in the river Ganges until we came out clean. I had mentioned that the river Ganges was the most polluted river in the world, but she gave me one of her looks, so I shut up. Anyway, that was why we had to meditate, chant Sanskrit and do Vedic things, so that we got clean inside. Also if you did bad things in your life, you might have to come back as a scorpion or something. I think the exact rules are in the Vedas.

'I don't know,' Amy said doubtfully. 'If you didn't believe in reincarnation, it would make life a bit meaningless, wouldn't it?'

'Well what's the point in Free Will?' Megan wondered. 'I wouldn't have done that, if I was God.'

'My Dad said to Uncle John that Free Will is God's greatest gift of all.'

'Why?'

'Because He hasn't got anything to prove,' she said, one eye shut, squinting as she measured the tree with her thumb.

We sat in silence and stared at the tree with its marshmallow blossom.

'I'd have forgotten to make skin waterproof,' I said, getting up and moving out into the gutter between two cars to get some perspective on the tree.

'Imagine! You'd get all soggy and heavy in the bath!' Amy laughed, grabbing a railing and leaning out.

'What do you call a swimming pool full of lepers?' I said.

'I don't know, Caroline Stern . . .'

It was Baker, he was back. He folded his arms. 'What *do* you call a swimming pool full of lepers?'

He was trying to show us that he had a sense of humour, which kind of spoiled the joke for me.

'Porridge!' I said, comparing the width of the tree to its height.

We were creating the Universe. We had just picked the fruit from the tree of knowledge and were now summoning up the four winds when Kate accidentally poked Joanna with the West wind. Joanna then accidentally poked Megan with the East wind and then Megan knocked the vase full of flowers in the fireplace as she gave birth to creation.

'Tay tattah tay tattah tattah tattah tay,' we chanted, rhythmically banging our heels into the ground as we danced, our flat palms slicing through the air as we divided the heavens from the earth, the bells around our ankles jingling and jangling. Megan managed to right the vase without Mrs Gentle noticing.

Mrs Gentle was not someone to be messed with. After Miss Fowler, she was the scariest teacher in the school. She had once laid me across her lap and smacked my bare bottom, hard, right in front of the window where normal people might have looked up and seen. She ruled Vedic dance with a blackboard rubber and would chuck it at us given half a chance.

She was standing on the rostrum, in front of the big windows. The light behind her was so bright it was impossible to read her expression, but you could pretty much guess that it would be grim. She was almost dwarfishly tiny and as thin as a stalk, with no bosoms, just two terrifying, accusatory nipples. Her red Brillo-pad hair was forced unwillingly into the obligatory bun. Instead of a mouth she had a slit, and her eyes were magnified behind her glasses like a goldfish. But she must have held some attraction; she was on her third marriage. She was on to her fourth name now, and if you got her new name wrong, even only a little bit deliberately, she went crazy.

She was also Jane's aunt. We didn't have proper teachers at St Augustine's; most of them were related to us and seemed to have been randomly allotted subjects. Except for Mr Steinberg, he was a real teacher. Out of the others, only one or two had any teaching qualifications, and I doubted there were many volunteers for Vedic dance. Everybody had a parent working somewhere in the building, be they cleaning or teaching or sewing uniforms. It meant that you didn't have to pay school fees. Teachers weren't given a salary, as such, they asked for 'what they needed'. So they all out-humbled each other with their low requests. I hated my dad for that. Often we just had Rice Crispies for supper.

'The next person to misbehave is going straight to Miss Fowler's study!'

Whenever those words were uttered, somehow I knew deep in my bones that it would be me. It was as inevitable as meditation. However random the words 'the next person' sounded, they weren't. It *would* be me. It was just a question of when. Mrs Gentle snapped her fingers and said, 'Circles.' We quickly formed our circles, one inner,

17

one outer, and stood awaiting her next command. The best thing about Vedic dancing was our long dancing skirts. They were colourful and made of satin. They were the most glamorous thing that any of us possessed, and we enjoyed swooshing into place, watching the fabric spin about around us.

'Lolitum!' she ordered in a Sanskrit-chanting voice.

'Lolitum!' we all echoed back before setting off, the outer circle going clockwise and the inner going anti-clockwise.

Lolitum was an awkward step that involved taking a pace forwards then a pace backwards and wiggling the toes of one foot in a circle, before moving forwards again. Jingle jangle went the bells around our ankles as one hundred and twenty toes circled in unison.

Jingle jangle. 'Lolitum,' we chanted.

The worst place to be was on the outer circle, where for a few steps you had to jingle past the window. Should anyone look up from the busy South Kensington street below, the embarrassment was acute. To be on the receiving end of that double-take solidified everything I suspected about the Organization.

A fundamental rule of Vedic dance was to keep your eyes downcast; they might only be raised for specific gestures. Every little flash of eyeball was significant. So we circled and circled with eyes so downcast it gave you a headache.

I knew everybody's feet as well as I knew their smells. Kate's pink, little, curled toes Lolitummed past me, followed by Emma's huge, white, long eagle claws, Sophie's dark brown, elegant feet, and – oh no – Megan was coming: there were her familiar splayed toes Lolitumming their way towards me. I had hoped she was on the inner circle safely behind me.

Megan was the only person in the world that could make me laugh just by looking at her. It was going to be a matter of chance which one of us would be facing Mrs Gentle when we crossed paths, and I noticed us both speeding up, hoping to have the advantage. However, I had Amy in front of me, snailing forwards, intent on perfecting the step. Damn it! It was going to be me facing Gentle.

I kept my eyes firmly on the ground as Megan loomed towards me and retreated back again for the toe wiggle. I clocked where Mrs Gentle was and risked a moment's play; my foot gave Megan's a little sniff as we neared each other. I knew she was trying not to laugh and, side by side now, I couldn't resist a flash of a look at her. She, of course, with her back safely to Gentle, was making the most of it; pulling her best retarded face, eyes crossed, tongue jutting her lower lip forward, making an only-just-audible spastic noise as she Lolitummed by me.

I have never managed to master the art of not laughing. However great the consequences might be, they always seem trivial in comparison to the joy of the moment. And this time, it was doubly funny because of the stupid Lolitum step that involved the backwards pace; it was the fact that I *knew* that she was going to reappear a moment later, with a minor variation on the retarded theme.

I could feel my shoulders go, followed by an uncontrollable nodding of the head.

'Is something funny, Caroline?' I looked up at Mrs Gentle's hands; she was playing with the board rubber, chucking it from one hand to the other.

I tried as hard as I could to sort my face out. I thought of dead babies and lifetimes of being a horse-fly.

I carried on with the Lolitum.

'Stop dancing when I'm talking to you!'

I stopped. Someone swerved around me.

'Obviously something is making you laugh. Perhaps you could share it with me.'

'Lolitum,' everyone chanted on the next wiggle.

She got down off the rostrum and walked around the outer circle towards the fireplace, hands on hips, nipples like barbed wire.

'Step out, Caroline!'

I made my way through the Lolitummers towards the fireplace but caught them just on the reverse and bumped into Catherine.

'Don't you think Miss Fowler has better things to do with her time than have silly girls bother her?'

This was a no-win question. I chewed the side of my lip. When in doubt, I always did this.

Unfortunately Mrs Gentle was standing at the place where the vase had fallen over; a small pool of water was bravely edging towards her bare foot.

'What's this?' she asked, looking down at it. 'Who did this?' Her goldfish eyes bulged up at me.

I shrugged.

'Are you going to tell me who it was?'

I kept silent.

'I'll assume it was you then. Get downstairs.'

My heart beat fast.

'Please! Please no!'

'I've had enough of you. Down to Miss Fowler now!'

My face was pressed into the corner of Fowler's study. I had been standing there for over two hours now and was feeling faint with hunger. I'd missed Vedic mathematics and most of Sanskrit. I didn't care about Sanskrit, but I liked Vedic mathematics; it was all about number tricks and short cuts. They'd worked it all out, the Vedic people thousands of years before the Egyptians. They were the ones who invented zero.

I could hear the gentle tread of sixty silent girls going down to the refectory for lunch. My stomach gave an envious rumble, and the scratch of Fowler's calligraphy nib on the paper paused for a moment. I could hear the chink as she dipped it into the ink and the scrape as she cleared the nib on the edge of the ink bottle. After a moment or two she swapped pens and picked up her Sanskrit nib – writing was a form of worship, and anything other than nibs and ink was insulting and sloppy. She made long confident strokes and I tried to guess which words she was writing.

In slow motion, I managed to rest my forehead on the wall without her noticing and I set about my usual occupation of licking the wall with the tip of my tongue. If I pressed really hard again and again, time after time, the paint began to come off. It was like a growth chart for me, that white streak on the moss-coloured paint. When I looked at how small I was when I'd started this marathon lick, I was amazed at how much I'd grown. But it also depressed me. I had never imagined I'd still be doing it a foot later.

I must have started the lick when I was nine. Up until then Fowler had quite liked me; I was bright, quick and happy, a perfect pupil. Sometimes she even used to ask me to sit next to her at lunch, not in a punishment kind of way. But that was before it all went wrong. At the back of the coach on a school trip to hear the Mahabarata being read out loud, she had caught me red-handed drawing rude pictures of the teachers in a little home-made magazine; a donkey weeing on Mrs Gentle's head, a robber chopping Mr Baker's willy off and other such hilarities. She'd snatched the booklet off me, dragged me down the coach, shoved me into a seat, sat down next to me and had slowly flicked through the pictures. They hadn't seemed quite so funny after that. Despite Joanna and Megan's creative input, I took the rap for that, and Fowler had seen me differently from then on; I was soiled, tainted, a bad influence. I would need a lot of washing in the Ganges. She grew to despise me and to suspect my every motive. And since then, I had become part of the sombre furniture of her study.

In the brass mount of the door handle I could see the reflection of the Masaccio painting that hung above the mantelpiece; pictures like this hung throughout the building and in most of our houses, presumably with the idea of turning our thoughts to the Divine. It didn't matter what religion anyone was or had been. The Organization was full of all sorts, Christians, Jews, Hindus, whatever, all meditating their way to nirvana, all discovering a new and better way. As far as I could tell, the Organization picked and chose its way through religions. The Bible was best for teaching us how to read (it was full of short easy words), but they never dwelled on Heaven and Hell. They couldn't get enough of Rama Krishna, but Megan and I only found out about the Kama Sutra by accident. Jesus and Buddha and the rest of them were all approved of, but you were never going to get the time to actually worship them. The Organization had made sure of that, they had you all hours, weekdays, evenings and weekends. In theory, anything that turned the mind to holiness was allowed. Renaissance paintings were the latest craze. Like Laura Ashley wallpaper.

This particular one had Mary in a blue dress on some sort of patio with an angel in a pink dress nagging at her. Mary looked like she'd had enough. 'Look, angel,' she was saying, 'I'm doing the best I can, so give me a break.' But the angel was having none of it; she was wagging her finger at Mary with a smug expression on her face. In the background, this miserable raggedy couple were being ushered along. They looked like they were really in trouble – I recognized their expression. You could see each and every flower on the lawn outside; I'd counted them lots of times but never come out with the same number. Three hundred and something.

I hated the stupid painting.

Suddenly the scratching of Fowler's nib stopped. I swiftly retracted my tongue. The gas fire made its usual clicking sounds as it breathed asthmatically into the room. I could hear the rest of the school having lunch. No noise except the occasional scrape of knife on plate. My right leg had gone completely dead. I had to move, so I shifted weight and gave it a tiny shake. The bells around my ankles jingled.

'Don't you dare move!' came her voice, vicious and icy as if she'd been waiting to pounce. 'Unless you're ready to apologize.'

I shook my head.

'Apologize now and then you can go back to class!' Fowler said to my back.

'I didn't spill it!' I said to the wall.

'So you say. Who did spill it then?' She didn't believe me. She was smug, like the angel. I could hear her shuffling her papers, straightening them on the desk.

'I don't know.'

A deliberate and final shuffle, then the brisk zip of her briefcase being opened. 'Then you can stand there all afternoon until you remember!'

I felt my eyes prick with tears at the idea, but I forced them back. My legs ached. Snot ran out of my nose and made a watery path over my lips, but I didn't wipe it. She'd have a little victory then. I would wait all afternoon.

There was a knock at the door, which made me jump.

'Come!' she cried. She always said it like that, as if she'd coined some catchphrase. The door opened ajar. I shifted my eyeballs as far as possible without moving the rest of me. It was the head of the boys' school, Mercer.

I was self-conscious, standing there in my Vedic dancing clothes, my white aertex shirt, my long red circle skirt, my bare feet and my dancing bells. But Mercer ignored me and stepped into the room, shutting the door behind him and leaning on it.

Then a strange transformation happened. I could sense

it before she spoke. She made little whelping noises like a newborn puppy. 'Come in! Come in!' she said, like she was hosting some party, all skippity la, in this horrible flirty voice. I could hear the sweep of her long dress brushing against the tin wastepaper bin as she bounced around her desk.

'I don't mean to disturb you. I was just wondering if we could discuss the new material from His Holiness,' said Mercer. He was right beside me. If I strained my eyes upwards I could see his large Adam's apple making gulpy movements. Personally, I never thought he was half as scary as Fowler, but the boys said he was lethal with the cane.

'Not disturbing me at all! No! Not at all. Take a seat, Mr Mercer!' she said, and for no apparent reason, she started laughing. The laughter didn't sound right, coming in cracks and bursts like faulty plumbing. I took the opportunity to wipe my nose.

'Back to the classroom, Caroline!' she said, not missing a trick. I turned around. Her face was unrecognizable; she was grinning at him. It was mystifying to behold, like a snake in a frock. The rare appearance of her teeth always surprised me; they were small and straight and neat. She wiped her inky hands on a piece of tissue and checked a stray hair, surreptitiously clipping it back into the severe, greying bun on the back of her head. Then she leant her stick-straight body over to turn the gas fire down, as if the room had suddenly become swelteringly hot.

'I haven't had any lunch,' I said, thinking this might be my chance to eat.

She looked at me, and to my relief the teeth

disappeared. Her face returned to its skullish normality. The headmaster leant on her desk and turned his attention to me. He had grown fond of me over the years. I was in that corner with such regularity that I suppose he had come to regard me as some kind of pet.

She walked towards me and opened the door for me to leave, letting her expression roam free with hatred now that he could no longer see it.

I turned to go, but he stopped me. 'Caroline,' he said, as if he were throwing some nuts to a monkey. He could tell I'd been crying. 'Do you think you could bring us some tea?'

He gave me a smile, and I saw her clock it. She looked pained by it, but kept the grin going.

'I've some mint tea in my cupboard,' she said to him, perkily.

'Thank you, I'll just have regular.'

'Of course. Some tea!' She almost pushed me out of the door.

I made my way down to the basement where the kitchen backed on to the refectory. Through a small interconnecting hallway, this building was joined to the one next door, where the boys' school was located.

The kitchen was full of our mothers swooping about in their long dresses, their hair pulled back into neat, identical buns, as if they were competing for drabness. No make-up, no flesh, no jewellery, no bright colours, no loud voices, nothing that might draw attention. They had been designed to deflect interest, to be invisibly servile. They glided about the place in their sensible shoes, knees slightly bent for that creeping, efficient, invisible ease.

Sometimes I wondered whether they had legs at all or whether they floated about on castors. They were journeying to and from the refectory where the girls were having lunch, carrying baskets of freshly baked brown bread, cheese boards, bowls of apples and pots of honey, with beatific smiles on their faces. I hoped my own mum wasn't there: she would know that I was in trouble again.

I slid through the women, past the large vat of retch-making yoghurt, shining creamy yellow like some jellied creature from the watery deep, and snuck into the larder, where I stole a roll and stuffed it into my mouth.

'Can I help you?' came a gentle, breathy voice that seemed to have followed me into the darkness. It could have been anyone since all the mothers had worked hard on their gentle breathy voices, weighty with spiritual advancement.

It was Kate's mum. She looked at me with one raised, disapproving eyebrow. She believed everything she was told about me, and I held that against her.

'I've got to take some tea up to the study,' I said. 'For Miss Fowler and Mr Mercer.'

I could tell she was impressed: sheepy devotion spread over her face. 'Then I suggest you get on with it.' The breathiness had undertones of steel.

I bit my lip. Her husband, Kate's dad, taught us geometry. I'd been at their house a few weeks ago, and Kate and I had found a pile of sex magazines hidden in his study. Women with their legs wide open clutching their enormous bosoms whilst doing things to each other. I tried to convey this powerful knowledge with a stare, but she elbowed me out of the larder.

Just at that moment, everything came to a halt. Lunch-time was over. The women stopped whatever they were doing, put down their baskets of food, paused in their washing up, stopped their floor-sweeping, their bread kneading. I looked through the glass of the refectory door as the girls put down their knives and raised their hands to their foreheads in prayer, thumbs brushing their third eyes. The mothers in the kitchen all did the same, but better, their elbows went higher and their third eyes weren't being thumbed. I lifted my own arms up and peeped around my forearms. I despised the way the mothers closed their eyes, in that reptilian manner, draw-ing the bottom eyelids up to the top so that they quivered as though in a state of transcendence.

'We thank thee, Govinda, for this table of food and devote it to thy service.' Then the same old Sanskrit chant that none of us knew the meaning of, even though we had said it before and after each and every activity all of our lives.

Through the refectory glass, I caught eyes with Megan. We had become experts at lip reading. She let me know that she and Amy next to her had smuggled some food for me. I mouthed thanks, and she wobbled her head as she prayed and crossed her eyes to make me laugh. Mrs Gentle slapped the back of her head.

I had never been sent to make tea before and had no idea how to make it. We didn't drink it at home. But I'd seen various trays of it carried about the building and I felt that I had the gist. I found a small white teapot and put it on a tray. I found a jar of tea leaves. I took the kettle off the hob. I couldn't reach the taps, so Kate's mum filled it for me and put it on the hob. The hob seemed a bit wasted; it was only ever used for boiling kettles. We weren't allowed cooked food or any mixing of foods at all; the Vedas said it was bad for the mind. Meat-eaters didn't stand a chance. So we were stuck with revolting spiritual food, like yoghurt and brown bread.

I couldn't find a strainer thing but, eventually, under the sink I came across a vegetable colander that looked like it could do the job. All the cups were located in the other building, so I went through the interconnecting corridor. Outside the parallel refectory next door, the boys were queuing up before going in for lunch. My dad was there, inspecting their hands. He was being typically thorough, bent over, examining them for dirt, sending boys back to the loos if they weren't clean enough. I grabbed two cups from the shelf, but I was too late, he'd seen me.

'Caroline?'

The boys turned to look. Marcus smiled at me. I loved Marcus, and Marcus loved me. Last week we had kissed for seven seconds on platform two at Gloucester Road station.

I caught eyes with Jason Winters and I tried to give him a sort of sorrowful smile; his sister had died at the beginning of term; she had jumped from the top of Putney car park, splat on to the pavement like strawberry jam. She was eighteen. Parents are saying that she had always been unhinged. I pictured her like a swinging door blowing in the wind, making a painful squeak. But we all knew why she had really done it; she'd only been married to Mr Gates, the law teacher, for six months. Anyone could have told her he was repulsive: hairs grew out of his ears. And he was over forty. But nobody was saying it; everyone was pretending it was her fault, and they were all being nice to Mr Gates. But it was Mr Wapinski's fault. It was all his idea. He was the head of the whole Organization, and his big new thing was to start betrothing people. It seemed to me that he was just making the rules up as he went along, because Fowler had been telling us for years that we mustn't even look at a boy until we were twenty-four. But now the sixteen-year-old girls were being paired off with teachers and Organization old men. Apparently the girls weren't forced, but we all knew what that meant. No one ever said no to Mr Wapinski. We only had three years before he'd be lining us up. Hannah and Kate were getting all giggly about the whole thing, but I'd do a Helen Winters if he tried it on me. I wouldn't go near an old man. Unless it was Mr Steinberg, of course.

Jason Winters didn't really know what to do with my smile and looked away. Dad told the boys to go into lunch and came over to me. He was no different towards me from how he was to the boys.

'What are you doing down here?'

'I'm making tea for Miss Fowler and Mr Mercer.'

He studied my face. 'Are you in trouble?' He looked so angry at the possibility that I shook my head.

I rushed back and spread everything out neatly on the tray and waited for the kettle to boil. I noticed that Jason Winters' mum was drying up in the kitchen. She had big, bulging, black eye-bags which I tried not to stare at. I felt sorry for her having a dead daughter but I hoped she blamed herself as well. There's no way I would have let my daughter marry Mr Gates.

I carefully made my way back up the stone steps and along the brown and black mosaic tiles towards Miss Fowler's study. I put the tray down on the floor and knocked on the door.

'Come!'

I pushed the door and held it open with one foot as I picked up the tray. Fowler and Mercer were seated either side of her desk going through some papers. She still had the rictus grin on her face, but it dropped pretty quickly when she saw me. As I approached, Mercer cleared a space for the tray. I carefully put it down and turned to leave the room.

'Caroline? What's this?' Mercer said, holding up the colander.

I looked at it and suddenly became aware of its ludicrous size; it was twice as big as the teapot.

'I couldn't find a strainer,' I said, embarrassed.

He looked up at me as if he were seeing me for the first time and beamed a smile at me. He held up the colander to Miss Fowler, inviting her to share his fun. She tried to smile, but I could see how appalling this state of affairs was to her; she was meant to be enjoying me.

He took the lid off the teapot and peered in. Oh God, I'd forgotten to put any tea in. This seemed to delight him.

'Have you ever made tea before?' he said, his eyes twinkling at me. I shook my head.

'I've got some mint in my cupboard ...?' said Fowler, turning towards it. She should just shut up about her stupid mint.

Mercer wasn't listening to her. His attention was on

me. It seemed that I was the funniest thing that had happened to him in a long time. He kept looking at the colander and inside the teapot as if I'd performed some sort of magic trick. He wiped his eyes and shook his head as he laughed. Then he touched my wrist as if to ground himself. Fowler stared at him with astonishment, and when she slowly looked up at me, I froze.

I was used to her anger and her hate, but this was quite different. I had triggered something new. It was evident that I had crossed some line, only I didn't know what that line was. She was repulsed by me. She looked at me as if I were one of those ladies from the sex magazines, legs akimbo. The coldness in her eyes shot straight through my bones and made the hairs on my neck stand on end.

I knew then that a new war had begun.

2

I hadn't had a nightmare for years and years. I woke myself up screaming, my body wet and clammy, the back of my T-shirt stuck to my skin. My throat was sandpaper dry.

I had been at a party in a big white, familiar, varnish-floored room. I was aware that I knew people there. They weren't total strangers. The atmosphere was jolly, and everyone appeared to be having a good time, but I was ready to leave, I'd had enough. So I made my way to the door, where a charming man in a white suit informed me that this particular exit wasn't being used. I snaked my way through the busy room and went to another door, where a woman with a smiling face in a long white dress told me that there was no exit from this door either. As I was politely turned away from the third and last door, it suddenly dawned on me that I was trapped, that it would not be possible to leave this party. Just as I felt myself begin to panic, a bell rang loudly, and the room fell silent. We were all ushered into a refectory at the back and invited to take our places at four carefully laid-out trestle tables. People started to take their seats. Everything was perfect, ready for a mighty feast: the white napkins were shaped into lotus flowers, the gleaming glasses and knives and forks were so polished that the light bounced about the room. But, when I looked closely, something wasn't quite right. It was clear that the place settings were all a means to an end. The glasses, the familiar Pyrex tumblers, were all placed upside down, and beside each one was an empty test tube and a hose full of carbon monoxide. I knew that the origamied napkins were wet and heavy with chloroform. On each blue and white patterned plate, four red pills lay in a diamond shape and the knives were large and wrist-slittingly sharp. It was a suicide feast. Someone pressed me into my seat on the bench. Everyone ceased their shuffling, and the room fell still. As one, all the diners, myself included, raised our hands in prayer, thumbs to forehead. Om Paramatmanaynama. I tried to speak, but my voice had left me, and I watched helplessly as the diners began to tuck in. People were picking up the glasses, holding them to their faces, closing their eyes and sucking in the poison, willingly. One woman cheerfully sliced her wrist, and her flesh was as smooth as butter. I watched the blood gush on to the table. Heads fell on to plates: crash, slump. I fled from the table, but the white-suited staff leant on the locked doors, still smiling. I knew there was no escape for me and I began to scream.

At first, I hadn't even recognized Joe; his black face, his bald head. He was just an unfamiliar shape, a stranger holding me, saying over and again, 'Hey, hey, Lol, easy baby, easy baby. It's just a dream.'

Lol? Lorrie? That's me. I'm here, in bed, in my house. I blinked hard. My eyes were dry, my mouth was dry. I was desperate for fresh air. I leapt out of his arms, out of the bed and pulled up the sash window as fast as I could. I stuck my head out and snatched lungfuls of the cold

34

West London air. In the distance somewhere I could hear a siren.

Joe turned the bedside light on. I could feel him checking the clock. He got out of bed and went downstairs. I heard a click-clicking noise and watched Tilly, the dog, trot sluggishly over the wooden floorboards, sleepy and confused. She half-heartedly wagged her tail, just in case there might be some unprecedented nighttime adventure.

I turned the light back off, kicked my clothes off the wicker chair and pulled it up to the window and rubbed my head. Tilly snuck up on to my lap, and I stroked her smooth temples, taking slow, deep breaths as I did so. I looked down at my fingers, all scratched, red raw. I hadn't done that for years. Oh no. I'd have to go to the doctor and get some pills, some proper knockout pills. I pushed Tilly off and leant on the sill and stared at the orange London street.

A fox sauntered across the road and rummaged in a dustbin.

Joe reappeared and placed a cup of tea on the window ledge in front of me.

'Thanks!' I said. My voice sounded feeble.

I glanced at him. He was naked. I looked at his chest, his dark skin shining coppery in the street light, but I didn't meet his eye. He shivered and grabbed a dressing gown from the back of the door before sitting down on the edge of the bed just behind me, and behind him I could see Tilly opportunistically burrowing under the covers. Neither of us spoke for a long while; we just sipped our tea. I stared at the street, at the parked cars.

'What was all that about, Lorrie?' he said gently. 'You frightened me!'

I didn't look round, I took another sip.

'I mean,' he carried on. 'Really . . . you scared me. Your eyes were wide open! You were terrified. I had to slap you. What the hell was going on?'

I blew on my tea.

'What was it, babe? Tell me!'

'Oh,' I said watching for the fox to reappear. 'I can't remember.'

He paused before reaching for his trousers and rummaging in the pockets. He lit himself a cigarette and opened the other sash window, leant on the sill and blew smoke out into the night. Somewhere down the Harrow Road an alarm went off.

'Lorrie, what's going on?' His voice was low and quiet, but deadly serious.

I said nothing.

'You're making it very difficult, you know that?'

'Making what difficult?' I replied. I couldn't stop myself being aggressive and defensive. Classic guilt.

'Making it very difficult for me to love you.'

I stared at my orange tea in silence.

'If you carry on shutting me out like this, I'm off, Lorrie, I mean it. I'm off. I can't take much more of this.'

I felt both a panic and relief at his words, but still I didn't speak.

'What's got into you?' he said, but he didn't say it harshly; he sounded like he was talking to himself.

'What is it you want from me?' I replied, as chilly as the

air. In chess they always say that when you're in a corner, you should attack. I grabbed his fags and lit one for myself, taking him in as I did so. He was pissed off.

'Why are you lying to me? Yesterday, you told me that you didn't recognize that woman at the farm, that you had no idea who she was. You said that "you'd never known anyone called Amy".'

My heart lurched. I blew smoke out into the street.

'That's right,' I said. I sounded pathetic.

'Then why've you just been screaming your lungs out, "Amy! Amy! For God's sake, Amy! We've got to get out of here! Amy! Amy! Amy! Don't sit down!"?'

Oh fuck. Jesus fuck. Oh fuck.

'Why are you lying, Lorrie? Or is that even your fucking name? What was it she called you, that woman at the farm? She called you . . . what? What did she call you?'

I could feel him facing me now.

'I can't remember.'

We hadn't always been like this. Oh, I'd always lied. I'd been lying for so long it didn't really feel like lying any more. But I had loved him once. I had really loved him and had dared to hope that it might just work, that I deserved a normal life, but right now I felt nothing except that I wanted to be on my own.

Joe flicked his cigarette out of the window, and we caught eyes. He didn't seem angry any more, just sad.

'Nothing's that bad you can't tell me. Maybe you underestimate me, Lol.'

I watched him pull the window shut and get back into bed. I looked down at the street and leant on my elbows.

There he was, the fox, standing still in the middle of the road, unafraid, staring straight at me.

Life's bullets strike with no warning. Flagless and silent, they knock you down quite unexpectedly. Days, weeks, months and years pass by and then, out of the blue, wham.

The day before the first nightmare, we'd had an appointment at Milford Farm at eleven thirty and we were running late. Well, I wasn't, I'm never late, but Joe was. From the corner of my eye, I watched him leaning heavily on the sink, his face pained, almost tearful. With great effort he turned on the tap and poured a glass of water, wincing as he sipped from it. He tightened the dressing gown cord around his waist with the ease of a man aged one hundred and three. He brought his hand to his brow and remained in a freeze of misery. All this was for my benefit, so that I could understand the uncharted pain of his man-bug.

'Look, you're obviously not well enough to come,' I said.

'No,' he replied, heroically. 'They wanted us both to be there.'

I knew I was no Florence Nightingale, but my lack of loving care shocked even myself. When I'm ill I certainly don't want to be tended to by someone like myself. I imagined other women being thoughtful and tender – basically just nice, but I knew I didn't have it in me. I like to think that, if he was seriously ill, cancer or something, I'd pull out all the stops, but this ostentatious parade of ill health I found deeply repulsive. Added to which, his body kept making noises from one end or the other; they rang through the house like fog warnings from a liner.

I flinched as he belched by the fridge.

'Oh, give it a break, Lorrie, I'm ill!' he said. 'You're such a bloody hypocrite!'

It's true, I was.

He shuffled across the room and flopped on to the sofa and with the strength of Samson managed to pick up the remote control and press the 'on' button. Mindless daytime drivel spewed out. I could feel my anger rising. He knew I hated it. I found daytime television truly depressing; it reminded me of hospitals and brain-dead institutions, of drugged morons lined up in rows, mouths hanging open, the jolly banalities of the presenters flying over their screwed-up heads.

'I'll be leaving in twenty minutes if you are coming,' I said crisply, leaving the room. Tilly's collar tinkled as she followed me out.

'Stop following me!' I growled at her and then felt guilty and patted her smooth, brown head lovingly. After all, it was her big day today.

Outside our house I had been conducting an experiment. I had deliberately not picked up a piece of litter that had flown into the front garden just to see how long it would take Joe to do it. It had been stuck on the path for three and a half weeks now.

'I'd better drive. It'll take my mind off my stomach,' he said, stepping over the crisp packet.

I lunged down at it and snatched it up, making a grand show of ramming it into the bin.

So we set off, Tilly in the back, head poking nervously between us.

Tilly was a middle-sized unidentifiable mongrel from Battersea Dogs Home. She'd been taken in by two families before us and returned twice. Understandably. She was a mental case. But a year ago, I'd looked into her brown, neurotic eyes and promised I wouldn't take her back, whatever. She was, however, truly testing me. She barked and chased anything that moved: bicycles along the canal, horses, cars, joggers. She barked at birds flying by, leaves falling, pollen bouncing about the air.

Not long ago, on Wormwood Scrubs, one particular jogger had proved irresistible to her. He'd had all the expensive gear on and at first I hadn't noticed that he'd only got one leg. The other one was a pole with a trainer on it. It was the most exciting thing that Tilly had ever seen – a stick that ran.

Inevitably she caught the stick and in her attempt to return it to me she had become embroiled in a scuffle with the stick's owner. By the time I got there the man was turning circles, fruitlessly trying to shake her off. When she saw me she looked almost proud, one eye seeking me out for approval as she snuffled, teeth clamped around the pole, her outstretched body flying around horizontally like a daring trapeze artist. I grabbed at her collar.

'Get off! Tilly!' I shouted with pack leader authority. She clung on.

'I am so sorry!' I said to the man.

'So you bloody should be! You shouldn't have dogs that you can't keep under control!'

I didn't respond but, to be honest; this whole one-legged jogging thing seemed a bit perverse to me. I mean, isn't life hard enough?

'Get the fuck off me!' he swore at Tilly, but it only seemed to make her more determined that the stick was rightfully hers.

I lowered my voice. I barked commands. I strutted about masterfully – all to no effect whatsoever. She spun about the stick as if she were dancing round a maypole, all the while demonstrating a remarkable lack of respect towards me, the pack leader.

There was only one thing for it. Tilly needed professional help.

I examined the directions to Milford Farm on my lap, 'Exit junction 3, first left at the first roundabout, second left at the second.' The motorway was surprisingly empty.

'Junction 3,' I said.

'Yes I know, Lorrie,' Joe replied. 'That's the third time you've told me.'

'Keep your hair on!'

Silly comment. He's bald as a coot. I thought he might have made a joke about it which I'd have been able not to laugh at. He was good at making jokes. Our relationship hung by the threads of humour. But no jokes today, not with him being at death's door.

'What is your problem, Lorrie?' he asked, turning to look at me. 'You're just so aggressive all the time!'

Tilly made whimpering noises and tried to get into the front to sit on my lap. I pushed her back.

Joe winced with pain, dealt yet another blow by his man-bug.

'I don't know why we're doing this!' he said.

'Doing what?'

'This! Going to see a dog shrink.'

My heart had lurched. I thought he meant us, he didn't know why we were doing *us* any more. But he didn't mean that.

'Yes, we all know that you think therapy is a waste of time.'

'I didn't say that.'

'No, but you meant it.'

Tilly tried to get into the front again, licking at me nervously, ears as far back as possible.

'She's a fucking dog, Lorrie.'

'That was it!' I shouted as we sailed past Junction 3. 'For God's sake!' I checked my watch. This session was not cheap, and we were going to be late.

Half an hour later, we sat in Dr Crawford's visiting room in silence. Dr Crawford was like an enormous hound himself. He had a big, shaggy beard and wild brown hair. He wore a suit of sorts, but it was crumpled and covered with hair, presumably dogs', and, incongruously, a white feather balanced on his lapel. Maybe he did bird therapy as well.

He let Tilly manically lick him all over the face as he rubbed her ears. Give her an inch and she'll take a mile. She tried to jump up into his arms. I was pleased she did this as it showed off her bad-dogness, which was why we were here after all.

I looked about the room. It was geared for the canine: low bean bag things, lino floor, dog bowls full of water. I was surprised, when he offered us a biscuit, that

42

it wasn't bone-shaped. He did serve Tilly first, however.

'Yes,' I said apologetically, 'and that's another thing, she's always jumping up!'

'Well, that's nice, isn't it?' he said turning to me. His eyes were sloping and brown with short, thick lashes; he might have been a dog himself in a past life, or possibly a cow. 'She's welcoming you!'

He looked into her eyes and made some dog whisperer noises and then he turned his attention to us. Tilly, quite at home now, sniffed about the room for a moment and then, miraculously, sat down at his feet.

'Do you mind me asking . . .' he asked, 'but did you two have a row in the car on the way here?'

He was very good.

Joe and I looked at each other, as if to get our stories straight.

'Er . . .' I said. 'A bit.'

'She picks up everything, you know, she's a very intelligent, sensitive dog.'

The implications were too obvious. Couple on the rocks – mad dog.

'What's she like with children? Do you have children?' he asked.

'No. We don't,' Joe said quickly, with what I thought was a hint of blame. We were no spring chickens.

'But she's good with children,' I said. I was still pissed off with him, otherwise I would have turned to him for verification.

'I bet you are, Tilly,' said Dr Crawford. 'You're a beautiful girl! Has she ever bitten anyone?'

'Not that I know of.'

43

'Only if they're very annoying,' Dr Crawford said to Tilly in a gruff, jokey, doggy voice. She gave him a French kiss.

'Separation anxiety, you say ...?' He was looking at some notes. 'Do you kennel her when you go on holiday?'

'No,' Joe said, pointedly. 'Lorrie doesn't do "abroad".'

'Well, I can't,' I replied, spikily. 'Not with Tilly the way she is.'

'Who would you say was her primary carer?' he asked, moving swiftly on.

'Me,' we said in unison.

'What?' I turned to Joe. 'Me! It's me who feeds her and takes her for walks.'

'Not always!'

I was aware that we were metaphorically laying out a therapist's picnic.

'You, yes maybe,' said Joe. I could almost have hugged him for that. We hadn't hugged for months.

'Right, so Lorrie ...' said Dr Crawford matter-of-factly. 'I have to ask these things, but ... er, does Tilly see you get upset much?'

'No,' I replied. Too quickly.

'Do you cry in front of her?'

He had a fountain pen in his hand now and was taking notes.

'I never cry,' I answered. He looked up.

'It's true,' Joe said. 'I've never seen Lorrie cry. Not once in the seven years I've known her.'

He said it like I was a freak or something, just because he blubs at the drooping of a flower. Dr Crawford looked as if he had heard too much human information.

'Well, you said on the phone that she chased anything that moved, so I thought we'd take her outside and show her the geese.'

'Hope they're insured!' I said, getting up, feeling fabulous that I was not going to be responsible for the outcome.

We strolled through a paddock, Dr Crawford holding Tilly on her lead. She tugged and pulled, which I was pleased about. A big, fat woman with a pitchfork was heaving piles of hay off a tractor and dumping them in a stable.

I stopped to pat a horse. They always made me rather nervous, but it was safely behind its stable door, just its grey face leaning over the top.

I could see Joe and Dr Crawford stop to talk to the fat woman. She had crouched down and was letting Tilly lick her face. These were seriously doggy people.

'Hello, girl!' She had a loud, farmerish voice. As I joined them, she was looking with concern at Joe. 'Oh, you poor thing! Food poisoning is just the worst . . .' I supposed he had to get a bit of sympathy where he could. I noticed she had a bit of hay in her cropped, fair hair.

'I'm being very brave, aren't I, darling?' he said with a wink as I joined them.

The woman laughed and then turned her big, blue eyes to me. She stared for a moment and then gasped.

'Oh my God!' she cried. 'Caroline! Caroline Stern!'

There it was; the bullet. It sliced through the air, hurtling towards me at an unstoppable speed, until it hit me in the stomach, right in the gut. I stepped back a pace. I needed a moment. My throat had clammed shut.

I could feel Joe and Dr Crawford turn their heads to look at me. I stared straight back at her, this big stranger with the blue eyes. Bemused, I shook my head.

'I'm sorry?'

'Caroline Stern!'

'No. My name's Lorrie Fisher.'

'Caroline!' she repeated. 'It's me, Amy! Amy Jones! A bit fatter but it's me! Caroline!'

I shook my head. 'Sorry! You've got the wrong person,' I said. 'People often think they recognize me. I've got that sort of face.'

I leant down and pulled Tilly away by the collar.

It's strange that after the bullet hits, you don't feel a thing, not a thing. You just wonder where all the blood's coming from.

The Jamesons were a pretty hopeless case. They made Joe and me look like Romeo and Juliet. They'd been referred to me by their GP because their teenage daughter Gemma was suffering from anorexia.

'Please sit down, all of you!' I said, as the three of them entered the room, Lesley at the helm, followed by the fragile Gemma and lastly Michael, who evidently felt that the whole family therapy thing was bollocks and didn't hesitate in making that obvious. He sighed heavily as he swaggered in. He had fine strawberry blond hair in a number-two haircut; it looked as soft as velvet, but his face was hard and angular. He was a thick-set working man, bewildered by the situation he found himself in. He preferred not to sit, not to partake, and he took his usual post over by the window and stared out at the trees.

Every part of him except his body was out there, up in the branches somewhere.

His wife, Lesley, clocked him with habitual irritation and then took a seat with her back to him, placing her gold handbag carefully and deliberately as far from her husband as was possible, as if he might nick her wallet. She flicked her over-dyed hair back off her face, shrugging both it and him off her shoulders. She sought in me an ally and over the hour tended to shift her chair nearer to mine giving the impression that she and I were ganging up against her husband.

Gemma, the little red-headed stick that she was, sat down next to her mother, eyes downcast, staunchly silent. She and I had just finished an individual session, and I felt that we had had a glimmer of a breakthrough. However, I had not yet heard her speak in the family session.

I was good with the anorexics. I understood the protest. I also understood the consequences; I blamed my inability to conceive on the anorexia. I didn't need the tests. I knew it and I would do all in my power to prevent this fate falling on girls such as Gemma. When I looked at her I saw the power of her frailty. Some part of me admired the fight, and another part wanted to slap her. But most of me just wanted to sort her out.

Had I really once looked like that? She had skinny jeans on that bagged around her thighs. Her fingers gripped her legs like talons. Her cheekbones stuck out like fists.

I watched her take a sip from her water in a show of normality, probably for her father's benefit, but I knew she would be counting the calories.

47

'Please, Michael. Join us!' I said, but he didn't move. 'For Gemma's sake!'

'Don't give me that,' he said, surly, his aggression masking his fear. He looked at me distrustfully as he took his seat, legs wide apart, arm around his daughter's chair, as if to protect her from me and her mother.

Something in me flipped. I hated men like him with their arrogant ignorance, with their victim mentality: 'Everybody's fault but mine'. I felt a surge of anger charge through me. The blood rushed to my head.

'Have you ever thought, Michael Jameson, that your behaviour is directly responsible for your daughter's mental and physical state? Have you ever thought that perhaps you should look at yourself and make an effort to change?'

I don't know what got into me. I have never lost it at work before. I pride myself on my self-control, my ability to pacify, to lull the client into expression. One of the primary rules of family psychotherapy is not to apportion blame. I was breaking an elementary tenet.

The atmosphere in the room changed from frosty to arctic. Even Lesley looked shocked by my outburst. I fumbled for the light switch.

'Okay,' I said, switching it on. It was dim in this room, I couldn't see a thing. The heavy skies outside had darkened everything. I coughed and pretended to look at their file for a moment. I changed my tone.

'Today, Michael, I'd really like you to tell me something. I want to ask you if you remember the first time that you met Lesley.'

Silence, they were all staring at me.

'Do you remember?' I asked. 'Or not?'

Lesley snorted dismissively. She was trying to help me, to get the session back on track.

'What?' he said, turning on her, leaning forward over Gemma to eyeball her.

'Nothing! Did I say anything?' She looked at me for verification of his paranoia. I ignored her. Gemma rocked about in her chair like the piggy in the middle.

'Michael,' I continued calmly. 'Please try and remember. Tell me about when you and Lesley first met.'

He shuffled in his chair. I listened with one ear, but inside I asked myself the same question. And was the question going to place Joe and me on the road to recovery?

I remembered when I had first met him. It was September the eighth, seven years ago. The health centre where I worked at the time had a project going with the local sports complex. In an effort to get families to spend time together, we held activity days. September the eighth was a Friday, and I was looking forward to getting back to my flat and splodging in front of the TV with a glass of wine. I had popped into the sports complex for the routine breakdown on a couple of families with Steve, the liaison officer, when this great big, bald, black man stopped me in the swing doors.

'Are you Lorrie Fisher?'

'Yes, I am.'

'I'm your new man! Joe Pearce.'

He smelt of chlorine. I watched a vein on his temple throbbing through his skin.

'Hi! Where's Steve?' I said.

'He was sick today so I took the McCauley session. Basketball. Then we did a bit of water polo.'

'Water polo?'

'Yes, it was the kids' idea, so I thought why not?'

'Shall we run through it at the café? I could do with a tea,' I suggested.

It wasn't love at first sight. For a start, he was younger than me, and I'd never gone for younger men. But I was curious. I liked his passion and his irreverence. So much so that when John, another co-worker, appeared and invited us to the Paradise for a birthday drink, I went. This was unusual, I never socialized at work; I quite enjoyed the way that people were a little bit afraid of me.

For a while, Joe and I had stood at the bar, talking to an interesting girl with an array of piercings on her face. I liked the attention he gave her; there was something genuine about him. And then later, I remember noticing him playing pool with John, his attention firmly focused on what he was doing. I got a good look at him then; he was leaning over the table, his cue poised, his expression serious and intense, his broad shoulders firm and strong, the defined muscles of his arm seemed carved and polished from smooth black wood. He looked like a cat about to pounce. I've always enjoyed watching men playing pool. I find it extremely sexy. It's something to do with the utter focus. It kind of makes me want to be that object of fascination. Inevitably, when I am it, I find it needy and irritating.

An hour or so and several gin and tonics later, I knew it was time to go. I have always been a good leaver. I have never been the dregs at a party. I'm the frothy bit that quickly disappears. The bar had got crowded, a load of John's mates had turned up, and I suddenly felt tired. I yearned for a bath and a book and bed. I could see Joe on the other side of the bar, holding a bottle of beer, engaged in an animated conversation with a pretty girl, so I slipped out of the club without saying goodbye.

It was dark but warm outside, and it felt right to have left. Serendipity brought a black cab into my sight, and I hailed it. Behind me the club doors opened, and a surge of noise spilt out on to the street, bringing with it Joe, still clutching his beer and looking a little bemused. Ushering him out was the girl with the piercings.

'You nearly left without him!' she said to me, grinning, making the embarrassing assumption that he and I were an item.

She turned around and went back inside, and Joe and I stood looking at each other on the pavement, just as the cab pulled up in front of me.

'Where to, love?' said the cabbie.

'Shepherd's Bush,' I replied, opening the door. 'Wood Lane end.'

Joe had got himself round to the other side of the cab. He leant down and smiled at the cabbie.

'Hackney, please,' he said, opening the opposite door. He looked at me over the roof, a glint in his eyes, 'Come back to Hackney with me!'

I laughed at the cheek of him.

'No,' I said leaning on the door. 'I'm going home. Shepherd's Bush,' I added to the driver.

'Hackney!' Joe repeated to the cabbie, who looked like

he'd heard it all before and leant over to turn the clock on.

'Come on!' said Joe, a smile on his full lips. 'Hackney! Say yes!'

'No!'

'Why not?'

'A million reasons.'

'Name one!'

'It's late.'

He looked at his watch, 'No, I can't accept that, it's only ten o'clock! Another reason!'

'You've only got one bed,' I said.

'Wrong again! I've got a sofa bed. Give me another reason!'

'Okay. I haven't got my contact lens solution.'

'I've got contact lens solution.'

'Oh yes,' I said suspiciously. 'For hard or soft contact lenses?'

He thought about it for a moment, 'Soft.'

Fuck it, I was feeling reckless, 'Okay,' I said, getting in. 'But I'm not having sex with you!'

He sat down next to me. 'Who said I wanted sex?'

Every relationship starts with a one-night stand – actually three nights in this case: we didn't leave the flat except to get papers and milk – but I never presumed then that it would go on for seven years.

Of course, in those very early days we swapped all that lover chit-chat that you have to get through: where you were born, where you grew up and all that. I told him the usual bullshit. Normal childhood, no siblings, local state school, blah blah blah, and then the sad bit – parents' death in car crash, no one in the world but me. Over the years, I had perfected the tone I used, factual yet with a hint of vulnerability to ward off prying.

'How shitty!' Joe said. Everyone said something like that.

'Yup,' I replied in a private, brave kind of a voice that usually did the trick.

I'd been lying for so long that it really didn't feel like lying any more; it had taken on its own reality. In some ways, I felt the loss.

Lesley and Michael Jameson had met in a pub on the Uxbridge Road. He had moved to London from Scotland for the construction work, and she and her sister used to drink in the Askew. So Michael and Lesley spent all their courting days in the same pub. The family therapy idea is that the couple try and repeat their early dates and in so doing rekindle those feelings that they had once felt for one another. It's not rocket science. However, it transpired that, on their first official date, Michael had beaten the shit out of some poor bloke for looking at Lesley's tits. Then later she found out that all through their early dates Michael had also been shagging her sister, Karen.

I shut the file. 'That's enough for today,' I said. I'd had enough. I needed some fresh air, some space. Michael got up, looking at his watch, still eyeballing me, but not giving me any lip. Lesley flung her bag over her shoulder and said pointedly, 'Tell him, Lorrie, that a relationship built on lies is fucked from the start!'

I walked home through Regent's Park. The sun was a

silver disc hiding behind a blotting-paper sky. A biting wind blew through my jacket. I sat down on a bench facing the zoo and lit a cigarette. I could see the elephants. Do we really need elephants in a zoo, for God's sake? It's bloody freezing. I watched two of them huddle together to keep warm and envied them their intimacy.

Lesley was right. What hope was there for a relationship founded on lies? Joe and I were on our last legs. We both knew it.

It had begun to seriously stagger six months ago. The day that was significant for the wrong reasons. I had known something was up: he had told me in the morning to make sure I was wearing something nice. He had picked me up from work and taken me for cocktails down Portobello. It was a good evening – margaritas and great music. We had even danced in the dimness of the candle-lit bar. When we sat back down at our table, he rummaged in his back pocket and brought out a little tissue-wrapped box. My heart flipped.

'Will you marry me?'

I hadn't seen it coming. Never, not once in the six years we'd been together, had I dropped the slightest hint that marriage was something I was remotely interested in. I'd heard friends of mine drop hints all over the place to their boyfriends, but me? Never.

'Oh Joe!' I said, shaking my head. It was a lovely ring. 'No, I can't!'

'Why not?'

'Because . . . I can't.'

'Why not? We love each other. We live together. Let's get on with it!'

'What about children?'

We'd been kind of trying unsuccessfully for months now, not counting days or anything, but not bothering with contraception.

'We can take tests. Maybe try IVF.'

'No, I don't want that!' I didn't want any unravelling of the past.

'I want you, Lorrie. I love you. It's not dependent on whether we have children. We'll get a dog.'

'I can't marry you.' I put the box on the table.

'Why not?' He looked hurt. 'What aren't you telling me?' And then he appeared to have a light-bulb moment. 'Are you married already?'

I laughed and shook my head, 'No! Joe, I'm not! It's nothing to do with you. I won't marry anyone. Ever.'

'Lorrie, why not?'

'I just ... don't see the point.'

Poor Joe. But I couldn't tell him the truth. Marriage was for people who want to wholly give themselves to each other, warts and all, and I won't do that. I would never do that. I would never give myself to anyone. I would never show anyone my warts.

Still, we'd struggled on for the last six months, both of us knowing it wasn't really going anywhere. That little question, those four words, had spoiled things. I'm not sure how much Tilly had helped either.

But I knew now that I had to do something about it, it couldn't carry on like this. I had to let Joe go or I had to let him in, and the implications of letting him in were just too immense, too impossible, so I had to let him go the way of all relationships. I shuddered at the thought of the inevitable mess of the ending. I would much rather just vanish.

When I got home, Tilly leapt up neurotically, her sharp claws catching threads on my jumper.

'I'm home!' I shouted, slamming the door.

'Are you all right?' Joe's voice came from the kitchen. I tried to gauge his mood. The welcoming smells that greeted me – lemongrass, palm sugar, ginger and garlic – seemed to say that things were all right.

'I walked home!'

'You might've rung.'

I went into the kitchen. His back was towards me. He was in his homey clothes, T-shirt and pyjama bottoms. I felt a surge of love for him, for us, for our life together. I didn't want to end this relationship, but I could see no other way. That trip to the farm had spoilt everything. Bloody lunatic dog.

He turned and kissed me briefly on the cheek.

'Smells good,' I said.

He was using the pestle and mortar to mix an aromatic concoction. A large glass of white wine stood at his side.

'I'm going to have a bath,' I said, taking off my coat and kicking off my shoes. I got out another glass and went to the fridge and poured myself a drink. Tilly, the relationship-wrecker, was still bouncing at my side.

'Stop it!' I shouted. Who would have Tilly when we split up? Poor Tilly.

She followed me upstairs to the bathroom, hot on my heels, needing me. I shut the door on her and leant on it. I crossed the painted blue floorboards, placed my glass on the edge of the bath and turned it on. I ripped off my clothes and climbed straight in.

I like to get into the bath as soon as it starts to run, to really appreciate the warming up process. The water always starts off cold before it turns piping. I sit down there in the tepid puddle, cold and shivery, in the sure knowledge that the unpleasantness isn't going to last. I turn the taps so that it runs almost unbearably hot and I fill it to my hip. Then I lie back, displaying most of my body to the cold air. I feel the water rise and rise as it covers up my goose-pimpling flesh. I make islands with my breasts, my knees, and rush tsunamis over my belly. The water rolls over me getting deeper and deeper until I am totally immersed in its glorious heat. The pleasure seems so much greater after the discomfort.

Our bath was large and deep. I lay back and let the water rise over my ears so that just my face poked out into the room. This was my favourite, my safest, position. The sound of the water in my ears, the thundering echoey quiet when the taps go off. I felt cut adrift, like an astronaut in space.

But it didn't feel right today. The peace quickly became uncomfortable. What was I going to say to Joe? I pulled myself up to sitting position and downed the whole glass. I could hear Tilly scratching at the door.

I washed quickly and got out and let Tilly in. She tried to lick the water off my skin lovingly, tenderly, and I let her lick my legs. Until it bordered on weird.

I put on my towelling dressing gown and came downstairs. It was dark now. Joe was still cooking in the kitchen. The effort he put into a meal always surprised me.

I wanted to come up behind him and rest my head on his back and tell him that I loved him, but instead I topped up my glass, then his, and pulled myself up on to the counter, resting my feet on the stool, and watched him chop up some ginger. I downed my glass and poured another.

'Oh Joe,' I sighed.

'What?' he replied, not turning, pretending that everything was okay.

I stared at the back of his shiny head, tongue-tied. I was so sorry that I'd made a fool out of him with my secrets and my lies. Surely I owed him more than this. Didn't he deserve a smidgeon of honesty, now, here at the end of our road together? Didn't I owe him that?

He turned to face me.

'What?' he repeated. I could see fear in his eyes. I held his gaze, but still the words didn't come. Relieved, I think, he turned slowly back to the chopping board.

There's a freedom in loss, once the fear has been realized. Now that we were here at the gates of relationship death, and nicely fuelled with a bottle of Sauvignon, I felt a wild recklessness take hold in me. And the words were out before I could stop them.

'My parents aren't dead.'

He turned sharply. 'What?!'

'I just haven't seen them for twenty-five years.'

I looked down at his hands; he had cut his finger. The blood seeped around the thick yellow clumps of ginger and then swallowed them up.

3

Dad woke me at five thirty. My bedroom door made a horrible crashing sound.

'Time to get up!' he said, opening the curtains to reveal the dead of night outside. He walked straight out again. I pulled the blankets tight around me and fought with the day. The house was freezing. My breath turned to smoke in the cold air.

I had to get washed and dressed twice, the first time in my sleep-foggy imagination. I always arranged my uniform on the floor in the right order the night before so that I could get dressed in bed. I darted my hand out of the warmth and grabbed my shapeless, navy blue knickers and Viyella tights and hauled them on. Then I wriggled out of my nightie and reached down for my vest and my off-white shirt with its ugly puffy sleeves and ridiculous long bow tie. I popped the cuffs together. Mum had made my uniform, and my poppers weren't aligned right, but I mastered it eventually. I forced myself to kick off the covers and clambered into the monstrous, purple tunic and made my way to the ice-cold bathroom, where I splashed water on my face and brushed my teeth. Then I woke up and had to go through the whole painful process all over again for real.

It was so cold that Mum had made porridge for me.

Dad didn't eat it, hot food not being approved of. In her own way Mum had her little rebellions.

They made the prayer, and I wolfed it down. Dad and I walked to Archway tube station in the rain, the yellow street lights doubling in the puddles. He walked really fast, and I always had to trot to keep up with him.

There was never a queue this early at the ticket desk. It wasn't yet six o'clock, Dad liked to get the first southbound train; he liked to get into school early. The little, old, black guard winked at me as usual as he clipped my ticket. Dad never met his eye, but I always did. I loved those brief exchanges with the outside world.

Down on the dark, dingy platform, there was hardly anyone else there, just a man up at the far end. We walked to our usual spot in silence, and I leant on the poster of a seated woman crying with a man standing behind her, putting a supportive hand on her shoulder. It was advertising the Samaritans or something, but overnight someone had put a thought bubble coming out of the woman's head saying, 'I wish this bloody man would go away.' I laughed, but when Dad read it, he moved us on a bit.

I preferred travelling alone. It meant I could scrape the date off yesterday's ticket and change the number with my Rotring pen, leaving Megan and me fifteen pence to spend on sweets. She did the same, so we would fantasize all day about what we would buy.

It was the first day back at school after half term, and I was filled with the usual dread. Half term had come as a great relief, just to get Fowler off my back. She'd had her eye on me the whole time since the teapot incident. If we passed the boys in the corridor, she made us all turn to face the wall, but me she physically pushed against it, pressing my face to the plaster, as if I might be unable to control myself at the sight of them and start ripping off my clothes. I thought about trying not to come back to school, maybe faking illness, but it wouldn't do any good. I had never had a day off school in my life. So I was never ill. Unlike Megan; she got asthma really badly. Sometimes she had to go to hospital in an ambulance. But she loved it there; you got cooked food, and they gave you meat, and there was even a room with a television in it. She once faked the wheezes to stay in a bit longer to watch *The Six Million Dollar Man*.

In the basement of the school were the 'dungeons'. They were windowless rooms probably meant for storing coal or wine, or whatever rich people did who once lived in those massive London houses. But they were our changing rooms. You had to duck to get through the door, and they smelt of feet and wet clothes, so the teachers tended not to get right in.

Mrs Gentle was hurrying everyone upstairs to Meditation, but somehow she missed me at the back, and I grabbed the opportunity to have a little lie-down. I kept very quiet until I was sure the class had gone and then I made a big pile of capes in the corner and lay down to sleep. But I soon got uncomfortable because I needed a pee.

I crept out of the door and checked that no one was about. The place was deserted. It was still only eight a.m. I dashed across the corridor to the loos. I left the light off, not wanting to draw attention to myself, so it was dim in there – just the grey daylight filtering down from the street through an opaque barred window. I rushed into the far cubicle and locked the door.

Just as I was about to leave the cubicle I heard the door swing open. Quiet as a mouse, I closed the lid and stood on the loo in case the person should bend down and spy my feet and report me. I crouched down.

It was a man. I could hear him peeing in the urinal. They were always changing the loos around. I thought perhaps I might be in the Gents. Last half of term these were the Ladies.

But my heart stopped when, instead of leaving the loos, he said, 'Hello?'

I hardly dared breathe. I could hear him approaching the cubicle.

'Hello?' he said again. I didn't recognize the voice.

I stood up on my tiptoes. It was the Sikh builder; I'd seen him about before. They were doing work in the kitchens. He wore white, paint-splattered dungarees and had a white turban on his head.

I pressed my finger to my lips and whispered, 'Please don't tell!' I begged. 'I'm hiding!'

He nodded and smiled. 'Okay!'

But instead of going away, he looked excited, as if we were playing some kind of game. In a pantomime fashion, he crept into the cubicle next to mine and locked the door and stood on the toilet.

'Who are we hiding from?'

His breath smelt of spices.

'Miss Fowler,' I said, rather wanting to get back to the dungeon.

'Don't go!' he said, sensing this. 'What's your name?'

'Caroline.'

'Well, Caroline. You look very nice in your uniform.'

'Thank you!' I said. He must have been mad. Our uniform was disgusting.

'What do you do after school?' he asked, still whispering. I wanted to leave now, but felt kind of responsible for us standing here, like when you've asked someone back to your house, but when they come you find them rather annoying.

'Nothing much. Homework, supper and bed.'

'Don't you go out? At the weekends?'

'Park Road swimming pool sometimes, with Megan.'

'Megan? Which is she?'

'She's in my class. She's little and she's got lots of freckles.'

'Oh,' he said, trying to recall her. 'Maybe you and Megan would like to go swimming with me?'

What a peculiar idea. I imagined him at the pool with Megan and me, blowing all the air out and sinking to the bottom like a corpse, letting the water roll us about or hand-walking across the shallow end or dying a gruesome *Jaws* death – not that we'd seen *Jaws*, but the poster had been all over the tube, and that was scary enough. I pictured him with a swimming hat on top of his turban doing the butterfly. Or if it was true that Sikhs never cut their hair, he might let it hang loose in the water, where it would float behind him, taking up a whole length.

Just as I was wondering what to say, he brought his hand up on to mine, which was resting on the partition between us. At first I thought it was a mistake, I pulled mine away, but he held on to it. 'We could meet after school?'

This felt all wrong. This wasn't Marcus.

He stretched his arm out and ran his hand down my chest and on to my left bosom. 'You're lovely, little Caroline!' he said. His eyes had gone all strange and dizzy.

I pushed him away and leapt off the loo and undid the lock as fast as I possibly could.

'Wait! Wait!' he was saying. 'Caroline!' And I could hear him undoing the lock of his cubicle.

I was a very fast runner. I was always used as a messenger because I ran at the speed of light. I sped up out of the loos, along the corridor and up the basement stairs, span round the corner, flew past Fowler's study, whizzed round the banister on to the red carpet, up past the mirrors, past Room 4 and Room 5, up another flight, picking up speed all the way. Up again, another flight, and up to the very top of the building. I flew into the room and slammed the door behind me.

Meditation had not finished. Everyone was in their seat, calligraphy boards folded down, palms upturned in their laps, knees apart. As one, the class looked round at me, my breathing the only sound in the room. Fowler had clearly been asleep. She rocked awake with a jerk and stood up and whisked me back outside the classroom all in one, swift movement.

'What is it?' she said, her curiosity pricked, my breathless state obviously overriding her irritation at my entrance.

I leant over the iron staircase and cautiously looked down to check that the Sikh hadn't followed me. No one was there. The thought flashed through my head that this wasn't such a good idea, telling Fowler about him. But I was scared to go back down.

'The builder, the Sikh builder . . . he touched me,' I said between breaths.

'What do you mean, he touched you?'

'He touched . . . my bosom.'

There would normally be no reason on earth to say the word 'bosom' to Miss Fowler, but I could see no way around it. Her face froze, and then she blinked with embarrassment. Her cheeks flushed pink circles.

'Where were you?' she asked.

'In the loos, outside the dungeon.'

I didn't offer an explanation, and strangely she didn't ask for one.

'Follow me!' she said. And when I didn't move, she grabbed my wrist and took me downstairs.

As we descended to the basement, my heart beat fast. He wasn't in the corridor. She took me to the loos. He wasn't there. She pushed open the kitchen door. Mothers were kneading bread on the central table; they stopped and looked up.

There he was. In the refectory, halfway up a stepladder, painting the wall with slow, careful, even strokes. Fowler gripped my wrist tighter and pulled me towards him.

She shut the refectory door. It was just the three of us and the intoxicating smell of paint.

'Excuse me,' she said politely to his back. He stopped painting and turned around and looked at her. Then he looked at me, blankly, as if he had never seen me before.

'Yes?' he replied, poised on the ladder.

'I'm so sorry to disturb you,' she said and coughed. 'But Caroline here says that . . .' and then she paused, '. . . says that you made a pass at her in the toilets.'

'I beg your pardon?'

She gave a sharp, nervous laugh. 'Caroline here says that you made a pass at her in the toilets.'

His neck jerked backwards a fraction and he looked deeply affronted. He stepped off the ladder, shaking his head, 'Oh no no!' he cried. 'Please do not say that! I have a wife, I have three children.'

Miss Fowler nodded, as if this was what she had wanted to hear from him, and she dropped my wrist.

'Please forgive me,' she said. 'I do apologize. Caroline is a terrible liar.'

I looked up at her, disbelieving. One thing I was not was a liar. My heart sank as she poked me out of the room and up the stairs, her forefinger prodding my shoulder blades as she pushed me into her study. The light was off, and the room was as dingy as a cave. I was an idiot, I should have known better than to have told her.

She shut the door hard and stood with her back to it. She stared at me, fire in her eyes.

'You are a despicable child!' She spat out the words.

'But he's lying!' I cried, backing away from her.

'You are evil!'

She walked around me; I turned accordingly.

'Look at yourself!' she said. 'What do you do? Do you get up early before school to curl your hair?'

I shook my head.

'Then why have you got these ringlets around here?' She flicked one at the side of my face.

'My hair goes curly in the rain,' I said.

'No it doesn't. Hair goes flat in the rain. You come to school with the sole reason to flirt with the male teachers!'

She jerked her chin high, keeping her eyes fixed on me.

'Don't you?' she spat, her lips tight with rightness. Evidently she had wanted to tell me that for a long time.

'You, Caroline Stern, are a slut!'

She said the word with such venom I had to will the tears not to come. I would not let her make me cry. I didn't dare speak, just in case.

'I've seen the way you are with men.'

She glared at me, chin jutting forward. It was frightening to be this hated, to be looked at with such disgust. But I returned it just as vehemently. I despised her with every atom of my being. I jutted my own chin forward.

Then she appeared to have an idea. She marched to her desk, got out her keys and unlocked her cupboard. She reached up for the big bible and carried it over towards me, dropping it at my feet.

'Swear on the Bible that you are telling the truth!' she shouted challengingly, her face flushed with anger, some of her pinned-back hair falling forward. 'You swear on the Bible that that gentleman molested you!'

She almost seemed to be enjoying it. I knelt down and put my hand on the Bible.

'Swear it!' she cried.

'I swear on the Bible that that man molested me!'

'You are a *lying* slut!'

She gritted her jaw. She went back to the cupboard and returned with the Bhagavad Gita in her hands. She knelt down close to me and placed it on top of the Bible.

'Swear on the Bhagavad Gita that you are telling the truth!'

'I swear on the Bhagavad Gita!'

'The Absolute!' she said, putting her face hideously close to mine.

'I swear on the Absolute.'

Then with the fear of God in her voice she whispered, 'Swear on Mr Wapinski's life!'

Her eyes searched mine, flicking from one to the other as if she might miss the truth escaping.

'I swear on Mr Wapinski's life, I am not lying.'

She looked rocked to the core; she sat back on her heels, 'Your soul, Caroline Stern, will suffer in Purgatory!'

The National Theatre was like a great big ship on the outside and probably as exciting as a ship on the inside, I couldn't be sure about that because I hadn't been on a ship. Organization people didn't really travel. My dad had told me once, when I had asked why we couldn't go to France for a holiday, that our journeys were all on the inside, and that through meditation I could get anywhere. He often gave me crappy answers like that.

Inside the National Theatre there were lots of people buying things and eating and drinking at tables. At first, there seemed to be no sign of a theatre at all.

We weren't allowed to talk when we were in public, which wasn't difficult because there was just so much to look at. We'd travelled by tube to Waterloo and we'd walked under the arches past lots of people lying around in sleeping bags who all looked up at us and stared. Mr Steinberg gave three of them money and had to say to the fourth, 'I'm outa pocket, guys.' One of them said, 'Where ya from?' And Steinberg said, 'The States.' And the man said, 'Not you, mate, the fucking Smurfs you've travelled with.'

It's because of our stupid uniforms, the hideous purple capes and bowler hats. The sleeping-bag man woke up his friend to have a look as well. When we all travel together, no one minds being stared at. There is safety in numbers; it's when you're by yourself that it's unbearable.

Bells started to ring all around the theatre, and we were so excited we wanted to get in straight away. We followed Steinberg to the Olivier auditorium. We were up in the circle in the front row. I wasn't allowed to sit next to Megan. Miss Fowler had told Mr Steinberg to keep an eye on me – it was a miracle that I'd been allowed to come at all – so I sat with Amy on one side and Mr Steinberg on the other.

'So, Caroline,' he said, in that exciting bit when every-one is taking their places but the lights are still on. 'You're going to find out what happens to Orestes in a couple of hours' time.'

I nodded excitedly. We'd studied Aeschylus' text for the last month, but Steinberg had deliberately not taken us through the ending. When the lights dimmed, I felt almost sick with excitement. Steinberg and I exchanged looks, and I knew that he felt the same.

I was a bit disappointed when the play began because all the actors had masks on and I'd rather be able to see faces and spit and stuff. If I was an actor I wouldn't like wearing a mask. You might as well get a robot to do it. But after a little while I got used to it. And after a little longer, it seemed as if they weren't wearing masks at all.

I had binoculars and I kept trying to keep up with who was talking on the stage, but it was almost impossible to tell. The chorus was the most difficult, there were lots of them, all with miserable masks on. If I was an actor I wouldn't want to be in the chorus. I'd want to stand out.

At one point, Mr Steinberg leant over to borrow my binoculars, and I was pulled in very close; it was like we were tied together. He smelt clean and soapy. I could see where the dark stubble on his cheek stopped and where his smooth skin took over. I felt like Clytemnestra when Aegisthus drew her close.

But I soon became completely lost in the world of the play. I was following it all until Apollo told Orestes that it was all right to avenge his father's death, and then I began to get confused.

'Is that Pylades?' I whispered to Steinberg, pointing at him.

He leant towards me without taking his eyes off the stage and I repeated the question. He nodded, the stage lights bouncing off his glasses.

When you know what's coming up in a play, the anticipation is almost too much to bear. I knew that Orestes and Pylades were going to return to the palace and murder his mother and her lover and I couldn't contain my excitement; it was impossible to sit still. I pulled up my legs and sat on my knees and gripped the sides of my chair.

Steinberg must have been feeling the same because a moment later he shifted in his seat, accidentally resting his hand against mine. And immediately, the action on stage began to feel rather less interesting than the action at my fingertips. I froze, transfixed by his touch, unable to pull away; for it was now as if my entire being had concentrated itself in my right hand alone. I tried to steady my breathing, but the heat from his body was passing into my own. It flickered up my arm, across my chest and into my core, igniting some new and unfamiliar fire within me, boiling up my blood, making it swirl and pump around until I thought I might faint with the giddiness. Worst and yet best of all, my thumping heart plummeted straight through me and landed firmly in my you-know-where. Throb throb throb, it went and sparks, like popping Space Dust in my knickers, turned my body into something electrifying and utterly thrilling. I wanted the play to go on for ever.

I didn't move a muscle but stayed like that, hands touching, blood pumping, Space Dust popping, all through the murders until the second interval when the black-out crudely broke the spell, and the harsh house lights brought the real world back.

I watched Steinberg's hands as he clapped and wondered whether he had been aware of anything at all. I myself was feeling bereft, as if something vital had been lost. Shaken, I kept my distance from him during the interval, and, when I returned to my row, Joanna, with her big, wide, plain face, was in my seat talking animatedly to Amy. I didn't reclaim it. I sat at the other end and waited to discover whatever mountain it was that Orestes was to overcome.

*

Fowler carefully and deliberately placed two heavy chairs either side of the gas fire, beneath the angel painting.

'Sit!' she said, pointing at the chair facing the desk.

I sat. It was a week or so after the toilet incident, or, as Megan was calling it, hide-and-Sikh. I was allowed back into class, but I still had to eat lunch by myself in Room 4.

Fowler lit two bars of the fire and stood up. She looked at my attire; I was in my games kit. She disapproved of this: too much leg was revealed even though it covered my knees.

'Why are your shirts always grey?' she asked.

This was a mystery to me and my mother. However much my mother tried, all our white clothes went grey. It wasn't as if she put them in a washing machine. We didn't have one. Everyone else seemed to have sparkling white socks, shirts and napkins, but mine were always off-white after the first wash. Only once had this worked in my favour. When you are initiated into meditation, you have to go and see a wise man who lives in a posh house somewhere in London. You sit down cross-legged by a candle in a little room, and he tells you your mantra, which you are never allowed to tell anyone else (turned out we all had the same one). He sprinkles some rice and flowers about the place and then he leaves you alone for ages to meditate. I tried the rice, it was hard but quite nice, and the flowers were real. When you arrive at the house, you give the man a napkin and a piece of fruit and when you leave you take away with you someone else's napkin and fruit. The best thing about initiation was I left with a bright white napkin and a beautiful big pineapple. Only someone like me, from a grey-wash family, would notice.

Some poor person left with a greying napkin and a mouldy bit of garden fruit.

'I don't know,' I said.

Fowler frowned and went to the phone on her desk and pressed a button, keeping her eyes on me all the time.

'I don't want to be disturbed,' she said, and replaced the receiver.

She was wearing a high-necked, long, navy blue dress. The bottom of the skirt was wet. It was still raining. Out of the window behind her desk I could see the rain bouncing off the glass roof of the refectory.

I had absolutely no idea what I was in here for. As far as I could tell, the day had gone smoothly. Exam results were coming through. I'd just come top in scripture, Vedic mathematics and Greek. I knew it annoyed her that she could never get at me academically.

I watched Fowler get a pair of keys from her desk and unlock her cupboard and transfer some books from her desk to the shelves: *The Bhagavad Gita*, *The Upanishads*, *The Book of Common Prayer*, *Holy Mother*, *Hermes Trismegistus*, yawn, yawn. The zip in the back of her dress had caught near the top. I could see a patch of white flesh. She wouldn't like that if she knew about it.

Her cupboard was meticulously arranged: sharpened pencils in various jars depending on their HB, three Quink ink pots lined up, two blues and one black, a glass jar full of wooden pens and another pot full of nibs of every width, depending on the task. All the shelves were labelled according to subjects.

In a little tray on the right I could see her stash of herbs, her see-through plastic bag with mint or red sage or dried daffodil or whatever it was Dr Fox had said she should drink for her chest. Dr Fox also recommended cold baths twice a day and ice compresses. I bet she did that as well. Mr Wapinski, also known as the Whopper, was mad for Dr Fox, so everyone had to be. Megan said Fox was a toady little man who lived in a plastic house in Kent with gnomes in his garden. He made her press glasses all over her body for her asthma. I'd just been staying at Megan's house for the weekend while Mum and Dad were on retreat. Her mum had made us all Dr Fox's nettle bread, and her dad had got up and walked out of the kitchen saying, 'Jesus, Maureen, if bloody Wapinski said we should all be eating camel for supper you'd be serving it up, wouldn't you?' Everyone just carried on eating, but I couldn't believe it, an adult questioning the Whopper. How I wished I lived with Megan. How I loved her dad for saying that, for the 'Jesus' bit and the 'camel' bit, let alone the 'Wapinski' bit. Megan said it was because he was Welsh.

I watched Fowler's back as she jangled her keys until she found the one she was looking for. She opened a long, flat box and pulled out some printed sheets of paper. I knew immediately what they were. They were the next exciting instalment from Sri Chabaransha.

I pictured him sitting cross-legged in a little hut in a village in India somewhere surrounded by tiger-filled jungle, his eyes closed in a trance as he dictated his wisdoms to an aide at his side, who frantically scribbled down his every word. As soon as Chabaransha's pearls ceased to flow, the aide would snatch up the papers and hot-foot it to the airport, where security guards would take the sacred pages from him, lock them in a briefcase and guard them during the long flight to Heathrow, where they'd be met by armed police who would hand-cuff themselves to the briefcase and jiggle and joggle along the Piccadilly Line towards South Ken, where they'd sprint the last couple of hundred yards until it had been safely delivered to the Whopper himself. I pictured Wapinski ravaging them in private, drooling as he read, before passing them on to Fowler and Mercer and ultimately to our deaf ears.

My mum and dad had a black and white framed photo-graph of Sri Chabaransha hanging above their bed, so I had studied him very closely. He was a fat, little man with long, shaggy hair, sitting cross-legged on the floor in a nappy thing with a big dot in the middle of his forehead. He had a drunken smile on his face, and his eyes went in different directions as if he were watching a complicated air display. But the rumour was that he could levitate and float all over the room whenever he wanted, so I was intrigued.

I watched Fowler lock the box again before chucking the pages on her desk, a bit recklessly, I thought, con-sidering she'd gone to all the trouble of locking them up. For a ghastly moment I thought she was going to give me my own personal philosophy class.

She locked her cupboard and put her keys away in the drawer before turning her focus back to me. She sat down in the chair with a sigh, as if we were going to be here for some time. She folded her hands in her lap.

She stared at me, and I stared back. The gas fire wheezed and clicked. I had nothing to say and felt quite guilt-free and was therefore determined not to be pressured into talking first. We were uncomfortably close, which presumably was the whole idea. I could smell the Dettol.

It was hard to guess Fowler's age; Deborah had once asked her at lunch, and she'd told us that she was seventy. No one had batted an eye, and a little while later Fowler had said, 'That was a joke by the way.' I examined her now. Her eyes were small and of a nondescript blue; she had hollow gaunt circles around them. I had seen a disturbing painting of a man on a bridge with his mouth wide open screaming, and she looked very like him. Her nose was long and thin, and her skin was sallow. Seventy seemed as good a guess as any.

I don't know how long we sat like this, but she began to get more and more uncomfortable. Her lips started twitching, and she gave in. She stood up and eyed me. I watched her change tack in her head. She walked around the room a bit, bouncing slightly, like a bad actress trying to be breezy, going nowhere in particular.

'Have you got any crimes of the land to confess to?' she asked.

I didn't understand the question.

'Have you?' she pushed.

'What?' I asked.

'Crimes of the land! Confess!'

I was blank.

'Oh I can wait, Caroline Stern, I can wait.'

'I don't know what you're talking about,' I said, feeling at an unfair disadvantage.

'I said, "I can wait."'

So we both waited. She underestimated my stubbornness. Eventually she got up and went back to her desk and marked a few homework books, but I could tell her heart wasn't in it. She stood up slowly and stared at me. I could see she was seething.

'Where do you learn this foul language?'

What was I meant to say? I chewed my lip.

'Where? On the streets? You disgust me.' She prowled around the desk, eyes on me all the while, like a taunted tiger.

'What am I meant to have done?' I was not going to be eaten without a fight.

'Oh yes! The innocent! You know what you are, Caroline Stern? You are a rotten apple in a box of healthy apples. You are rotten to the core. You are like a poison seeping into anything that you touch. Anyone that you go near, you contaminate!'

How I hated the fact that she could get me. I could feel the tears pricking my eyes, and she saw them.

'No, I don't,' I said, but I'd lost some of my spirit, and she could tell.

'Yes, you do.'

'No, I don't.'

'Yes, you do.'

'No, I don't.' Damn the stupid tears.

'Confess, Caroline!'

'Confess to what?'

'You're not going to get away with this. I'll get the police involved, I can promise you that. And they'll find you and they'll prosecute you, and you'll go to prison!'

What the hell had I done?

'What have I done?' I willed the tears to stop.

'Yes. What have you done?'

My head was racing with possibilities. There were one or two. She sat down and pulled her chair even closer to me, searching my face.

'Confess!'

I glared at her.

'I know you. I know you!' She was really shouting now. 'I've known you for years. Did you think I wouldn't recognize your voice on the telephone? You have been ringing me up twice a week for eight weeks now saying obscene things down the telephone! I've got the dates. I've got the times.'

I was genuinely amazed, 'No I haven't!' I said and I wondered who had; it was a stroke of genius.

I was feeling powerful now, because she had shown me her humiliation. Her hair was hanging down in strands, her cheeks were red. She was really losing it. She was blowing out through her mouth like you're meant to do when you have a stitch, trying to calm herself down.

'What did I say on the phone?' I asked, milking it.

'You know what you said, you foul-mouthed child. I would never repeat those words and I can tell you that you are not leaving this room until you confess.'

She got up and leant over and turned the gas fire off and went back to her desk.

On the third day she took me down to assembly with her. The school stood as we came in, and she told me to stand on the podium without looking up. I could feel

78

everyone's eyes on me. I stared at the wooden floorboards, the indoor sandals of the girls in the front row.

She started with the Sanskrit prayer as usual.

'Sit!' she instructed the school, and everyone sat quietly in anticipation.

'Not you!' she spat at me. My hands had gone clammy.

'I want you all to take a good look at Caroline Stern . . .'

I could not resist looking up. Maybe a hundred girls were looking at me with blank expressions on their faces. I scanned the room for Megan, but I couldn't see her.

'Do not look up!' she shouted at me so loudly that, when she carried on, her voice was hoarse. 'Take a good look at Caroline . . . because this is the last time I want to see anyone looking at her. If, however, you do, or are seen talking to her or communicating with her in any way at all, you will be severely punished. This is for your own good, girls. She is the Devil. Be warned. She will contaminate you if you are near her.'

That was the last contact I had with any of my friends. I spent all day in her study, face in the corner by the white streak, and, if she was teaching, I was outside, face pressed to the pipe, and there I had to remain until I confessed to the phone calls.

A note went out to the parents of my classmates, informing them of my dangerous influence and, according to Fowler, mothers were falling over themselves to report instances of my insubordination; someone had heard me swearing, somebody else had seen me wearing 'a shiny garment'.

And so the real punishment began. Younger children scurried away from me when I arrived the following morning; they stole looks and whispered. I tried hard to ignore them, but inside I felt both furious and embarrassed. The grown-ups, people I barely recognized, gave me icy glares and shortness.

It was quite something to be such a pillar of poison; it felt powerful in all the wrong ways. I'd imagine the poison seeping out of me, through my breath, through my eyes, through the tips of my fingers, sizzling like caustic soda, destroying everything in its path.

That first afternoon, I felt a tap on my shoulder and I turned round from the pipe. It was a brave person who dared speak to me. It was Deborah's mother.

'You don't belong here any more,' she said, smugly, as if she could now tell people that she'd had her say. It quite threw me; I had thought she was going to be kind.

'Good,' I said to her. 'I hate the lot of you.'

And I did. I despised the whole pack of them. I turned back to the hot pipe, pressing my forehead to it until it burnt. Inside, I was boiling like a volcano, bubbling with red-hot hate, and every now and then I could contain it no longer. It would spew out in a cry, and raging tears would burn down my cheeks. I despised every single sheep-brained grown-up who swallowed what they were told, unquestioningly. I swore to myself that I would never ever respect age or authority.

When I could bear it no longer, I would close my eyes and imagine I was floating out of my body, like a kite, drifting up to the top of the building, out of the window into the sky, away from this horrible street, up over Hyde Park, off over London, up higher and higher through the sky into space, free at last.

One afternoon, outside the study, face pressed to the pipe, I heard a familiar voice behind me.

'Caroline?'

I didn't move an inch, 'Hey, Caroline?' I turned an infinitesimal degree. It was Steinberg looking down at me, his lovely face a picture of concern.

'Hey darlin',' he said with his gentle American twang. 'Don't cry, what's going on?'

He'd never called me 'darlin'' before, but then again he'd never seen me cry. As discreetly as possible I raised my finger to my lips and pressed my face hard into the pipe.

'Hey, Caroline!' He sounded really worried – he only knew me as a joker. He put his hand on my shoulder. 'This isn't like you . . . what's up?'

'She thinks I'm lying!' I whispered, panicking, eyes flicking, checking she wasn't about. 'That builder with the turban, he touched me . . . and she doesn't believe me.'

I could tell by his face Steinberg knew what I meant straight away. He didn't know what to say. I shook my head. 'You're not allowed to talk to me. No one is. She'll kill me.'

'The Sikh guy? Downstairs?' he asked, and I gave a quick nod.

'I believe you. He was working at my apartment. My girlfriend said she didn't like the way he looked at her.'

My heart skipped a beat. For two reasons. Someone believed me. And he had a girlfriend.

Just then, out of the corner of my eye I could see the long home-sewn skirt of Fowler swooshing up behind him. I felt sick, 'Get your hand off me,' I wanted to say. And 'Keep it there, please.'

'Tell her!' I whispered.

'Mr Steinberg!' Fowler snapped at him like he was a schoolboy, and I actually saw him flinch. 'Leave that child alone!'

He stared at her, his mouth slightly open as she roughly grabbed my shoulders and pushed me into her study. She shut the door on him.

The next day Amy tried to make contact with me, but I was silent now. I didn't want to talk to anyone. She came into Fowler's study under some pretext and blew me a kiss on her way out. I looked away, for her sake. I kept pretending to be the kite drifting higher and higher.

Fowler knew she'd won. She had a skip to her step. She was in a good mood all the time. On the fifth day, I caught sight of my face in the brass door mount; my eyes were slits, bloated and puffed with crying. I couldn't take any more.

I whispered to the white streak on the wall, 'I did it.'

'What?' she said from her desk.

'I did it.'

'Louder please!' she said chirpily.

'I did it. I made the telephone calls.'

I stared into the brass mount, at the reflected Mary in the Masaccio painting above the fireplace. You could tell by her face she'd had enough of the stinking, old angel. Just give me a break, she was saying, leave me alone and I'll say whatever you want. Poor old Mary was tired and hungry, delirious with lack of food. She wasn't listening to the angel. She was thinking about Joseph and the weight of his hand on her shoulder and the way he had said, 'Hey, darlin', don't cry' in his lovely American accent. She was remembering how his kindness made all the difference in the world. How she wanted him to keep his hand on her shoulder, to lift her up and take her away from all this.

4

I was behaving distinctly oddly. On passing one of the antiques shops on Golborne Road, I had, in a fit of uncharacteristic extravagance, purchased an eighteenth-century, silk-upholstered, German sofa, which, miraculously, had fitted through our front door. Joe wasn't around. He was at a training day, so the man and I had heaved it into the sitting room. I spent the next hour or so sitting on it, staring out of the window, with Tilly eyeing me covetously from her lowly basket.

Despite what I advised my clients, 'avoidance' had worked very well for me for a long time. And then I'd gone and blown it all with four reckless words, 'My parents aren't dead.' I'd had a constant stomach ache and nausea ever since. I was demonstrating such blaringly obvious triggers and reactions, I could have been a case study in a Cognitive Behavioural Therapy manual. Highlighted with little pictures of me, hair all messed up, clutching my tummy on an eighteenth-century, silk-upholstered, German fucking sofa. Next thing I knew I'd be having a panic attack, spazzing out in Tilly's basket.

'That's sick,' Joe had said to me. 'The whole car crash thing. Why couldn't you just tell the truth? Say you don't see your parents any more?'

The truth? He had no idea. I'd sat there, gormlessly staring at the floor watching the worms wriggle out of the can. At the time, I'd felt that telling him they weren't dead was almost an act of kindness; giving the condemned man a blindfold before I shot him, kind of thing. The only trouble was, after the blindfold was on, I couldn't pull the trigger.

'They were God-botherers,' I'd added feebly. 'I couldn't take it any more.'

'What sort of religion were they?'

'Does it matter?'

'Did your parents cut you off, or did you cut them off?'

'Jesus! Joe! What is this? *Twenty Questions*?' I'd busied myself in the fridge. 'If you must know, *I* cut *them* off,' I'd said, unable to keep the disdain from my voice.

'Why?' he'd asked.

'Because they were weak.'

He had laughed, disbelieving. 'Weak? Should we be punished for being weak?'

I'd turned around then and stared at him, deadly serious. 'Oh, yes. We should.'

I stopped gawping out of the window, got up off the sofa and began to wander aimlessly about the house, seeking out distraction, rootling through drawers for no particular reason, chucking out ten-year-old mascaras and trying on pale blue eye-shadows, tipping shelffuls of clothes on to the floor, pulling out the odd brightly coloured garment and wondering what on earth had possessed me to buy it. Then trying it on and deciding that it wasn't so bad, and popping it neatly back in the cupboard, where it wouldn't see the light of day again, until I did my next sort-through. I had been trying on so many peculiar pieces from the past that I resembled a children's TV presenter – horribly jolly with a touch of the buffoon about me.

In that attractive state, I answered the door to one of those hawkers who never leave when you're politely telling them to piss off. But today I let him get out his wares on the doorstep; I needed the company. I even bought some overpriced oven gloves, a pet hair removal thing and a cheeseboard. Any old rubbish. I didn't really care. I nearly asked him in for a coffee, but he looked kind of keen to get away.

For a while I returned to the sofa and groomed Tilly, but I kept getting that kick-in-the-stomach feeling, so I took my cheeseboard into the kitchen to make myself some cheese on toast. To which there is an art.

The toast must be grilled on one side only, the butter thinly spread on to the uncooked side, followed by a layer of thinly sliced tomato (with no overlapping edges) placed underneath the cheese, which must be Cheddar and be all of the same thickness and pieced together as snugly as a jigsaw, not doubling yet leaving no gaps. Most importantly, it has to go all the way to the edges of the bread before the entire thing is grilled to melting point, but not burnt. Today, however, I was all over the place. It was undercooked and overlapping, and I'd forgotten the thin layer of Branston pickle. I wolfed it down without tasting it, gazing out of the kitchen window at the neighbours' brick wall.

My lies had become the backbone of my life. And up until now, that had worked just fine. But suddenly I felt as fragile as a house of cards. One little truth and I was beginning to collapse. Why had I told him the truth? What had changed me? I knew, of course. I knew exactly what and when everything changed. It was her, the fat woman holding the pitchfork, the split second when I recognized Amy. My beloved Amy. I couldn't get her out of my head, standing there with her short hair and her big blue eyes so full of love when she saw me. And then her bewilderment when I blanked her. How could I do that to her? How had that made her feel?

'Fuck!' I suddenly screamed, chucking my crusts across the kitchen. '*Fuck!*'

Tilly trotted in, staring at me with victim eyes, wagging her tail nervously as if it were all her fault. Although, now I came to think of it, is *was* all her fault. Fucking psycho dog.

'Come on! We're going out!'

I marched down Portobello to Westbourne Grove with Tilly tugging on the lead. I sat on a bench on the island by the flower stall and watched the woman selling her flowers. She looked happy, lucky cow. Really happy. What a nice job being a flower seller, apart from the cold fingers and the weather, but everyone's happy to give you their money. My mind began to calm down a little. I could smell the leafy sweetness of her stall. By my reckoning, the average customer was a woman in her late thirties with blonde hair and nice clothes. Me, really.

A dark-haired girl in great boots picked up a beautiful bunch of lilies. The boots were just what I was unknowingly after: a low heel, a bit bikery, borderline dykey. I tended not to wear heels; I always liked to feel that I could run away if I had to. Boot woman was just paying for the lilies when another woman in trainers tapped her on the shoulder. She turned around and they both started yelping with delight, squashing the flowers between them as they hugged.

I saw it then, the problem. I was desperately lonely. I missed Amy. I missed my school friends. I had friends these days, of course, but not ones like those, not friends who really understood it all.

By the time I got back, it was five o'clock, and Joe still wasn't home. A gleaming, glossy Tilly and I lay in a luxurious kind of embrace on the eighteenth-century, silk-upholstered sofa. I was pretending to watch the telly, but my stomach ache had come back, and my mind was whirring again.

Then, quite suddenly, as if I were observing someone else, I watched myself swiftly get up off the sofa, go purposefully over to the telephone, pick it up, flick through my address book and dial a number. I caught up with myself just as someone answered the phone.

'Hello?' said a male voice.

'Hello? Would it be possible to speak to Amy Jones, please?'

'Amy Jones? Do you mean Amy Johnson?'

'Oh . . . yes, probably.'

'Hang on! . . . Amy? For you.'

I waited as a dog barked in the background.

'Hello?' Amy's voice had grown surprisingly husky over the years.

'Amy Jones . . . it's me.'

She paused.

'Caroline!' she said, quietly. She didn't even sound surprised. 'I've been expecting you to ring.'

It was pissing with rain. The Heath was almost deserted except for the hardiest of dog walkers. I was cold and wet as I walked through the naked, glum trees on this, the bleakest of days. Even Tilly didn't want to be here: her tail was hunched between her legs, and her head drooped; she hated the rain.

Whenever we passed another dog walker I would inevitably be drawn into conversation due to Tilly's peculiar new look. She had been fitted with a large black canister that hung around her neck on a thick black collar, like a suicide bomber. The very moment she set off in pursuit of a bicycle, a horse or a jogger, or at the merest whiff of a dog fight, I was under strict instructions not to call out her name; all I had to do was raise my arm and aim my remote control at her. When I pressed the button, a jet of citronella squirted into her face from the canister and her dog-brain related the unpleasant shock of it to the dog or the bike or the horse or whatever, and she'd stop immediately. Only I'd been finding it really hard not to yell out at the same time, and Tilly had soon begun to relate the squirt to me rather than the moving object. She had started to look back at me with the same expression Joe made, wounded and hurt by my meanness.

If only my own behavioural problems could be solved with a squirt of citronella. I was still having the bad dreams and had moved myself downstairs to the sofa, which didn't make much difference to our non-existent love life. I still wasn't sure that I could carry on with the whole relationship and I could tell he didn't trust me now. He knew there were more lies, and it made me prickly. It wasn't really fair; he had no idea what he was up against.

The rain was getting through to the back of my neck, so I pulled my collar up. The next thing I knew, Tilly was in a whirlwind of a fight with two Dalmatians. I fumbled around in my slippery wet pocket for the remote, aimed it at the growling mass and pressed the button. Nothing. It was soaking wet. Damn! I pressed again and wow! The three of them flew away from each other suddenly and violently as if someone had shoved fireworks up their arses.

The Dalmatians' owner looked mightily impressed and started asking me about the contraption, but I didn't feel like talking, I was too edgy. I put Tilly on the lead as a punishment and walked towards Kenwood House. But she soon tugged and pulled, and I let her off.

We'd said we'd meet outside the café, but in the downpour I presumed she'd have gone inside.

As I walked towards the house I wondered what the hell I was doing. It wasn't too late, I could go back, I could get myself back on track, get back to Joe, to the secrets. But some part of me knew that I had no choice, that I was already on the roller-coaster and I couldn't get off. Not yet.

I was right. There she was, sitting by the window in the tea rooms, the only person there. I saw her before she saw me, her face in repose, her features still beautiful but more rounded now like her body. Her short, cropped hair was much darker now and had lost its nylon shine.

She was staring out at the pouring rain, and I could see that the years had taken their toll. There was a sadness in her eyes that I didn't remember; the corners of her mouth sloped downwards as though there had been little laughter in her life.

Then she turned and saw Tilly and me, and I let the lead go. Tilly ran over, and Amy welcomed her like the long-lost friend that I was. When she'd finished with Tilly she looked up at me, and we held each other's gaze. I think neither of us moved for a very long time. But then somehow I found myself in her arms with her squeezing the living daylights out of me. I felt indescribably safe, there against her soft body, scooped into her being, replete with her unconditional love. I didn't want to ever move. I could have died there in her arms, in the peace that I craved. I felt like a circuit that had just been completed. Everything was going to be all right.

But a woman came over and told us that Tilly wasn't allowed inside, so the three of us went and sat outside in the rain under a large umbrella in the garden. The strange thing was, we didn't talk at all: twenty-five years and the rest of it seemed too impossible to put into words, so neither of us bothered. Amy held my hand, and we just watched the rain falling around us.

'Are you still in it, Amy? Are you still in the Organization?'

'No,' she said, flatly. 'I left twenty years ago.'

I sighed with relief. 'I don't talk about it,' I said. 'I never talk about it.'

'That's okay,' she said, soothingly. 'I don't really either. Most people don't. Not those who've left.' I leant my head on her shoulder and sighed again. The rain was showing no signs of letting up.

After a while, she turned towards me and said with some detachment, 'What do you do these days, Caroline?'

I paused and leant on one elbow to face her. 'I'm a family therapist,' I said.

She sat bolt upright and then she began to howl with laughter. We laughed until the tears rolled down our cheeks.

Two days later, when I got home from work, I was greeted by a sheepish Tilly and found Joe in a pair of washing-up gloves cleaning a pile of white, transparent puke off the eighteenth-century sofa. On the floor at its side was an empty, thoroughly licked wrapper of lard.

'Oh no!' I said.

'Bloody dog! She's going back to Battersea.' Joe was swiping at the sofa. 'Battersea, you fucking mutt!' he said, directing his gruffness towards the kitchen table. I saw a quivering brown thing underneath it. Joe was pissed off; he never swore at the dog. A few weeks ago, he would have made light of it and said something like, 'Well, it's all good preparation for having kids.'

'*You* can do it!' he said, ripping off the gloves. What did I expect? I wiped up the greasy mess. The sofa was ruined. Fucking dog.

Joe disappeared upstairs, and I could hear the shower go on. When he came back down he didn't say anything. He went straight to the kitchen and got a beer out of the fridge. He would never have done that a few weeks ago either. He would have automatically brought me one as well. He sat down on the other sofa and put his feet up and picked up the paper.

'Are you all right?' I asked.

'Fine,' he replied, tight-lipped.

'Well you're obviously not.' I'd assumed a self-righteous tone, which even I found irritating.

'Oh, so we're communicating now, are we?' he said, putting down the paper. 'When it's convenient for you?'

I went to the kitchen and got myself a beer.

'What's your problem?' I was using my best therapist voice, calm and deceptive.

'There's a message on the answer machine, if you want to listen.'

His tone was so accusatory, for a moment I had to ask myself whether I was having an affair. I went to the machine. He'd obviously already listened to it, the light wasn't flashing. I pressed play. I didn't recognize Amy's voice at first, it had grown so husky. She sounded excited. 'Caroline, Joe! It's Amy. Caroline, it was so lovely to see you on the Heath. Look! I'm going down to Cornwall next week. Dad's just lent me the farmhouse. Please come down, you guys. Come on, Caroline, no ifs, no buts. Joe, you've got to come. Make her come! Ring me!'

I looked at Joe. He was standing up now, swigging his beer from the bottle, one hand on hip, ready for a battle.

'How nice!' he said, sarcastically. 'Funny how you never mentioned that you'd met up with her on the Heath. Or, in fact, acknowledged to me that you even knew her!'

What could I say? I chewed my cheek. I was finding his whole sarky cop routine distasteful. I wandered over to the window and watched the woman over the road putting out her rubbish.

'Tell me something! One thing ...' he said. 'What is your name?'

I answered calmly, trying to placate his rising anger. 'It used to be Caroline but now it's Lorrie. I changed it when I left home.'

He was leaning against the kitchen doorway, arms folded. 'Lorrie, Caroline, whatever you're called. I can't do this any more. I can't. I've had enough of your bullshit. God knows what other lies you've told me. I'm off. I'm moving out.'

He went into the kitchen and started pointedly tidying up. I was speechless. He was dumping me.

'What?' I said, aghast.

'You heard.'

No, this wasn't right. Joe was finishing with me. I couldn't lose Joe. He was essential to me. I loved him.

'Oh wait, Joe. Please!' I cried, stumbling into the kitchen behind him. 'Just a little longer. I'm sorry. Yes I met up with her. We were at school together, Amy and I.'

'You were at school together? So what's the big deal?'

I looked into his eyes. He was properly cross.

'No big deal.'

He sighed and looked down, wiping his brow, weight on one leg.

'You just don't get it, Lorrie. Why all the secrecy?'

'You don't want to know.'

'I do!' he said, raising his voice. 'I do want to know!'

'Bad things.'

94

'What? What bad things? Is it about your parents?'

'Don't, Joe!'

'Was your dad sexually abusing you, Lorrie?'

I was tempted to say yes, that could nicely plug the flow of questions.

'No.'

'Then what?' he said.

'It was a strange school, Joe.'

'Strange how?'

I begged him with my eyes not to keep probing, and we held that pose for a good half minute.

Eventually he sighed. 'You don't have to tell me,' he said, gently. 'But I'm at the end of my tether, Lorrie.'

'Don't give up on me yet, Joe. Please. I need you.'

He leant against the counter and bowed his head.

'Do you want to go to Cornwall?' he asked.

Oh my God. No. Yes. I don't know. Would it be safe? Amy was nothing to do with the Organization any more. She didn't talk about it either. Oh shit, I don't know. If it would stop Joe leaving me, yes.

'I think so. With you. Will you come?'

He rolled his eyes at me. 'You are a fucking fruitcake,' he said, but he said it as if he quite liked fruitcakes.

The A303 is a beautiful road: villages with quirky names, country roads cupped by trees, branches kissing up above, green, hilly English countryside at its best. The late afternoon sun cast long shadows across the fields, and everything glowed in a golden light. I like travelling by car. I like the dreamy otherworldliness of a long car journey. I looked at Joe at the wheel, his bottom lip jutting out, lost in a driving limbo. I twisted round; there on the back seat, lying across our duvet, tummy exposed, was Tilly. I couldn't resist a little rub of her hot digestive-biscuit-smelling flesh. To all intents and purposes we looked like a happy little family.

I plonked a load of wine gums on Joe's lap and munched my way through the rest of the packet.

Joe and I had made love that night when he told me the relationship was over. I had initiated it. I needed it. He had pinned me down with an urgency. We both knew we were in last-chance saloon, and it was all a bit desperate and clawing. During it he'd said, 'I'm going to get through to you one way or another, Lorrie Fischer, Caroline Stern, whoever the fuck you are.' I'm a sucker for that sort of macho crap.

'Wow!' he said, as the road forked, and Stonehenge appeared on our right.

'Mmm,' I agreed, my mind wandering. I was nervous about staying with Amy, nervous yet excited. I could feel it in my belly. I was monitoring exactly which thoughts were resulting in which physical response.

The sky was dark by the time we got off the A30, just a yellow moon beaming. I wound down the window, and the cold air rushed in. Tilly got up and stuck her head out next to mine. I could smell the sea. My spirits soared as we hit the coastal road and got our first glimpse of the Atlantic: black and pounding, white horses glinting in the moonlight. I'd forgotten how completely beautiful it was here, how the landscape could take your breath away.

The cottages were situated on a cliff at the top of a hill, where the sea gives the rocks such a hammering that they tumble down quite frequently – living proof that everything ultimately collapses under too much pressure.

'Where now?' Joe asked.

Shit. It looked different in the dark. And I hadn't been here for twenty-six years. 'Er ... it's one of these turn-offs. Maybe we've gone past it. Turn around.'

We drove around a bit, but I still didn't recognize anything. I decided to ring the cottage, but couldn't get any reception on my mobile. Jesus. Bloody country life. What did they do, send smoke signals? Eventually, at the top of the previous hill my mobile signal came on. Joe stopped the car, and I rang the cottage.

'Amy?' I said. I could hear lots of people in the background. I knew she had six kids, but it sounded like a party going on.

'Caroline! Where are you?'

'We're about two minutes away, at the top of the hill by the sign post. Which turning is it?'

'Oh fab! It's third on the right. Megan and Co. are here. And Marcus.'

'What?' I said. Kick in the stomach. I suddenly needed Joe not to be listening. My heart began to pound. I opened the door and got out. The air was freezing and hit me like a wall. My legs felt numb from sitting down for so long.

'Amy ...' I whispered into the receiver as I walked around to the back of the car. I could see Joe getting out to stretch his legs. 'Amy, listen to me. You never said there'd be others. I can't talk about it ... You promised. If anyone mentions "her" I'm leaving. Okay?'

I was beginning to panic. I couldn't even bring myself

to say Fowler's name, as if saying it might make her real again.

'Yes, I've told them that you don't want to talk about the past. Look, I'm sorry, Caroline. Marcus asked them yesterday. Listen, it's the third little road on the right. Shall I come down and get you?'

'No. We'll be fine.' I closed my mobile, feeling shaky. I lit myself a cigarette and got back in the car.

As he restarted the engine I said, 'Joe. Can we go home?'

'What?'

'Can we go home?'

'Why?'

'I can't do it.'

'Is this to do with "her"?' he asked. He'd been listening. I didn't reply.

'And no, we are not going home. I didn't drive five hours to go home. Which road is it?'

'Third on the right,' I said. 'Confront,' I said to myself. Confrontation was the only way now. I flicked down the passenger mirror, checking my reflection to see how much damage there had been in the last twenty-five years.

'This is it!' I said, as we got up the hill again. The lane was easy to miss, backing down on itself.

'Stop!' I said as we turned down it. He did so.

I looked up at the courtyard of cottages lit up by four old-fashioned lamps. Grey flint stones, grey slated roofs, wooden slatted doors. They were once pig sties, Amy's dad had converted them. They were utterly unchanged. In the middle of the courtyard hung a set of swings, ropes with wooden seats on a wooden frame. They too appeared untouched by the years. Behind the cottages, silver clouds whirled across the moon, eager to get somewhere else.

'Drive as far as you can down here!'

We drove past a few new cottages that I didn't remember and then we stopped outside the farmhouse. A porch light came on. I got myself out of the car, as did Joe. Tilly made a run for it. The farmhouse door opened, and two tiny people came running out, then two more, slightly bigger, and then some big people.

The littlest person, a tiny kid, was running towards me down the path. I didn't know what I was meant to do; children were an alien species to me. The child just kept running and threw itself into my arms until I had no choice but to catch it and swing it up into the air. It clung to me and hugged me. I don't think I had ever held a child before. I didn't realize that they could be this disarming. She was a girl and she looked at me with big, brown uncomplicated eyes. I held her away from me and studied her smooth, open, happy face, her hair shining in the lamp light, little freckles all over her nose. Oh my God. She was Megan. She was my beloved Megan. I was four years old again. I felt a lump in my throat. I thanked God for the darkness.

'You've got to be Megan's little girl!'

'My mummy!' she said and pointed towards the house.

I looked up, and standing in the farmhouse porch was a small, plump woman. She ran straight towards me, screaming with delight, and we embraced so hard we nearly squashed her little girl. How can twenty-five years vanish in a flash? How can those years suddenly seem

99

insignificant and dreamlike? How familiar she was to me! How good it was to feel her in my arms, to smell her again; dough and milk! She pushed me away, and we examined each other. Her mischievous brown eyes were wet with tears. We put our hands on each other's face like blind people. I knew her face as well as my own; I could read her every expression.

She dragged me into the light and stared at me hard. She still had that wide, innocent face, a few crow's feet, but otherwise just the same. Her face told the tale of a happy, uncomplicated life. I could detect no tragedy there.

'Oh my beautiful Caroline,' she said, quietly, but with a sorrowful undertone. Clearly my face didn't read quite so positively.

'Oh Megan, look at you! You look just the same!' I said, not even self-conscious that Joe might see me being so ... emotional. All my nerves had gone. This felt good and right, like coming home.

'No I don't! I found a grey hair the other day!' She laughed and squeezed me to her. Then she turned and saw Joe.

'Joe? Are you Joe?' I had forgotten how charming she was. 'Nice one Caroline!' she said raising her eyebrows at me. And he did look like a 'nice one'. Briefly I saw him through a stranger's eyes, this big, black, cool dude. And I felt a surge of love for him. This was good. This was all good.

He laughed as she bearhugged him, and I was glad that he was here, that I too had some sort of family. I was still holding Megan's mini-me, and it all felt like the most natural thing in the world. I almost wished that I had been able to conceive and had my own little mini-me running about.

Joe was shaking hands with all the kids and introducing Tilly as we piled into the farmhouse.

The farmhouse had not changed a jot – the bare necessities, nothing extraneous: two sofas, an armchair, a wooden table, a piano, a desk. It still had a faint whiff of the Organization, but minus the holy paintings. A few friend-drawn watercolours hung about the place instead. A fire was roaring.

'How many of these are yours?' I asked Megan, looking round at the kids.

'Just two!' she said beaming. 'These two!' She pointed at one of the teenagers, a tall attractive boy of about fifteen. 'And the afterthought,' she said, ruffling the hair of the little girl in my arms. 'Caroline.'

I stopped in my tracks, but I didn't want to be presumptuous. After all, so many years had slipped by.

'Named after you,' she smiled. I nodded. I didn't know what to say. I didn't mention that it was no longer my name.

'The others are all Amy's and Marcus's.'

'Are they?' I looked about me. There is nothing like the children of friends to make you feel the whizz of the years gone by, the brevity of our little lifetimes.

'Where's Amy?'

'She's lighting a fire for you. In your cottage.'

The door opened again, and a man came in. A tall, good-looking man with dark hair and glasses carrying a bundle of logs in his arms. He was smiling at me, a broad, warm, familiar smile. My heart flipped a somersault.

'I don't believe it!' I said. 'It's Mr Steinberg! What's he doing here?'

Everyone laughed. I was not in on the joke. I could feel all eyes in the room on me.

'He's my husband!' Megan said.

I can honestly say that I was completely speechless. When I tried to analyse it, I knew there was a huge mixture of feelings, but the predominant one was disbelief at Megan's treachery. Megan marrying Steinberg? He was surely out of bounds. She knew how much I had loved him. I was his Greek gal.

I know similar thoughts were going through her head because there was a brief moment, just as everyone was laughing, when she couldn't meet my eye and, when she did, she said something daft.

'Nate! Caroline and Joe are here!'

Nate. She called him Nate. Not even Nathaniel.

'So I see!' he said, his eyes locking mine.

I couldn't stop staring at him. Time had barely changed him. He was as beautiful as I had remembered him, if not more so. Age suited him, although I supposed he was probably only forty-seven. The age gap had completely vanished. He came towards me, shaking his head with disbelief.

'Caroline Stern!'

He said my old name with such relish in his beautiful lilting accent that I almost wanted to reclaim it.

Then it was my turn to say something stupid. 'You've got new glasses!'

Everyone laughed again, but he didn't. He kept smiling at me and said, 'That's right, I do,' as if I'd said something mightily clever. 'I used to have those old social worker specs, didn't I?' They were clearly a fond memory for him.

He was leaning forward now as if he were going to kiss me, as if that was the most natural thing in the world, like we'd been meeting at fucking dinner parties for the last twenty years. And he did. Mr Steinberg kissed me. It was awkward, made more so by the logs, and little Caroline and we ended up in a strange embrace, his daughter slipping into his arms as we parted.

'Mr Steinberg,' I said, the feeling of his flesh against mine still burning on my cheek. 'This is Joe!'

'You can't call him Mr Steinberg!' Megan laughed, as if I'd said something hysterically funny.

'Well, what am I meant to call him?' I said turning to her. 'I only know him as my teacher.'

I had meant to hurt her. She should stop laughing at me.

'Your teacher?' said Joe, who just at that moment was shaking Steinberg's hand.

'Caroline,' said Megan, grabbing my hand, pulling me into her arms. 'It's so good to see you.' She squeezed my cheeks, a little too hard. I remembered that she'd always done that, 'What happened to you?' she said, shaking me like I was a rag doll. 'What was it like in Scotland?'

I had absolutely no idea what she was talking about.

'Scotland?'

'With your relatives in Scotland? Why didn't you ever get in touch?'

So that's what my parents told them. It turns out we're all fucking liars.

There was only one thing for it. I was going to get drunk. Arse-bendingly drunk.

I did just that. I was way too gone to walk back to our cottage unaided. Joe was kind of carrying me, but I think he was pretty drunk as well. I kept slipping on the muddy ground and I could feel warm blood dripping down my knee where I'd tripped on a rock. My only navigation in the darkness was the white flash of Tilly's bum.

I'd been holding myself together in there, in the farmhouse, I was amazed at myself, how jolly and amusing I'd been, falling straight back into the joker Caroloony role, when inside a part of me wanted to beat them all to a pulp. They were still in it. Megan, Steinberg, Marcus and his wife were all still in the fucking Organization. Only Amy had seen the light.

So whilst joking on the outside, inside I'd been dealt a double whammy. Megan had married Steinberg. And they were all still there. Thanks a bunch, Amy.

All through the evening I had kept referring back to Megan's betrayal, try as she might to change the subject.

'Have you been there all these years?' I asked. 'Never left?'

'No, I've never left. Don't look at me like that's so odd!' she laughed. 'Marcus has never left! And Kate and Joanna. There are lots of us still there.'

'Who's not there, then?'

'Oh, Deborah went a bit screwy,' she said blithely. 'Anna left; she turned very strange.'

How could she talk so flippantly? I couldn't ask any more. I knew I was treading a fine line.

'Megan,' I said. 'Why are you still there? Have you never wanted to think for yourself, to find out what you actually believe in?'

I should have known better. She had never had a particularly curious mind, quirky and quick but never curious. After another few glasses, I had warmed up. There was something else preying on me.

'So . . .' I had to ask, otherwise it was going to hang in the air, and, to be honest, for the first time in twenty-five years I needed to know whether they were still alive, perhaps because here were the only people who could tell me.

'Are my parents still there?'

Megan nodded, 'Yes, your mother is . . .'

Well what an idiotic question that was; as if they could have existed without the Organization, as if they would ever have had enough gumption to leave. I didn't want to know any more.

'But, Caroline, didn't you know? Your dad died.'

Didn't I know? How on earth would I have known that?

My father was dead. I realized that the words should have had a momentous effect on me, but they didn't. He had been dead to me for a long time. I didn't feel anything about it, nothing at all. Analyse that, Lorrie Fischer.

'When did he die?'

'Only recently. Last summer.'

'What did he die of?'

'A heart attack. I'm so sorry, Caroline.'

'Why? Did you like him?'

She was shocked by my heartlessness, I could see.

'I'm just saying I'm sorry.'

'Well, don't be. I'm not.'

I knocked back the wine fast and shortly began to feel a little high, a little less wound up, a little bit freer, a little bit wired. Death's release, I suppose.

Perhaps it is the nature of reunions, but I started to feel thirteen years old again. I looked about the room. Marcus and his wife had turned up. Marcus, who I used to kiss on the lips at Gloucester Road tube station, until it had begun to feel a bit of a chore – his dry, chapped lips were getting a bit off-putting. I couldn't help but notice that they were still a bit dry. His wife was an overly hearty presence; she had a galumphing happiness I found both endearing and dim. I remembered her from school: she was a brainbox a few years my junior. One of his children, a sombre-faced eight-going-on-fifty-year-old called Lakshmi – do me a favour! – was playing the piano with surprising alacrity, and people were singing. The wine was flowing.

It was clear, looking about the room, that the Organization people, in their spurning of the material world and all its vanities, were not looking as good as we fugitives. How pleasing. They were make-up-less and dowdy, grey roots and wrinkles. I revelled in my own looks, maintained with lotions and potions and all that the material world had to offer.

The more I drank, the more waspish I became. I was talking with Amy, I didn't yet feel safe with Megan. I still wanted to shake her to her senses. All the while, my antennae were out; I knew exactly where Steinberg was in the room. Maybe he felt a little odd surrounded by us girls, us schoolgirls. Joe and he were by the fire, talking about American football, nice safe male territory, but they both had one ear on us. I could tell, I could almost see their ears flapping.

I couldn't take my eyes off Steinberg's boy. He was the spit of his father, only with his mother's colouring. He caught me staring at him.

'I'm sorry,' I said. 'You ... just take me back, straight back. You look so like your father.'

'Great!' he said sarcastically. Oh yes, I wanted to say, it is great, just you wait.

'How old are you, Cameron?' I asked.

'Nearly sixteen.'

That made Megan twenty-two when she had him.

'Where do you live? Where do you go to school?'

He was holding a bottle of beer, which he was twisting in his hand, fast, deftly. He had it, whatever it was, he had it.

'St Augustine's, but we live in Chiswick.'

'What?' I cried. 'They don't send you there, do they?'

He laughed. 'Why do you say that?' He really had no idea. We were joined by the middle-aged child, who kept staring at me. I was struck again by how shocked I felt. How could they do that to me, to us, to all the people who had suffered there? How could Megan do it?

'And you?' I said. 'Where do you go to school?' Although, did I really need to ask, with a name like Lakshmi?

'Same!' she said, smiling, as if it was all just a game.

'And how do you like ...' I hadn't said the words for

so many years. I felt my tongue go dry as I turned to Cameron. 'How do you like . . . St Augustine's?'

'It's okay.'

Okay? Okay?

'Really?' I said, searching his face for telltale lying signals, but found none. 'What about you, Lakshmi?' I said turning to the middle-aged child.

'Yes, I thoroughly enjoy it,' she replied, with an incongruous maturity. Perhaps she really was fifty in an awful miniature frame, the punishment for some terrible Karmic crime. Megan joined us, casually fondling the child's hair.

'She's a great student!' Megan said. 'She's top of my class.'

'Your class? You teach there?' I said, astounded.

I stared at Megan. I felt an incredulity and fury at her weakness. It made no sense. She had always been a rebel. Had nothing meant anything to her? Had we been through totally different experiences? How could she have become complicit with the enemy?

'It's such a different place now, Caroline. Since Mr Wapinski stopped running it. It's completely different. You wouldn't recognize it.'

I glared at her. She'd spoken so heedlessly, as if, now that the school was different, that made everything all right, the past counted for nothing. I wanted to slap her. But we were in dangerous territory; I needed to get off the subject.

The girl put her arms around Megan and leant on her, easily, like a child on a parent. Here lay the crux of the Organization school: a teacher had the same form from four years old until they were eighteen; they became their guardians; they took on a parental role. In fact I would say they were considered more influential and more powerful than a parent. It was just luck of the draw as to who your form teacher was. Or unluck of the draw.

'So,' I said to the kids, trying to provoke, to upset their happy-clappy apple cart. 'Do you still do a lot of singing?'

'Yes, we do,' said Cameron, it was clearly not his favourite activity.

'Still singing that old favourite, "Pull out the golden stopper?"' I asked.

In his boundless supremacy, the Whopper had fancied himself as a composer and had set the Upanishads to music. I use the term loosely. We numpties had had to sing his works in public. Obviously not in public – mixing with the public was actively discouraged – but we had had to sing it in front of all our peers.

Lakshmi and Cameron shook their heads; they didn't know what I was talking about.

'Didst thou bring forth this Universe? Pull it, Lord! Pull it, Lord!' I sung, trying to jog their memories. Aware, as well, that I was getting a bit pissed now. They shook their heads. This made me cross; they should have to sing the same ridiculous, humiliating songs that we had had to. It wasn't fair on the rest of us.

To my surprise and annoyance, Megan started laughing as if I was the funniest person in the world. If it was so laughable, why had she sent her children there?

But I had forgotten what a brilliant mimic she was, what a talent she had. Who knows what would have become of her in the real world? She did an impression of the useless music teacher, Mr Crane, and despite myself, she made me laugh so hard that I ached. Amy started remembering more. 'Holy is Govinda,' she sang in the tuneless monotone Whopper style, 'The father of all!' Only, for some unknown and, frankly, foolish reason, we had had to pronounce the word 'father' as 'farter'. Hilarious to a bunch of eight-year-olds, and, evidently, thirty-eight-year-olds.

It *was* funny, those stupid, stupid songs.

'Correct me if I'm wrong,' I said quietly, turning to Amy. 'But it *was* a fucking madhouse, wasn't it?'

She nodded. 'Oh yes,' she said, raising her eyebrows. 'Don't ever doubt that.'

Once that was settled, I began to feel a surge of immense happiness, of warmth even, of belonging and, dare I say it, of safety. I looked about me. There were all the kids singing around the piano, like we were on a cumbaya-me-lord bloody campsite. I looked at Joe, suddenly wondering whether he might be feeling excluded. I caught his eye, and he winked at me. He was looking at me afresh, as if I were new to him, and as if he liked what he saw.

Then, nicely lubricated by a bottle of Sauvignon, I briefly let go my guard and my judgements and found myself joining in on the inevitable 'do you remembers?'. Not too much, just a little. No one had mentioned Fowler.

Steinberg was next to me now. I could feel him watching me, charmed by me, and it gave me a thrill, as it always had. He was shaking his head in that same way he once did: a reluctant half grin, a slight lick of his lips and a flash of blue eye, and it went right through me. But I was still angry with him.

'Childhood,' I said to him when he topped up my glass. 'A series of mortifications and embarrassments.'

He laughed.

'I don't know what you're laughing at,' I snapped, half cheeky, half serious – it was liberating being a grown-up. 'You were the cause of a lot of it.'

I hadn't meant to sound quite so aggressive; I surprised myself and felt obliged to take some action. Like an exit. I went upstairs to the loo.

The drunkenness happened in a flash.

The bathroom was as functional as every other room in the farmhouse, still with shades of the Organization; Amy's family had been pretty fundamentalist at one time, though they had left a long time ago. I shut the door and locked it. I drew in a great breath and shook my head, as if surfacing from a dream.

I looked straight ahead. Above the bath was a framed painting, the white paper yellowed by time. It was piercingly familiar. I leant over the bath. 'By Amy Jones, age thirteen today'. It was her painting of the cherry blossom. Oh my God. I could immediately recall every detail of that tree. Fancy that – keeping it all these years. Fancy that – framing your memories, as if they were a good thing.

I looked at myself in the corroding mirror. I looked good, I looked alive. My eyes were shining.

'Hello, you!' I said, like I hadn't really seen myself for a long time. I could see Caroline Stern in there, the cheeky, happy girl I had once been. Laughter and music wafted up the stairs – anyone would think that this was a normal party. I hitched down my jeans and sat on the loo and stared at my legs. What had my legs been doing for twenty-five years? I looked at my hands, no longer those of a thirteen-year-old. The skin wasn't elastic any more. I suddenly remembered my mother's hands – raw, dry from all that scrubbing. My mother. My father was dead. I banished them from my mind.

I gazed at the green lino floor between my knees, and the little thrill darted back through me. I was reliving the look Steinberg had given me, the appreciative glint in his eye, the look he had always given me. A look that said I was special to him.

But then to my disgust, I dribbled, like I was mentally ill or an old person or something. I dribbled a string of spit on to my leg. It was definitely time to leave.

I pulled up my jeans, washed my hands, hurriedly unlocked the bathroom door and nearly walked straight into Steinberg himself. He steadied me in his arms.

'Hey!' he said, holding me there. 'Caroline!'

I concentrated hard on trying to appear sober. He paused as if he'd forgotten what he was going to say. His hands were warm against my flesh. 'It's so wonderful to see you!'

I was surprised by the intensity in his voice. He said it as if he had been waiting to see me for a long time, his eyes full of nostalgia.

'You too,' I said, but I couldn't hold his gaze for long. I had not recovered from the fact that he had married Megan. I felt betrayed by the pair of them. I went down-stairs and grabbed Joe, and we left.

'Look up at the stars!' Joe said as we staggered back in the darkness. I looked up and fell over in one swift movement. How on earth had I got so drunk?

'Fucking countryside!' I was kind of laughing and kind of moaning. I'd banged my bum on something hard. 'Why's it so dark?' I had gone from being witty and glamorous to a foul, slurring drunk in the space of about two minutes.

'Yes. What we need is a nice bright, orange street light!' Joe said, pulling me up.

'Well, country people are so in your face, you'd think they might want to see it.'

'That's right, Lorrie.' He was humouring me. 'You mean like when you're walking the dog minding your own business and someone says, "Morning!" or "Hello"?'

'My point exactly,' I slurred. I needed to get my anger out on something. '"Ooh, we're from the country, we're so friendly." Leave me alone, you inbred!'

I tripped on a stone, but Joe had me.

'Careful, Lorrie!'

I was on a roll, 'What about that guy at the petrol station? I didn't even know there still *were* petrol attendants. Did you hear him? "How's the traffic on the A39? Here on holiday? What sort of dog's that? Hope the weather holds. Visiting relatives?" Fill ... My ... Tank ... And ... Fuck ... Off.'

And I slipped right out of Joe's supporting arm and down the path. Tilly sniffed at my muddied face and got a blast of alcohol fumes. I stopped bothering trying to get up. I lay on the ground and looked up at the stars, feeling all sorts of things wash over me. Stars, love, happiness, rage, fear. But most of all, I just felt alive.

'What are we doing here?' I yelled. I didn't mean it existentially, but once I'd said it, it seemed that I did.

Somehow, a bit later – and I've no idea of the logistics of the process – Joe and I lay side by side in our lumpy, bumpy, damp bed. Tilly was somewhere at the other end, and I didn't have the strength to turf her off. Besides, the cottage was freezing, and she was serving as a nice little hot water bottle. Joe had wiped the blood and mud off my legs and my face. I didn't think he'd ever seen me like this, but these were exceptional circumstances, even if he didn't know it. We had an electric fire on in our room, and I rested my eyes on the red glow that shone on the ceiling of the little bedroom, which was not as easy as it sounds, because the ceiling was spinning furiously in an anti-clockwise direction.

'Stop the ceiling!' I said to no one in particular and then I wondered where Joe had gone.

I managed to shift my eyes from the fairground orbit. Ah, he was right next to me. I didn't like the way he was looking at me with his eight eyes: crafty, scheming. The bugger was going to take advantage of me. He leant on one elbow and stared at me.

'I don't know what to call you any more,' he said quietly.

'Drunkard?'

'Why did you change your name?'

'Lorrie, I'm Lorrie. Call me Lorrie. Red Lorrie, yellow Lorrie.'

'Let me get this straight. Nate was your teacher?'

I winced. 'Don't call him Nate, Joe. You can't call a

teacher by their first name. You'll get into trouble. He's Mr Steinberg.'

'I can't call him Mr Steinberg. He wasn't my teacher.'

'I can't call him Nate.'

'Anyway, he was Megan's teacher and he married her?'

'He was our teacher, affirmative.'

'How old were you when he started teaching?'

'What is this? The Spanish Inquisition?' Only due to all the 's's, I hadn't said it like that, but I think he got the drift.

'It's just not normal!' he said.

And there I had to change my focus and pinpoint two of his eyes.

'Normal? Normal? What the fuck has normal got to do with any of it? Normal is a relative term. You've just got a different normal to our normal.'

'So it's us and them, is it?'

'I'm with us. Not them,' I said quickly. But I wasn't really sure where I was.

'Joe?' I was serious now. 'Joe, you know what the worst thing is?'

I know I must have sat up here because I watched the eiderdown slip off the bed and on to the electric bars.

'They're grown-ups and they chose to send their children there. The traitors.'

I watched Joe pat out the flames.

I woke up with a start. I had not been dreaming. This was reality. Joe was fast asleep next to me. Tilly was under the covers, uncomfortably trapping my legs.

I slid myself quietly out of bed, evidence of last night

all over the place. The singed, wet eiderdown was hanging up over the door, the bathroom towel was covered in blood and mud; I must have pulled down the clothes hangers. I looked down at my knee: a dark red gash. I grabbed Joe's jumper, pulled out some socks from my bag, and crept through to the main room. The remnants of the fire were still warm, and I chucked another log on. It looked as if it might catch; I wasn't really a fire maker. I used to watch my father make fires. We didn't have central heating, and in the winter he said that, if I could breathe smoke, he would light one. Mean git. Mean dead git.

I wandered through to the open kitchen and put the kettle on.

Miraculously, I had no headache at all. I felt fine. More than fine; I still felt a little exhilarated. I gazed out of the window. The sky was white, and the valley below was foggy, but the horizon was clearing. Like the landscape, I felt a little as if a cloud were lifting. It was a truly beautiful view; it sent me into a daze. I sipped at my coffee and stared out of the window, feeling strangely calm and tranquil.

I watched Amy come into the courtyard. Once again, I caught her face in repose, an unhappy turn to her lips, a frown etched into her forehead. She moved slowly, still gracefully, but she had none of that confidence she used to carry. I'd asked her the previous night how she dealt with Marcus still being in the Organization. She said she'd never known any different; she didn't see him that much, and besides, her life had been so busy bringing up the kids, she barely gave it a thought. But I wondered.

I noticed how much she'd enjoyed taking the piss last night. But it was true that she was busy; she'd spent the last twenty years bringing up six children, living in a hippy commune and married to the commune founder. She had jumped straight out of one frying pan into another. I think once you've been brought up being told how to think, you need it. Her husband, whom she had once thought was such a catch, turned out to be a bit of a ladies' man, and she had eventually got herself together to leave him. But only recently, which is why she said bumping into me had been a sign: a sign that she had to get her own life back, see her 'people' again. That was the trouble with us lot; we had to see meaning in everything. We had been trained from four-year-olds to spot signs, to look for the higher purpose, and it was impossible not to once you'd been pre-programmed.

'Hey, Ames!' I said, opening the door.

Her face immediately lit up. She came up the steps, swinging an empty coal bucket. 'Did you sleep all right?' she asked.

I gave her a hug. 'Thanks for all this,' I said. I don't know why I said it and I didn't even know if I meant it, but she looked in need of a hug – she was endlessly looking after everyone else.

'Do you want a coffee?' I asked.

'They're waiting for me back at the farmhouse for the coal . . .'

'Oh sod everyone else. Have a coffee.'

'Yeh, okay.' She hugged me again and looked searchingly into my eyes. 'Caroline, what happened to you? In Scotland? What were your relatives like?'

How easily my parents had disowned me.

'Amy, please,' I said, ending the conversation.

'All right! No questions!' she said and came in.

A few hours later, I said I fancied a walk to Bedruthan steps. Tilly needed a run around, but also I wanted to be on my own. Joe said he'd stay in the cottage and watch the footy.

Before I knew it, it had been decided that everyone was going to Bedruthan steps. That was very Organizational; everything was always done in groups. I can't stand being in a 'party', all that waiting around whilst so and so hunts for their other glove and then so and so goes and locks the car. I hate all that communal business. This was even worse, what with children needing pees and juice bottles and God-knows-what.

In the meantime the sky had turned an ominous dark grey. I zipped up my waterproof. 'I'll set off, I'll see you there,' I said, in as friendly a manner as possible.

Megan and Amy laughed at me. 'Oh Caroline! You're always so impatient!' It made me smile, to be so known. And so unjudged. They made me feel good.

The walk to Bedruthan steps has to be the best walk in the world. It must be the only bit of Great Britain left that isn't cordoned off with 'Mind the cliffs' and 'Look where you're going' and 'Danger Danger' and 'No children' signs everywhere and barricades and handrails, despite the fact that, if you didn't keep your wits about you, one false move and you'd be tumbling hundreds of feet to your death. When the wind blew the other way, from land to sea, you could quite easily get blown over the cliff. You could take your life in your own hands.

There was nothing to see but sea and cliff; no trees dared to grow here, where the elements were unforgiving. The salty, wind-beaten grass stopped suddenly at the edge of the cliffs, which were sheer, inverted from the relentless pounding the Atlantic gave them hundreds of feet beneath. Today the waves were enormous, mesmerizing in their power. The tide was on its way out, and the seagulls circled at the same height as us. I loved this view even more in the cold and blasting rain.

We took turns lying on our stomachs and crawling towards the edge to appreciate the magnitude of the sight whilst someone else sat on our legs to keep us from tumbling down. All of us were made quite giddy by the elements. There was something magical about this landscape. I wanted to bottle it and give it to my clients to blow away the cobwebs.

Somehow, little Lakshmi had attached herself to me.

There was a moment, about halfway there, before the rain started in earnest, when Steinberg and I were side by side, Lakshmi still holding my hand between us.

'So . . . how is my mother?' I asked him. I had surprised myself with how much I needed to know the answer to this. I didn't want to ask Megan; I didn't want to go there with her; she'd read me like a book. I hadn't needed to know about my parents for so long, but suddenly, surrounded by people who knew more than I did, my curiosity had been roused. I did, however, ask in as casual a tone as I could muster.

'She's okay,' he replied carefully, implying that she wasn't.

'She must be getting on now.'

'She's coping,' he said.

I turned my head seawards and breathed in the rainy, salty air.

'I heard about the old Turkey.' Again, casual, as if I couldn't really give a toss. No, worse than casual, dismissive.

Lakshmi laughed. 'Who's an old turkey?'

'My father,' I said, smiling sweetly at her.

Surely Steinberg knew my father's nickname, or maybe he was just shocked by my lack of respect. Either way, I didn't care.

'I'm sorry about that,' he said.

'Why's everyone so sorry?'

He looked at me with surprise. He didn't know how to respond to my callousness. Lakshmi let go of my hand and skipped back to find her dad, who was battling the rain, behind us. We watched her go. Steinberg and I were facing each other now, the wind blowing in my face.

'Why are you looking at me like that?' I asked him. 'Oh! I forgot. You lot all worshipped the Turkey, didn't you?'

I could tell by his silence that they did. My dad was one of the Whopper's chosen people. 'I bet you all stood up when he came into rooms,' I added, rolling my eyes.

Steinberg looked out to sea, slightly evasively.

'Oh my God! You did!' I cried. They were like bloody school kids. 'Why?' I asked him, serious now. 'Why did you stand up?'

'Well ...' he replied with a false note of cheer, hands in pockets, eyes on Marcus lifting his daughter up in the air, '... we did so, for the traditional reason, as a mark of respect.'

'We? We? I wasn't asking about "we". Why did *you*? You personally.'

All he had to tell me was why he, personally, respected the Turkey; not that I would have let him get away with it, mind you. But instead, he stared at me, confused, a furrow on his lovely brow.

I set off, backwards, facing him, Dalek-like. 'Malfunction . . . Malfunction . . .'

He laughed. He liked my teasing. He always had. He hurried a little to catch up with me.

As we neared the top of the steps and stopped to wait for the others, he leant in towards me. 'I'd forgotten how refreshing you were.'

I was quietly thrilled by the force with which he said it.

Lakshmi and Marcus caught up with us, Lakshmi grabbing my hand. 'My old turkey said he had his first kiss with you,' she piped.

'That's right!' Marcus said, putting his arm around me. 'And she dumped me like a hot potato.'

He had rounded out like Amy, but not unattractively. The Organization had left its mark on him, on them all; they swamped you with niceness.

'Did you two use to . . . go out?' Steinberg asked. He was smiling but blushing, I noticed, or was it just the wind in his face?

'I think "going out" might be overstating it; we never went anywhere,' I said.

'I wouldn't dump a hot potato.' Lakshmi was looking up at me. 'Why would you want a cold potato?'

The view was even better than I had remembered: ten

massive boulders marking the giant Bedruthan's steps across the sand. Far behind the opposite cliff stood a lighthouse on a headland, a beacon of man's hope against nature's might.

It took a good ten minutes to get down on to the beach; there were a hundred and seventy-odd slippery, uneven steps to clamber down. I could see some of Amy's kids ahead of us on the sand, running towards the mussel rock, their footprints being eaten up as they ran.

Tilly was looking a bit miserable, considering where we were. She didn't like the rain, but the kids dragged her with them, and she barked at the sea a bit and peed in various rock pools.

Someone found a piece of timber, and Marcus made a ball out of seaweed and we had a game of rounders, but Tilly got too annoying, barking all the time, and the rain began in earnest, so we headed back pretty sharply.

Tilly and I were the last to get to the steps up the cliffs. The sky had turned almost black, and the rain was getting harder. I could see Marcus and Megan up at the top with the kids. They waved down at us from the cliff, and I watched them disappear along the cliff path back towards the cottages. Steinberg, Marcus's wife, Amy and two older girls were halfway up the steps, trudging slowly upwards; it was hard work on the legs. I was delayed by Tilly, who had not stopped barking at a dead jellyfish over near the mussel rock. I'd forgotten to bring the gas canister away with us, and she had reverted to her usual troubled self.

I had to go back and get her and put her on the lead. I stared out at the sea; I still had that exhilarated feeling in the pit of my stomach. I was dragging her back to the steps and over some boulders, when she shrieked suddenly. She had stepped on a sea urchin and was making a great deal of fuss. To make matters worse, at that moment the blackening skies above let loose their load and it started to bucket down. Damn it.

Tilly was giving it the full tragic treatment, holding out her paw to me, looking deeply wronged, her mournful brown eyes beseeching me for help. I looked at the paw: three brown needles were sticking out of her forefinger pad. I tried to pull the brown prongs out, but my fingers were clumsy due to the cold and wet. I picked her up and carried her towards a little cave and sat us down on a boulder out of the rain. I held her in my arms like a baby. I loved her like this, all pliant and needy. I carefully tried to pull them out but I wasn't getting very far; she kept struggling. I was going to have to use my teeth.

'Can I help?'

I looked up. Steinberg was in the cave, rubbing his hands together to warm them up.

'Thanks!' I said. He was soaked to the bone; the rain behind him was like a waterfall. He took off his glasses and rubbed them on the hem of his jumper. He looked different without them, a bit naked. I felt like I shouldn't stare, and yet I knew that I could because he couldn't see me.

'She stepped on a sea urchin. Maybe you could hold her still while I try and pull out the needles.'

Steinberg knelt down in front of Tilly and me and tried to hold her firmly while I operated. We were very close. I could feel his knee against my leg. Our foreheads were almost touching. Occasionally, we used to be this close when he was reading my class work. I would look behind his glasses then. I always enjoyed that, seeing his real face, his eyes suddenly so much bigger, his lashes surprisingly long.

His hair was drenched, black strands clung to his face, and drops of water dripped on to Tilly. I managed to get the needles out and I put her down. Neither Steinberg nor I moved, only now that we were Tilly-less it seemed inappropriately intimate. We both watched her limping about the cave until she got distracted by some fishy smells and forgot to limp.

Outside, the lashing rain was flying almost horizontally across the beach. The sky beyond was a thick, dark grey with streaks of black.

'Move up!' he said, not getting up but turning his body around and joining me on the little boulder. 'We'd better stay here for a bit.'

'Okay, Caveman!' I said, my heart pounding fast.

I would have been quite glad to stop the world and get off there and then, just sitting in a cave with Steinberg, watching the rain. It couldn't get any better. But then I went and broke my own promise.

'Mr Steinberg?'

'Nate, please.'

'I'll drop the mister.'

He smiled.

'Steinberg?'

'Yes, Stern?'

'I need to ask you something.'

'Fire away!'

'Do you remember the Sikh builder who molested me?'

'Yes,' he replied, as if the question didn't surprise him.

'Why didn't you tell ... her ... that the guy was a creep?'

He kept his focus on the pouring rain. 'I thought we weren't allowed to mention "her".'

I bit my lip. 'You haven't answered my question.'

'Tell her what, Caroline? What could I say? My girlfriend didn't like the look of him?'

'You could have said *something*,' I said fervently, turning on him.

He seemed surprised by my vehemence. He was trying to work me out, studying my face, his sea-blue eyes blinking at me behind his glasses. But I couldn't hold his gaze for long; he made me feel too exposed.

'I *should* have said something. You're right.'

Good. I was glad he said that.

'Hmm,' he said. 'You don't think much of me, do you?'

I flicked him a glance. 'What does it matter what I think of you?' I asked. He looked back at the sea, pushing his glasses up his nose and we sat in the loaded, rain-filled silence for a while.

'You always asked pertinent questions,' he said. 'I missed your questions when you left.'

He'd missed me. What music to my ears.

'Where did you go so suddenly, Caroline? We were told that you went to Scotland.'

'Well, if that's what you were told, then it must be true.'

'Was it true?'

'God forbid you should be questioning something you've been told to believe, Steinberg!'

He laughed. 'God forbid it. But I think I am.'

'Careful!' I said, risking a smile. 'That way disaster lies.'

He sighed and shifted his weight. 'Well, perhaps, just perhaps, one might learn something from the odd "disaster".'

I wasn't quite sure what he meant by that, but it made my heart beat so loudly I thought he must be able to hear it.

The most God-almighty crack of thunder broke across the heavens, and forked lightning zigzagged into the ocean. I grabbed his arm instinctively in a rather pathetic, girlish way. But he was just as surprised as I was; he'd put his arm around me and was clutching my wrist.

'Wow!' we both said, in unison. The power of the elements was truly humbling. We stayed like that: stock still, mesmerized by the bucketing rain, flesh on flesh, Tilly aquiver at my side.

'How Virgilian this is!' he said eventually.

'What do you mean?' I asked softly, keeping my eyes out front, not wanting this moment to ever change into the next.

'*The Aeneid*. Remember Dido and Aeneas?'

Oh yes, I did. I remembered all his stories. Dido and Aeneas were set up by Venus. She made Dido fall in love with him when they both took refuge from a storm in the same cave.

I smiled to myself. Dido was, after all, the beautiful Queen of Carthage, and Aeneas the Trojan hero. Of course it all ended tragically, but just by mentioning the lovers, Steinberg had, knowingly or not, turned up the heat. And although my eyes were glued to the wild sea, every single particle of me was focused on where our bodies were touching.

'Do you remember …' I said, '… going to see *The Oresteia*?' He was quiet. I thought perhaps he hadn't heard me.

'Yes, I remember,' he replied in a voice so hushed, I didn't dare move.

I turned at the same moment he did, and we were so close I could feel his warm breath on my face. But this time I held his gaze.

'I was in love with you, Steinberg.'

'Really?' he whispered. 'I thought you were in love with Marcus.'

'Oh no,' I said. 'That was just a silly schoolgirl crush.'

I hate it when couples that have got together through adultery say, 'We just couldn't help ourselves. It was bigger than us, we had no choice.' It's not true. We're not helpless. We're not animals. There's always a choice. And Steinberg and I made ours.

He, oh so gently, brought his hand up to my face and moved a bit of wet hair from my temple, his eyes on mine all the while. There was nowhere to hide now. He had me. I was his. Tenderly, he lifted my chin and pressed his lips against mine. The kiss began tentatively, sweetly, and then all the longing from all those years took over and turned it into a desperate, profound desire.

There in the cave, Mr Steinberg unzipped my waterproof, placed his cold hands on my flesh and sought out my breasts.

'Oh Caroline, my sweet Caroline,' he said, in his beautiful lilting accent, breathless for me now. And I gave myself to him there in the darkness of the cave with Tilly limping about around us.

After Steinberg and I had made love, we straightened out our clothes slowly, not taking our eyes off each other and not saying a word. Then, satiated and reborn, we stepped out of the cave and wrote our names in big letters in the sand and watched them get swallowed up as fast as we wrote.

We took our time getting back to the cottages, both of us aware of the fragility of these moments, reluctant to let them go. Oblivious to the rain, we ambled along in a haze of completion as if our love-making had been as inevitable as the rising of the sun.

No one commented on our late arrival. No one even noticed. Steinberg went his way and I went mine, parting with a glance. My cottage was empty, and I made myself a cup of tea, listening to the whelps and shrieks coming from the back. I took the tea to the back door and leant on the door frame and watched Joe playing football with a gang of kids, unaware of the seismic shift that had taken place in his relationship.

5

The moment I heard the front door slam and felt the kitchen shake, I knew Dad had heard about me and the Sikh and the telephone calls. I watched the wind from the door-slam eventually make the Sanskrit prayer on the wall flap up. Mum looked up from her washing up, and I froze behind my calligraphy board. I had been waiting for this moment all week, and there was almost a sense of relief as it actually arrived.

Dad came into the kitchen. When I peered out from behind my board, his face said it all. The muscle at the side of his cheek was pulsating. He flashed me a look and dropped his battered, bulging briefcase on to the floor. It rolled on to its side like a fat, old dog.

'Hello, dear,' Mum said and began to dry her hands on a dish cloth. He undid each button of his fawn mackintosh with a deliberate and violent twist. He took off his coat and shook out the creases. He opened the cupboard. His face grew irritated by what he saw – presumably it was over-full – and he flashed me another look as if it were my fault, before finding the hook on his coat and hanging it up. He pushed the door firmly shut. We could all hear the coat falling off the hook, but we all pretended it hadn't.

My father was a tall man with a long neck and hair that grew in crinkles like those crisps you could nibble at. At school they called him the Turkey behind his back because he kind of jutted his neck backwards and forwards as he moved. This was accentuated when he was angry, like now.

'You, young lady, upstairs!'

Mum turned away silently and started to do the drying-up. Her shapeless cardigan had rucked up at the back of her long skirt.

'Now!' He sounded scary.

I dashed out from behind the calligraphy board and hid under the table.

'I'm warning you!'

He went around the table, pulling the chairs out, and I quickly made my escape. I scrabbled out of the kitchen and ran up the stairs as fast as I could. I could hear him coming up behind me – heavy, even footsteps. I could hear the swift, smooth noise of his belt coming off.

I ran into my room and pushed hard against the door to stop him coming in. But it was useless: he was much stronger than me and he easily forced it open. I ran across my room and picked up my chair and held it up, legs out, like a weapon.

He slammed the door shut.

'Mum!' I shouted. 'Mum! Help me!'

But, of course, she didn't come.

His face was a blotchy red; a lock of crinkly hair had flopped forward, his heavy breathing making it jiggle. 'How dare you jeopardize that man's future, Caroline Stern!'

Spit flew out of his mouth. I pulled my little desk nearer to me with one hand, hoping to corner myself.

'But he touched me, Dad!'

'Don't lie to me!'

'I promise! He touched me!'

'He did not!'

'He did!'

'He did not! And I suppose it's not true that you made those phone calls?'

'It's not true!'

'Are you calling Miss Fowler a liar?'

I glared at him.

'She's had the calls traced. She said you got out at Leicester Square tube and used a public phone box!'

'But ...'

The very idea seemed mad to me. I would have to have got a new ticket. I didn't have the money.

'Are you calling Miss Fowler a liar?'

'Yes.'

We grappled with the chair, but he tugged hard and threw it across the room. He swung the desk away from me and he grabbed my arms and jerked them roughly behind my back. He dragged me to the desk and pushed me over it.

I kicked my legs like a donkey, but he overpowered me. He lifted up my tunic and pulled down my tights and pants in one fast movement.

He began to thrash me with the buckle end of the belt.

Kate had told me that the best thing to do when you were being beaten was to say, 'I bet you love doing that, don't you, Dad?' She said it always worked on her dad, but, to be honest, it hurt too much to say anything,

I was just screaming. He must have been very angry with me; he didn't stop for a long time.

Afterwards I lay on the floor where he dropped me, my bum and my back burning and bleeding. I could hear his heavy breathing; he sounded as if he'd just sprinted a mile. I opened my eyes. I could see him on the edge of my bed, his head hanging, his body had gone almost as limp as mine. He wiped his forehead.

With great effort, he began to strap his belt back on.

'Please!' I begged him in a small voice from the ground. 'Please take me away from school!'

He said nothing.

'Please, I hate it so.'

He was breathing tightly out of his nose. I pulled myself on to my hands and knees and crawled towards him. I looked up at him, 'Please, Daddy!' I hugged his ankles. 'Please, Daddy! I'm begging you!' I was getting snot all over his trousers.

'You've chosen this lifetime, Caroline!' he was trying to sound kind. 'You've chosen everything about this life. You've chosen your mother, you've chosen me, you've chosen your school!' He was having trouble threading the belt.

'Did I choose for Thomas to die?' Thomas was my baby brother. He died from meningitis when he was two.

'Yes! You did. We all did. It was for the good of us all!'

'It wasn't for my good!'

'It was the will of the Absolute.'

'I hate the Absolute!'

'Don't ever say that. The Absolute is pure love.' He was getting cross again.

'You can't keep me there, Daddy!' I was snotting and sobbing all over the place. 'You can't! You have to take me away from school! Please!'

He tugged back my head and looked down at me. The veins on his forehead were sticking out. He was trying hard to get through to me. He spoke very slowly.

'Don't you understand, Caroline? Asking for me to take you out of school is like forcing me to cut your throat!'

That's when I stopped talking altogether. There was nothing left to say.

It was a Saturday and my dad was away on a teachers' retreat at Riversmead. I didn't know what they did to him, but he always came back worse; even holier and colder than usual. It always took him a couple of days to revert back to his regular level of holy coldness.

All of us had to spend weekends or weeks at Riversmead, the Organization's big house in the country. We used to go as a form. It gave us an idea of what St Augustine's would have been like as a boarding school. Awful. If you were a girl, you'd be up at five o'clock in the morning for a day full of preparing food, serving, washing up, washing the male teachers' clothes, scrubbing flagstone floors with milk, cleaning, tidying, prayers, meditation and Sanskrit. We wouldn't get to bed until eleven o'clock. The Whopper didn't approve of sleep: six hours was more than sufficient. The next morning it would be the same again. You were always hungry, and there were always more things to do before you would be allowed to eat. And then it was only bread and fruit and the usual rabbit food from the garden. Sometimes the women had to climb trees in their long dresses and pick fruit all day long. I'm not sure what the men were doing. I suppose they were getting on spiritually in another room somewhere.

So with my dad away at Riversmead, my mother and I were facing a weekend alone together at home. I had just come back from another silent morning of school, and I had taken to lying on my bed and staring at the ceiling of my bedroom whenever I was at home. I had to lie twisted on my side because the bruises were still painful, and two of the stripes were full of pus and had gone a luminous green as they crawled up my back. If I twisted around in the mirror, I could see my back, stripy like a strange beast.

I watched the spider that had made its home in the corner above my bed; I wished I was a spider. I started to pretend it was my pet. I called it Thomas, after my dead brother. No one had talked about Thomas in this house for years. It was as if he had never existed. But I used to imagine him: he was strong and brave and he didn't let bad things happen.

My mother called me downstairs to lunch. She knew I wasn't eating, so I don't know why she bothered. I didn't move. I could hear her coming up the stairs. She pushed open the door.

'Caroline, you heard me. Come downstairs! It's lunchtime.'

I swung my legs off the bed. I was still in my foul school uniform, but I couldn't be bothered to change.

I sat in front of a bowl of muesli and listened to Mum

eating hers next to me. I could hear her chomping. It sounded disgusting.

'Eat it, please!' she said.

I stared at it. She put down her spoon.

'Why are you doing this, Caroline? I just don't understand you at all.'

I said nothing.

'You don't have to make your life so difficult, you know. If you just did as you were told everything would be so much easier. Eat it!'

I looked up at her. She was a stranger to me.

'Don't look at me like that!' she said. I think I frightened her. She pushed her bowl aside, got up, walked over to the window and looked out at the garden, leaning on the window pane. Her shapeless purple corduroy skirt was creased around her bottom.

'I'll give you one last chance!' she said, turning around. 'Eat it!'

We stared at each other. Her glasses were filthy, her hair was wiry; she looked a mess.

'I'll ring your father ... I'll ring ...'

Then she burst into tears, not dramatically or anything; they were quiet, suppressed tears. She brought her clenched fist up to her mouth.

'Why do you have to be like this? I must have done something very bad in my last life to deserve all this.' But she wasn't really saying it to me; she was saying it to the garden.

She put her hand into her cardigan pocket, pulled out a grey handkerchief and blew her nose forcefully, like a man. She went over to the telephone and picked up the receiver. I watched her dial the number. She didn't need to look it up, so I knew *where* she was dialling, I just didn't know *who*. In between the clicks of the numbers she glanced at me and wiped the tears away, fitting her fingers behind her smudgy glasses.

'Hello?' she said, sniffing away her unhappiness and replacing it with false cheer. 'Is that Anthea? It's Judith. Hello. Would it be possible to speak to Miss Fowler? ... Thank you.'

She waited a long time. I pictured Anthea, who was Kate's aunt and lived at Riversmead, putting the phone down and swooping up the big staircase in her long skirt, her sensible shoes padding along the red carpet until she got to a door, knocking gently on the dark wood saying, 'Sorry to interrupt!' in a breathy, calm, meek voice, 'but it's Judith Stern on the telephone for you, Miss Fowler,' Miss Fowler, flashing her teeth, irritated by Caroline Stern once again disrupting her life, but nevertheless getting up from her Sanskrit session and making her way down the stairs.

'Hello!' said my mother into the receiver. 'I'm so sorry to disturb you, Miss Fowler,' she said, in a grovelling voice. I despised her lack of dignity; I had to turn my head away.

'I didn't know what else to do. It's Caroline ...'

She was silent for a moment. I could tell she was trying not to cry.

'She won't eat anything, she won't speak, she lies on her bed,' she was working herself up again. 'I don't think I can cope, I'm at my wits' end.'

She nodded into the phone and then said almost happily, 'Thank you, Miss Fowler, thank you so much.'

And the next thing I knew, Mr Wilson, the Organization's dentist was at the door, ready to drive me up to Riversmead in his car. I didn't really care though. I didn't care what happened any more. I felt like I was floating face down in a swimming pool. I'd go wherever the water took me.

He wasn't very used to children, it was obvious, and after I didn't answer any of his questions he stopped trying. We spent the rest of the journey in silence.

When we got there it was dark. Mr Wilson parked the car on the crunchy gravel and he carried my bag to the house for me. We went through the front door, which I had never done before, through the two big pillars. He let me go ahead of him as we entered. Perhaps he hadn't heard that I was the Devil. Or maybe he was better off keeping the Devil in front of him.

There was always an air of nervousness and excitement at Riversmead amongst the adults because the Whopper spent a lot of time there. If he wasn't actually there, he was just about to arrive, and everyone scurried about with whispered voices. Personally, I had never actually come across the Whopper; he was always behind a closed door; high-ranked women, his handmaidens, would be going in and out with urgent, breathy instructions to other women. I once saw the back of him, though, and he was a bit disappointing: squat and balding.

Years ago, when I was happy, I had once asked Fowler why we had to wear long dresses when we got to sixteen, and she had turned white with fury and said mockingly, 'Perhaps you'd like me to arrange it so you could ask Mr Wapinski that question?' And I'd said that I would like that very much. But she never did. He was a bit of a mystery, because, on the one hand, all the girls getting betrothed had to be virgins before they got married and then, on the other hand, he knew full well that Joanna's dad was having an affair with Mrs Michaels and he did nothing about it. In fact, he must have actually approved of it or they would not have been allowed to carry on. It wasn't nice for Joanna, or her sister, who was in Mrs Michael's form.

Mr Wilson left me on a chair outside the kitchen and told me to wait there. I heard Fowler before I saw her; I knew that cough anywhere. When I looked up she did not look pleased to see me. Her nose was red.

'You are under Anthea Warner's charge and you are to do whatever she tells you and you are to do it immediately. If you are wilful or surly she will send you to me.' And with that she disappeared again.

I followed Anthea Warner up the stairs; she had a large bottom and wavy red hair up in the obligatory bun but falling floppily down, in a country way. She took me to a little room with a boiler and a camp bed in it.

'Are you hungry?' she asked. I shook my head.

'You're probably tired,' she said. She didn't like me. She didn't know me, but she'd heard about me.

I was tired. I took my clothes off, changed into my long, appropriate nightie, turned the light off and lay straight down and stared into the blackness until I fell asleep.

I was woken in the middle of the night. A bright overhead light was switched on.

'Get up! Caroline! It's four thirty, time to make tea.'

At first, I didn't know where I was or who she was.

Then I remembered and dragged myself sleepily out of bed into the cold and pulled on my dressing gown. I had forgotten my slippers in the last-minute packing.

I made my way down the swooping staircase. The hall was dark, cold and silent. We went through to the kitchen, which was large and square with a massive table in the middle, like you see in places like Hampton Court. The stones beneath my feet were ice cold, and my toes had turned white.

Anthea Warner had already put two kettles on. They were steaming into the cold air. About ten cups and saucers, in the familiar blue and white pattern, had been lined up on the table, with ten small trays, ten little jugs of milk and ten little teapots. My job was to take them round to all the teachers' bedrooms and wake them up.

I yawned. Anthea Warner gave me a disapproving look. I gave her one back. I felt it was quite unfair of her to have taken such a dislike to me based only on hearsay. I despised the lot of them.

Mr Gates was my first port of call; he was staying in the Ficino Room. I knocked on the door politely, but he didn't hear me, so I knocked a bit harder. Still no response, so I opened the door. I could see a hunched figure in a small bed. I brought in his tray and placed it on the bedside table. He didn't stir, so I turned on the bedside light.

'Thank you!' he said, sitting up and blinking at me like a big water rat. I thought of poor Helen Winters jumping off the top storey of the car park. I imagined her waking up to his twitchy nose and his little dark eyes. I wondered what she was doing now in a new life.

I went downstairs to get the next tray. 'This one's for your father,' said Anthea Warner. 'He's in the Shiva Room.'

The Shiva Room meant that my dad was important; the Whopper's favourite guests slept there. In some way I felt sorry for my dad, that I was always ruining all his hard work.

I knocked on his door. I didn't think I'd ever woken my dad up before.

'Come in!' he said, not sounding sleepy at all, raring to get on with the day. I opened the door. He had already turned the bedside light on and was reading his Upanishads.

People look different in their night clothes, they look like children.

'Thank you very much . . .' he said, clearing a space between his Bible and his Bhagavad Gita. 'You can put it on the table.'

He must have been so used to being served that he didn't even look at me. He hadn't even noticed that it was me. I flicked him a look and left the room, relieved.

Downstairs, Anthea Warner had been joined by Mrs Garing. She was the Organization's vet. She looked at me and snapped, 'You should have got dressed.' She didn't like me either.

'Come on! Come on! It's getting cold. This is to the Ganesha Room for Mr Steinberg.'

I drew breath. It hadn't occurred to me that Mr Steinberg would be here, but of course, pretty much all the teachers were. I suddenly became aware that my hair was loose.

I carried the tray back up and stood outside his room. I knocked. No reply, so I opened the door and went in. It was very dark, the curtains were drawn, but I could make him out. He was on the near side of a double bed. I put down the tray on a table and went over to open the curtains. He stirred, leant on his elbow and turned on the bedside light.

'Thank you,' he said sleepily, rubbing his face with one hand. I could hear the sandpaper noise of his chin-rubbing. He fumbled for his glasses.

'Hey!' he said when he had put them on. He stared at me. 'What a surprise!'

I brought the tray over from the big table to his bedside.

'Thank you,' he said, making some room for it. His hair was all messy and he was wearing a black T-shirt. I had never seen him look so young.

'A nice cuppa!' he said, in an English accent.

I smiled a little and poured him a cup.

He checked his watch, which lay beside the tray, and he pulled himself up to a seated position. I could feel him watching me, and it made me nervous; I dropped the spoon and bent down to pick it up.

'Whoa!' he said, as I did so. I stood up. He was looking concerned. 'What's happened here?'

He was pointing behind me and it took me a moment to realize that he meant my back; the yellow and purple bruises had spread almost up to my neck.

He was waiting for me to say something.

'May I see?' he asked, quietly.

I nodded and came a little closer. He smelt of warmth

and night-time. I turned around and pulled the nightie off my shoulder so he could see my back. He gave a little intake of breath. 'That's ... terrible!' he whispered. 'Caroline, I'm so sorry!'

How odd, I thought, that it's the physical marks that people should find so disturbing. They seemed irrelevant to me. Steinberg knew exactly who'd done it. There was nothing he could say. People were beaten all the time at school. Every time he sent a boy to the headmaster, he knew what the likely outcome would be. I pulled the nightie back over my shoulder and picked up the tray.

'Caroline?' he said. 'You still not speaking?'

I nodded, and he leant back and stared into his tea, cradled in his lap.

'Not even to me?'

I paused before nodding again.

'I admire your fight.'

I smiled at him. Yes, I thought, I do still have some fight in me. I mustn't give up. There must be something I can do.

Suddenly, he reached out his left hand towards me and pressed his curled fingers to my cheek. I wanted to turn my face into his palm and cry. Instead I stared at the dark floorboards.

'I don't believe a word they say about you, Caroline. They've got you so wrong.'

I think people could be killed by kindness. It's sharper than any blade.

I quickly left his room.

*

The train pulled into Bayswater station for the third time, or was it the fourth? I had been sitting on the Circle Line going round and round for several hours now, just getting my head together. It was past rush hour on the tube; most of the city people with their hats and briefcases had got off on the last circuit, and now the carriage was filling up with tourists and people dressed up to go out for the evening. Suddenly the train smelt of perfume, lipstick and chemical stuff, not sweat and feet and coffee. The doors pssshhhhed open, and a load of new people got on, I stood up to give a lady my seat and I leant against the glass panel. My bum was still a bit sore, some of the scabs had come off but most of the bruising had gone now, so I didn't mind losing my seat.

Some normal school children were staring at me, not unkindly, but staring all the same. I was so sick of people staring at me. I wished Megan were with me, I hated the attention our uniforms attracted. I never wore my hat, Megan and I made sure at the beginning of every summer term to go down on to the tracks at South Kensington, District and Circle lines, and place the boaters on the rail. We'd watch with joy as the train split them in two, knowing it would take ages to order another. The blazers were bad enough, but were nothing in comparison to the capes. Winter was just one long embarrassment; we were so identifiable we might as well have had sirens on our foreheads.

But it was bearable with Megan, maybe we just didn't notice the looks, we were so busy doing things. You could see our efforts all over the Underground; on the inter-connecting doors of the carriages of the Northern

Line trains we would get to work with our Stanley knives, changing, 'To increase ventilation lower this window' to 'To increase the nation love his widow', or our favourite: on 'Please let passengers off first!' we'd scratch out the word 'passengers'. We thought we were the best thing since sliced bread – something we knew about, only being allowed disgusting, wholemealy, crumbly, brown bread that was impossible to slice.

We never ever went past a chocolate machine without pulling all the handles. Once, when we were about eight, I had pulled and a free bar came out. We had pulled and pulled and pulled and we went home with fifty-seven bars of chocolate. We sold one to her brother – a nasty fruit and nut one.

Megan and I had a private game we never told anyone about, Surfing. This game was best during a really long tunnel like the via Bank branch between Euston and Camden Town. Surprisingly, it was best when the train was really crowded – no one ever noticed you then. You had to take all the clips and bands out of your hair and then you had to open the carriage doors and stand on the little movable silver platform that joined carriage to carriage. We'd wait until the train was really thundering along, and one of us would give the other a foot-up and we'd take it in turns to cling on to the roof of the train and feel the wind blow us away. You could scream as loud as you liked and not a soul could hear you. We had surfed the Northern Line since we were seven.

But none of this mattered any more.

Fowler had won the war. I had been completely silenced. I hadn't spoken to anyone for weeks now – I'd built a wall around myself so that nothing could get out and nothing could get in. Megan kept trying to get through to me despite the punishments. Fowler had caught her sliding me a note across the floor and she'd dragged Megan out of the room and made her write out Vedic sutras. But still Megan tried to make me laugh, pulling faces and things. She didn't understand that there wasn't any laughter left to come out. Fowler tried to get through my wall; she would force me to eat. She'd put a plate of bread and cheese in front of me and she'd tip my head back and hold a glass of water to my lips. I'd count the flowers on the Masaccio painting and let the water slide down my chin.

At night, I kept waking up downstairs. One night, I found myself sitting at the kitchen table. I'd put my uniform on back to front and tied my hair up in a pony tail. Another night I must have woken my father up because I remember him dragging me out of the coat cupboard and taking me back upstairs. Twice I'd woken up in the garden. I was getting tired and weak. When I looked in the mirror I barely recognized myself; big black rings around my eyes and my cheekbones sticking out of my whiter-than-white face, my jawline harsh and angular.

I slunk down the glass panel and tried to make myself invisible as the train pulled out of Victoria. I knew what I had to do. I picked at my Typexed initials on my little brown briefcase. I got out at Embankment and made the walk from District and Circle to Northern Line.

The platform was empty enough; I must have just

missed a train. I walked up towards the far end, where the trains come in, and gave a habitual pull at the chocolate machine. Nothing.

I looked up and saw the normally disappointing words 'Edgware branch'. All those times Megan and I had run our fastest through the passageways to catch a train, only for it to be an Edgware branch. But it didn't matter today. An Edgware branch was just fine.

I sat down on the empty bench. I was ready. I was prepared. I knew that what I was about to do was my only option. Yet it was much more than that, it was my final card. This should win me the trick. This way surely questions would have to be asked. I had visions of Fowler being handcuffed and taken off to the police, pleasurable images of her wailing for my forgiveness.

In my briefcase on my lap was a long, strictly confidential letter to Sri Chabaransha. In it I explained what had happened to me and how he had the wrong people running his school and how I felt that my subsequent actions were the only choice I had and might even help prevent situations like this from arising in the future. It was a heroic sort of letter.

I took it out and folded it neatly underneath the handle of my briefcase and drummed my fingers on the case. A few new people arrived on the platform, but no one came up this way. It was perfect.

I had chosen this particular platform at this particular station for specific reasons. Aside from the fact that hardly anyone from school travelled home this way, a bit of a guessing game happened on this platform. I always enjoyed watching tourists get up at the first roar of the approaching train and shuffle to the mind-the-gap edge only then to have to shuffle back again with surprise when the train never appeared – it would roar into the platform next door. It wasn't until the very last moment that you could tell whether the train would be arriving here. Also, for some reason, perhaps because the platform was extra long, the drivers never seemed to start braking until they were well into the station, so the trains were always going at full pelt as they appeared.

All this was ideal for my purposes. I would have only a split second to make myself jump, there would be no chance to chicken out, and the speed of the train would make my death as quick as possible.

I was filled with a mixture of excitement and terror as I heard the beginnings of the roar. I took the briefcase off my lap. I wished suddenly that I had written a note for Megan. Told her how much I loved her and how sorry I was to leave her. But it was too late for that.

I walked to the edge of the platform as the roar got louder. I placed my briefcase just behind me with the letter on top where somebody would discover it. I gazed at the dark tracks in front of me that were now zinging with electricity. My legs began to shake as the sound got nearer and nearer, my feet right on the edge. I wouldn't need to jump, I could just fall forward. I was ninety-nine per cent sure the train was coming into this platform and I felt the most alive I had ever felt in my life. Look what you've done Fowler! Look what you've done! I could feel myself rocking and then somewhere above the noise I heard a man shouting.

'Caroline! Caroline!'

With my heart pounding, I turned towards the voice along the platform just as the train whipped by my nose.

There, walking towards me in his fawn mackintosh was my dad. 'Caroline!' he called cheerfully, tucking his Hermes Trismegistus under his arm. 'I always thought you took the Picadilly.'

'Shall we play the piano?' my mum said cheerily about a week later. She was pretending to be happy. She didn't like scenes.

We were doing the washing-up. She was washing, I was drying. Our crockery, like everyone else's, was that same royal blue and white china: we all had it as if it had been made in bulk for the Organization. I stared at the plate in my hand, the pictures on it; a tree, some little birds, a boat, a bridge, a mystifyingly happy parallel crockery world where I spent a lot of my time, staring through my food.

'Caroline? What do you say?'

She was also pretending that she hadn't noticed that I was silent. Life seemed easier for everyone since I'd stopped talking. I hadn't spoken a word for weeks now. Not since the scene upstairs. We didn't have scenes in our house. We didn't have anything in our house. Not a telly, not a radio, not a fridge, not a washing machine. The Whopper had it in for electricity. But we did have a piano.

'A Mozart duet?' she carried on as if I'd said, 'Great, just what I fancied.'

Mozart was the bee's knees. The Whopper had said so, and that was that.

But I didn't move from the kitchen table. If you don't talk the strange thing is you slowly become invisible.

'How about the garden, shall we go into the garden?' She said it as if she didn't really expect a response any more, like she was talking to a baby or something. Sometimes I caught her looking at me strangely, although she had adjusted to my behaviour surprisingly seamlessly. My sleepwalking had just become part of the nightly routine. Mainly, I jumped off the sofa and I normally woke up when she was putting me back to bed, which she did very matter-of-factly, not cosily. She never tucked me in.

My mother opened the back door, and I heard her sigh. She went out. The warm air came into the cold house. I felt it on my skin. It was hard for me to feel anything in particular since I hadn't jumped under the Edgware branch. Of course I could try again, but it required quite a lot of energy, and I didn't seem to have much any more. Fowler had won. She had triumphed in my downfall, her teeth were making frequent appearances; she smiled as she came into rooms. Even my hatred for her had mellowed into a bog of nothingness. Hatred required a passion, and I was numb to it all now.

The fact that I was still alive when I should be dead was killing me slowly, unkindly. I felt like I was living someone else's life now, that the real me had got out and moved on to something better. I felt that my father had cheated me of my rightful death. Ever since I'd missed that jump, I had been floating about, observing but not partaking in life. I was weak and floppy too because of not eating. Sometimes I felt as if the back of my mouth had sealed up; nothing had come out or gone down for so long except water through a straw.

'Caroline!' I could hear Mum shouting from the garden. I put the plate down like an automaton and followed the sound. The garden was all overgrown, and it seemed that spring must have arrived, because where there hadn't been anything, there was greenness. The neighbours' houses had suddenly disappeared behind blossom-filled branches. Although we barely talked to our neighbours, them not being in the Organization, a great sadness filled me, the fact that I could no longer see their houses and get glimpses of their normal worlds: Arsenal flags in windows, jeans and frilly knickers on washing lines, flickering televisions, a burst of pop music when a window was opened, the comforting sound of a washing machine, I missed them already. I felt sad that I would be cocooned in this house, cut off from them, these lovely normal strangers. At least there was still the hole in the fence, where I spied on Carol Watson hanging out the washing in her pink dressing gown, not that they used their garden much. It was all overgrown, and they chucked things they didn't want into it, like old armchairs and mattresses. One day, I'd have a garden like that.

I could see Mum at the back by the gooseberry bushes crouched down, looking at something. She was in a dappled light under the pear tree.

'Oh Carry! Look!'

She never called me 'Carry', it surprised me. We weren't allowed to use nicknames. We had to call the hunger striker Mr Robert Sands.

I went to her. The Patels' tortoise had emerged from

his long winter's sleep and had ambled into our garden. The Patels were a little old couple; they lived on the other side, and Mr Patel spent all his time tending his roses. I would have thought my parents would have been friends with them because they were Hindus and knew about Krishna and Vishnu and everyone. But no, they never talked to them. Someone had once scribbled on their gate post 'WOGS OUT', and I had asked my dad what a Wog was. He told me that it was a Western Oriental Gentleman. But the Patels weren't in their garden today, the day their tortoise woke up.

I crouched down next to my mum and tapped the tortoise hello on his shell. I thought how nice to be a tortoise, to shut everything out for six months and to get up on a sunny day.

'Isn't he beautiful?' she said.

I nodded. She looked at me; we were close. Her glasses had slipped down her nose. I could tell that she wanted to take my hand, but that wasn't her way.

'For Pete's sake stop this, Caroline!' she said, quietly, as if she were at the end of her tether. 'Say *something*! You're being as stubborn as a mule.'

I waggled my finger near the tortoise's head. He retreated into his shell and then cautiously came out to examine my finger.

'I'm going to get him some cucumber,' she said and got up and headed back into the house, her long, home-made, flowery dress making swishing sounds in the overgrown grass.

I watched the tortoise for a bit. I put my hand on his back. His shell was all warm. He kept sticking his little pink tongue out; it was dry and scratchy. I went to the nearest flower bed and picked him a few leaves. He sniffed at them.

I could hear Mum's skirt swishing back out.

'Not that, Caroline! Don't give him that!' she said, running towards me. 'That's foxglove! It's poisonous. Those leaves would kill him!'

I looked at the innocuous-looking leaves and rubbed them in my fingers. I smelt my hand.

'Could they kill a human?' I asked her.

I had unsettled Fowler. She hadn't been quite so perky with me for the last couple of weeks, not since I was talking and eating again, smiling even, my eyes no longer glued to the ground. She knew it had something to do with the fire burning back in my belly. She didn't like me like this; she much preferred me silent and emaciated, a fine example of the misery that badness brings. I caught her looking at me now and then with alarm. Keep your enemies close by. She needed me by her side, so instead of face in the corner, I had to sit at the very front of every class, back to everybody, so that she could keep a sharp eye on my every move.

What she didn't know was that I had a plan, and all I was waiting for now was the opportunity to execute it. I had picked the leaves from the foxglove: every single leaf from one long stalk. I wasn't taking any chances. That weekend, I had closed my bedroom door, put my chair up against it and laid out every beautiful, elegant leaf on my bed, where the sun shone in through the window. I'd lovingly watched them dry out over a few days, changing from a dark to a dirty green. I'd turn them over like biscuits, smelling and caressing them, careful always to use my mittens. It was hard to believe these ordinary-looking things were killers. When they were completely dry I carefully scrunched them up and scooped every last bit into an envelope. I sewed a piece of fabric inside my big navy gym knickers then popped the sealed envelope into the pocket and wore my gym knickers over a clean pair every single day, waiting for the right moment. I carried around the lethal leaves, warmed by the heat from my slutty loin, for three whole weeks. She was right. I was poisonous. She didn't know the half.

And the opportunity eventually arose. Fowler was reading Sri Chabaransha's latest instalment to the twenty-four of us. It was vital, before philosophy class, that everyone had something to fiddle with: elastic bands, Blu-Tack, Sellotape, those little games where you had to roll the balls into hollows, marbles, anything to while away the boredom of the next couple of hours. Not me, though. I had been stationed, as usual, not one foot away from Fowler, my back to the rest of the class, my hands most visible.

A favourite pastime of ours in a philosophy class was to see who could come up with the most ridiculous observation. Each week we were given an exercise to carry out. This week we had had to observe ourselves in situations where we were being asked to do something against our wills, and when we felt ourselves becoming irritated we had to take a step back from the situation, from the irritation, and sound the Sanskrit word *aham*, the Absolute, and watch the effects.

Kate got off to a good start. Out of the corner of my eye I saw her hand go straight up. Fowler asked her for her observation.

I could hear the scrape of her chair as she stood up. 'Well, I was helping my mum do the washing-up and I really didn't want to, so I sounded the word *aham* and then I did.'

It was an inspirationally pathetic observation, and I could see Fowler was deeply unimpressed. She flashed her teeth and gave me a quick once-over as if I had been responsible for it in some way. I looked down. I knew the class was trying to cheer me up, and their support was my only other life-line. That and my secret.

'Anyone else?' she asked, looking about the room.

Someone must have raised their hand. I watched Fowler nod curtly and I heard the scrape of another chair, this time right at the back.

I could tell it was Deborah by the way she cleared her throat. 'I was at home in the garden feeding the birds in the birdbath, and one of them landed on my head, and I sounded the word *aham*, and it flew off.'

Deborah never quite got the gist of the observations and I, amongst others, couldn't help myself: I snorted with laughter.

'Outside!' Fowler snapped, poking my thigh. I got up and let myself out of the room, catching eyes with Amy, who was doing her utmost not to laugh, her face pallid and twitchy as if she had a mouthful of vomit.

I shut the classroom door behind me and leant against the wall.

I looked at my watch. There were twelve more minutes

left of class; she wasn't going to bring me back in. This was it. This was my opportunity. My heart began to beat fast. At last, the moment had arrived.

I peered over the staircase; the building was deserted. I could hear monotone singing coming out of the classroom next door,

'... Didst thou bring forth this Universe!'

I crept past the two doors and down the first flight of stairs. Sarah Martin was outside her classroom. I felt a strong allegiance to her; she too spent most of her school time outside classes. Although she was younger than me, we met a lot in this fashion. We exchanged 'Hi's as I passed her.

Down the next flight, past Room 8, where they were chanting Greek, I could hear Mr Steinberg chanting with them: 'Andra moi ennepe, Mousa, poloutropon hos mala polla'. The Greek merged with the Sanskrit from Room 7: 'Ak, ach at, aan, aam, eek.' I passed Room 4, the unmistakable tinkle of Vedic dance bells and girls dancing and chanting 'Ta taah ta tahh tay tat a tay tat a' as they stamped their feet in unison.

I peered over the railings and sprinted down the last few flights of red staircase. Not a soul about. I knocked quietly on her study door, just in case. I opened the door. I went straight over to the desk and pulled the drawer open and took out the bunch of keys. I knew exactly which one I was looking for. I went to the cupboard and opened the door. I couldn't reach the shelf so I pulled over her chair and stood on it. There were two plastic pouches full of dried herbs. I opened the big one and smelt it. Minty. I put it back. I opened the other one. At the bottom was a small amount of leaves that smelt musty and not too good: definitely a Dr Fox potion. I got out my envelope and tipped the scrunched-up dried foxglove leaves into the musty pouch, mixing them up with the other herbs. I closed the pouches and replaced them, jumped off the chair and pushed it back into place. I quickly locked the cupboard and put the keys back in the drawer and left the room. I could hear footsteps coming up from the kitchens, but I darted across to the staircase and up and up. Sarah Martin had rejoined her form. Out of breath, I got back to the top, leant against the wall and checked my watch. Eight minutes of the lesson left. Silence from my classroom: they must be practising an observation. I steadied my breathing. I'd done it. It was too late to change my mind.

6

Hyde Park is my least favourite of the London parks, for its mere proximity to St Augustine's. As schoolgirls we had spent inordinate amounts of time running around the Serpentine. However, I had to admit that today the park was looking pretty good. It was the end of a glorious spring day: buds had just budded, leaves had just burst forth, limp and green and exhausted with all the effort of being born. The sun shone sharply in the icy blue sky.

I was late, but I was in good spirits. I'd just had a break-through session with the Jamesons and I had a spring to my step. At last I felt as if we were getting somewhere. Since coming back from Cornwall, I had felt renewed in different ways, at home and at work. I had opened the gate to childhood and peered in, and in so doing I had known what to do with Gemma.

I'd been watching Lesley and Michael bickering across her, the poor little thing perched in between, head bowed, invisible, and I had asked Gemma to move her chair and join me and make some suggestions that she thought might improve her parents' marriage. She had gawped at me, amazed that I thought her opinions might be worthwhile, but she had joined me and pretty soon, to her parents' bewilderment, she was nailing their problems on the head. She, who had been observing them all her life, knew just what to say. I think we had all left that session on a little high.

Cornwall had helped me shed some baggage; I had felt lighter in some way, as if I were emptying the wardrobe that I have carried around on my back for so long. The wardrobe would always be there – of that I was guaranteed – but at least I was clearing out a little bit of the junk. And with it, my back was just a little straighter, my head a little higher, and the pressure inside a little less constricting. Suddenly I was looking up: if not at the horizon, at least not at the ground.

Objectively, I'd say that I was going through a manic episode. The effect of this at home with Joe was surprising. We were getting on well, the house was harmonious, and Tilly was behaving.

Cornwall already seemed like a lifetime ago, a weekend of sheer madness, a false world, a dreamy, sexual unreality. I'd never had an affair before and hadn't anticipated how extremely titillating it was going to be: the occasional brush of an arm, a finger meeting a finger as a cup of tea is passed, a lingering look, the delicious traces left by the desired one – a warm seat, a borrowed jumper, a taste of his beer. It had felt like Steinberg and I were living in some kind of twilight zone. There had been one foolish moment in the farmhouse where I'd gone upstairs to get something and he had followed and caught me and shut the bedroom door and pushed me up against it to kiss me, to touch me, to feel me, to take me in his mouth. It was reckless and dangerous, which, I presume, is what had made it all so painfully erotic.

Steinberg and I had made it through the rest of the

weekend avoiding and pin-pointing each other at the same time. We had exchanged numbers along with everyone else, making promises, false or not, of meeting up. He had rung me pretty much every day for two weeks, but I had not been returning his calls. I could see it for what it was. I did not want our affair to continue. It was good and necessary to have done what we did, but that was no reason for it to carry on. I didn't believe in destiny and all that crap. The only thing I knew with any certainty was that I did not want to have the Organization back in my life, in any shape or form. It was too risky. There are some things which should never be unearthed. I would see Amy again because we had both turned our backs on it, but I would not see anyone who was still in it. A line had to be drawn, and I knew exactly where to draw it. So that was what I was here to do.

Steinberg had obviously seen me before I saw him. He was seated on the agreed bench overlooking the Serpentine. I noticed that his hair had grown, making him look boyish and unkempt. He was wearing a long, blue, woollen coat and had one of those stripy, studenty scarves tied around his neck in that way everyone is wearing them now, loop-and-through, like a uniform. Organization people just shouldn't do it – attempt to be fashionable; somehow it was unseemly, this merging of Jurassic mentality with an *à la mode* vestment. I hoped he hadn't made this effort for me. Megan had probably put him in it.

He was watching me in the way only a lover can do, proprietorially, like the proud owner of a new car, only Organization people weren't allowed attachments to the material world. They disapproved of ownership full stop, so should I say he was looking at me as if I were a fresh page of Sri Chabaransha's wisdoms? No, the hypocrite, he was looking at me with all the lust and desire the physical world could muster. He yearned to possess me.

I sat down next to him, and we kissed each other's cheeks like acquaintances. As we did so, I noticed that we both had a guilty glance about. We looked shifty, like two KGB agents in our long dark coats. He moved a little closer to me.

'You're even better in the flesh than my imagination,' he said, that sweet half smile upon his lips.

'Is that so, Caveman?' I replied.

'How you doing?'

'Fine.'

He caught my eye properly now; new lovers need these verifications.

'I've thought about you non-stop,' he said.

'Yeh?'

'Oh yeh. I'm almost deranged.'

It's a strange thing, requited passion. It was almost as if a third party was present; a rabid animal sitting on the bench between us, drooling and desperate. I kicked it off.

'This can't happen, Steinberg.'

He sighed audibly and pulled away. 'I knew it!' he said, his face wincing. 'I knew you were going to say that.'

He leant back on the bench stretching out his long legs. He crossed his ankles and joined his hands behind his neck and turned to me, 'Tell me why not, again? I keep forgetting.'

'Oh, you know,' I said, getting out a cigarette. 'Little things . . . children, wives, husbands.'

'Are you and Joe married?'

'As good as!' Interesting, I thought, that I said that. I lit the fag.

'You should quit.'

'Yeh, yeh,' I said.

He reached over to take my hand, but I moved it away. 'Steinberg, this can't happen.'

He turned his body to face me, one arm resting on the back of the bench, leaning in towards me, the half smile. 'I want you,' he said, quietly. 'I want you! I want you!'

I took a deep drag.

'Blow your smoke at me!'

I did so and he breathed it in. 'See? I even love the air you pollute.'

'Stop it!' I said, as if he were an annoying schoolboy.

'Tell me you don't want me! Go on! Say it!'

'I don't want you!'

'Look me in the eye and say it!'

I crossed my legs, angled my body towards him, sighed and looked him in the eye. 'I don't want you.'

He smiled and shook his head with mock despair. 'You're lying!' he said. 'Shame on you, Caroline Stern!'

Ah! I'd forgotten that, I'd forgotten that he said that. I believe those words could bring me back from the brink of death itself. I couldn't help it. I laughed. Then, despite myself, I leant forward and kissed his lips. I didn't care who saw.

He kissed me back, intensely. He knew I wanted him.

He grabbed my hands and pulled me off the bench and marched me through the park.

We got a small, overpriced room in a hotel opposite Hyde Park. He led me by the hand through the busy reception to the lift, where we glared at each other like hungry dogs, across two fat Arabs. He led me down a corridor, key in hand, head turning to check room numbers like Arnie on a killing spree. He found the room, opened the door, let me in, and we barely made it to the bed.

Then a little while later, we made love again, but this time tenderly, lovingly as if we had all the time in the world. And afterwards, as we lay there entwined in the hotel sheets, my body lying on his, I gently kissed his face a thousand times, not missing a single pore, while he lay there with his head back, his eyes shut, just seeping me in.

Outside, the London sky slowly turned pink.

'You know I could never love you,' I said, as I laid another kiss on his temple, breathing in the sweet smell of him.

'No,' he said, not stirring just receiving. 'I didn't know that. Why not?'

'Because you're weak.' My lips brushed his hairline.

'Is that right?'

'You're still there,' I whispered.

'Ah, the Organization, that's what this is about.' He moved his head slightly, as if to say, I'd missed a bit. 'Is this because I didn't tell about the Sikh?'

'Partly.' I kissed the same place again just in case I had missed a bit.

'Boy,' he said dreamily. 'You sure can hold a grudge.'

'Yes, I can.' I moved my lips across his cheekbone. 'You're no better than any of them.' I kissed the hollow between cheekbone and jaw. 'You were scared and you were just another sheep. You believe what you're told!'

Between each phrase my lips moved down his face, intent on covering every piece of him. 'You're a puppet. They pull your strings. They say "dance", and you dance. You question nothing. And you know what the worst thing is?'

'No,' he said, raising his chin a minuscule amount so I could kiss his neck. 'What's the worst thing?'

'You send your children there.'

'Okay!' he said and reluctantly he opened his eyes and looked up into mine. He rearranged the pillow behind his head so our faces were level. I rested my chin on his chest.

'One accusation at a time! I should have said something. I can see that now, but would it have made any difference?'

'It might have,' I replied, twisting the hairs on his chest.

'Ow! Caroline, I had no idea what was going on between you and her and I still don't because, although you're quite happy to point the finger at everyone else, you don't talk! We're not even allowed to mention her name in your company! And guess what? We don't! Every time I mention your folks you just give me the silent treatment! Or what ever happened to you when you quit? You know what, Caroline, my sweetheart, I think you're more obsessed with the Organization than anyone who's in it.'

I slid off him and leant on my elbow, 'Just to let you know, Caveman, I think all of you – Megan, you, my mother, all of you who are still there – are traitors to the rest of us, to all those ex-pupils whose lives have been trashed.'

'And secondly,' he carried on, 'yes, I send my children there, because I want them to realize that there is more to life than this physical world. I want them to develop their spirituality. I want them to be of some use to this world. I want them to know they have a purpose. And I can't find another school that does that. Is that so wrong? Caroline, you have to understand, it's not the same place it was when you were there!'

I looked him in the eye, serious now. 'I should bloody hope not!' I lay back and focused on the peeling ceiling.

'Caroline. It is different now. It was extreme then. It was way too extreme.'

'Oh, *now* you say that. Why the fuck wasn't anyone saying that then?' Even I was shocked by the ferocity of my anger.

He pulled himself up and leant against the headboard.

'Why are you *so* angry?' he asked, gently.

'You probably are too, Steinberg, you've just never noticed, you're so bloody brainwashed. It's the children I can't take. It's just not fair on the children.'

'I wouldn't put my children there in the school how it was.'

I laughed, outraged. 'But it was okay for us? It was okay to teach there?'

'We believed in it then. We thought we were doing something really important.' He sounded quite passionate.

'I came from a family who had no spiritual life whatso-ever. I never felt I belonged and then I heard about the Organization, and it was just what I had always been looking for. I jumped like a shot, Caroline, at the chance to be in it, to teach at St Augustine's.'

I sighed heavily.

'But, I don't know,' he said, looking out of the window, as if the purpling sky might hold the answers. '"Power tends to corrupt. And absolute power corrupts absolutely."'

'Wapinski?'

'Yes. Everyone grew to realize that. And Fowler ...'

'Don't!' I said, turning to him. 'Don't say her name!' I was deadly serious, and he knew it.

'Okay, okay. But you have to know that things changed when Howard took over.'

'Oh please,' I snapped. 'Whatever you do, don't give me any more of that crap about it being "different" now. Don't blanket over my past, over other people's pasts with this "it's so different" shit!' I could hear my voice begin to wobble. 'Don't negate my life like that. Things happened, and that fact cannot be changed.'

I kicked off the sheets and got out of the bed, but Steinberg grabbed my arm.

'Come here! Come here! Come here!' he said pulling me back into his arms. 'SShhh ...' He held me tightly, as if I had been crying. He was right, really. I think if I could cry I would have been crying.

'What things, darling? What can't be changed?' he whispered into my ear, his hand gently brushing my cheek.

Perhaps it was the warmth of his breath in my ear or the lilt of his accent on the word 'darling', but for some unfathomable reason I almost told him. Instead, just in the nick of time, I pulled myself away and began to get dressed.

I knew something was up when both Lesley and Michael Jameson sat down together, their chairs almost touching. It didn't feel right, Michael not standing by the window gazing outside. It seemed as if the day was calling him and he was rebuffing it.

I offered them a biscuit. I was absolutely starving. Lesley refused; she waved them away rather grandly. She'd had her nails done, perfect little American flags on each one. She'd also had her hair done: it was black underneath with white streaks through it. She looked like a flag-waving skunk.

'How's it going?' I said, rummaging on my desk for my notes.

'Very well, actually, Lorrie.'

'Sounds intriguing,' I said, my hand flapping around my desk furiously looking for a pen.

'We've come into a bit of money, actually,' Lesley said, trying to suppress a big grin. I instinctively looked to Michael, who wasn't giving anything away.

'Lucky you!' I said. I knew better than to ask how they'd come into it.

'We're going to go on holiday. Florida.'

'Lovely, Disneyland?'

'Yes, staying in a five-star.'

'Wow!' I found my notes and my pen and opened them.

'So we won't make the next two sessions.' They actually smiled at each other. Who said money can't buy you love?

'Okay,' I said, smoothing down the pages of my pad.

'And . . . the big news is we're going to go private.'

I was rather offended, 'Are you not happy with our sessions?'

'God no! I didn't mean therapy,' she said.

'We'll screw the state for all we can,' chipped in Michael. Cheers. I'd never seen him so jolly. I wanted to rub his velvet head.

'No, I mean we're going to send Gemma to private school,' Lesley carried on. 'It's something we've always wanted.'

'Oh?'

Obviously, in my opinion, a private education is thoroughly overrated.

'Well, she certainly isn't thriving at her present school, I agree,' I said.

'Exactly. And at her new school, you'll be pleased to hear, Lorrie, their school dinners are really healthy, very Jamie Oliver. That was probably half the trouble with Gem: she's very health conscious.'

Right. That'll be why she weighs five stone.

'Is it a local school?' I asked.

'No, actually, not at all, it's an independent school,' she said proudly, as if 'independent' meant it had wandered off somewhere. 'Top of the league table. She starts beginning of next month. St Augustine's.'

I stopped taking notes; my pen hovered above the page.

'I'm sorry?' I said, looking up. 'Where did you say?'

'St Augustine's, South Kensington.'

I was so gobsmacked I lamely echoed her words, 'St Augustine's, South Kensington?'

'It's got a ring to it, hasn't it?'

'But you can't!' I said, totally inappropriately.

'I beg your pardon?' Michael replied.

I backtracked: '. . . it's such a long way away.'

'I believe my child is entitled to a good education, and it is worth travelling for. You should see it! It's gorgeous, not like a school really: plush carpet, indoor shoes, real china, chandeliers, posh paintings everywhere. They do all sorts of classes. You wouldn't believe it, Lorrie. The usual stuff, but other stuff too. They do Veddic dancing.'

Vedic, Vedic. Pronounced Way-Dick.

'That's like Indian Bollywood stuff. Gem loves dancing.'

My mouth must have been hanging open.

'Get this! They learn Sansklit.'

Oh my God. Sansk*rit*, Lesley. Sansk*rit*.

'They love Indian stuff. It's sort of an Indian school, I think. Without the curry.'

I was nodding my head, keeping my eyes down. Poor Gemma, poor Gemma.

'The head, short, red-headed woman without a bra, she was ever so nice. She said they'd had anorexics before, and she'd keep an eye on Gemma. It's a very special school, Lorrie. Celebrities send their children there and everything. She'll be mingling.'

I don't know how I got through the rest of the session.

I kept having visions of little Gemma getting thinner and thinner with her face pressed to a pipe.

I sat on the bench in Regent's Park where you can see the elephants. I felt as if I were walking on a tightrope, at any moment liable to fall, to come crashing down. My life had suddenly become dangerous. I couldn't help Gemma without opening doors. I had spent all these years shutting them, keeping things separate, and now, it seemed, all my worlds were colliding out of my control. I wished I'd never bumped into Amy at that stupid dog shrink place. I wished I'd never gone to Cornwall and met Megan and Steinberg and their children. I wanted to chuck everything back into my wardrobe again and sling it on my back.

When I got home, Tilly greeted me at the door half-heartedly before returning to the sitting room. She'd been guilt-tripping me a lot since the escapade in the cave. She had probably seen things a dog shouldn't really see, and ever since I felt that she had been looking at me accusingly with those dark, knowing eyes of hers. She had been deliberately favouring Joe ever since we got back from Cornwall: whenever a choice of laps came up she would get on to his with a little curt nod in my direction once she was safely perched as if to say, 'Scrubber.'

'Hi!'

'Hi!' I dumped my bag in the hall and kicked off my shoes.

Joe was on the sofa, watching Sky Sports whilst playing Football Manager on his Playstation, whilst listening to Five Live on the radio and apparently reading the sports pages of the newspaper all at the same time. Usually I'd

169

find this deeply irritating: how much noise and flickering imagery could one person take? But today I found it comforting. I think I really did love Joe, for his complete and utter normality. I would stick to his world; it was where I belonged, away from these Organization people. All I had to do was not see Steinberg.

I went into the kitchen and turned the radio down.

'I was listening to that!' He was joking.

'Cup of tea?' I shouted.

'Yes, ta,' he said, looking up.

I made the tea and joined him on the sofa. He stopped playing Playstation, put down the controls and turned the volume down. The little men carried on running around in silence.

'What's up?' he asked. 'Bad day?'

'Yes.'

'Why?'

I wasn't used to opening up to Joe. For so many years I had backed out of corners like this. But, for God's sake, if I wanted him and me to function, I had to start putting the work in.

'One of my clients, she's this little fragile thing, skin and bones, really breakable, parents fighting all the time. Oh Joe,' I said turning to face him. 'Guess what school they're sending her to?'

His jaw dropped. 'To the funny farm?'

'Yes.'

I loved him for that. What the hell was I playing at with Steinberg?

'I don't know what to do. I don't know how to help, how to stop them.'

He sighed and opened a packet of Silk Cut that was on the table. We were half-heartedly trying to give up. He put two in his mouth and lit them both and passed one to me.

'What should I do?' I said. I thought that this was perhaps the first time that I had ever asked him that question. It seemed extraordinary that only a few weeks earlier I could not have ventured into this territory with him.

He blew smoke out slowly into the room; we both watched it churn around and vanish.

'Lorrie,' he said gently. 'One day, you'll tell me whatever it is you're … not telling me, whatever it is that happened.'

I bristled. He put his hand on my thigh and rubbed it absent-mindedly. 'I don't know what went down there, Lol, but what I do know is that your people from there are good people.'

He was looking at me now; he meant every word. I loved him so much for not asking questions.

'I've liked everyone I've met,' he continued. 'They're a bit … removed, maybe, no that's the wrong word … they're a bit dreamy … absent, maybe, but that's okay. That Cameron boy, I would be proud to have a son like that. Listen, baby, I know you did some weird shit there, but they are doing *something* right if they're turning out kids like that. So I imagine she'll be okay.'

I flicked my ash. I leant my head against him. Maybe this was how other couples lived. No secrets. Well, only one or two. My eyes were caught by his Playstation; his players were in a line-up.

'Joe?' I said. 'Have you made the whole West Ham team black and bald?'

'Aren't they gorgeous?!' he said, putting his arm around me. I smiled and rolled my eyes.

'Hey,' he said. 'How about we go upstairs, you and me, you put on my West Ham shirt – it's clean, I promise – lacy knickers, fishnets, nice pair of heels . . .?'

I laughed.

'You know you want to, Lol,' he said, kissing my neck.

And we did. I don't mean I dressed up as a Hammer whore, but we did go upstairs and have sex, nice and familiar sex. It was surprisingly rewarding having two lovers.

Afterwards, when Tilly had thrown herself at the door a few times and I was rummaging through the covers looking for my pants, Joe said from the bed, 'By the way, before I forget, Megan rang, inviting us to supper on Friday. I said yes.'

What? Alarm bells started ringing in my ears.

I delayed calling her until much later, until Joe was out of the room, and then she didn't answer her mobile, so I had to ring the land line, thinking hopefully Steinberg would be out at some Organizational thing.

But, no, he answered. 'Hello?'

I had caught him unknowing, in his happily-married-family-man-answering-the-telephone voice.

Joe wandered into the sitting room in his boxers and a T-shirt. I thought of putting the phone down, but it would be too embarrassing if Steinberg pressed ringback. It was hateful, this deceit.

'Hi, Steinberg,' I said; his intake of breath was just about audible. 'Nate!' I added for Joe's benefit, which was a giveaway if ever there was. 'How are you?'

'Caroline!' he replied, changing his tone to both intimate and formal all at once. I could tell that Megan was in the room.

'About supper on Friday, we can't come.'

'Right,' he said. 'I'll pass you over to Megan.'

'Okay. Bye.'

It was all horribly stilted, and I could hear Megan saying she'd take it upstairs, so I was left with him for a moment longer. Neither of us said anything, but I could feel him in my ear. Joe kissed my shoulder on his way out of the room with the paper.

'Caroline!' Megan said, and then she yelled downstairs. 'Nate! You can put it down!'

Click went the phone. I pictured their house, their bedroom, their phones.

'Hi, darling,' Megan said.

'We can't come on Friday.'

'What? Joe said you could! Why not?' She sounded disproportionately disappointed.

'Oh, I'd promised this friend at work we'd go to the cinema.'

'Get rid of her! Caroline, you have to come! I need to talk to you!' She spoke as if we were still best friends, as if a lost twenty-five years meant nothing, as if she had some right to me.

'What about?' I caught eyes with Tilly from across the room.

'Something's wrong.'

'What's wrong?'

She lowered her tone, 'I think Nate's having an affair.'

Organization families had always congregated in certain areas of London, for no apparent reason. Chiswick was one of them. The very word 'Chiswick' mustered up a hundred pictures in my head: gloomy houses with lights left off until way past dusk, cold rooms, religious Renaissance prints on walls, pianos with Mozart pieces left open, scrubbed wooden floorboards, polished wooden chairs, dark furniture, perhaps a sculpture of Vishnu or Ganesha alone on a bare mantelpiece, blue and white crockery on the dresser in the kitchen, a plain wooden table, a calendar with calligraphic quotes from the Bhagavad Gita, Holy Mother or – how modern and risqué – Shakespeare, the smell of baked bread and milk, a chill in the air, indoor plants, nibs lined up on desks, holy books on bedside tables, long skirts in cupboards. And silence, silence everywhere, broken only perhaps by the ticking of an old inherited clock or the swish of a skirt.

It was disconcerting to find that Megan's and Steinberg's house wasn't like that at all. Steinberg opened the door. He looked homey and preppy, and it felt all wrong to be here, like climbing into a baby's crib.

'Come in! Hi Joe!' he said shaking Joe's hand and taking the bottle of wine from him. 'Thank you!'

He and I kissed cheeks and didn't look each other in the eye. I stepped in.

Music drifted down from upstairs, something edgy and urban, not befitting a house in Chiswick.

'Cam!' Steinberg shouted upstairs. 'Turn that down,

can you?' The volume decreased almost immediately.

My eyes gave the hall and the living room a quick recce as we went through to the kitchen. To my surprise the house was lively and colourful and strangely normal. One or two things gave them away; the obligatory framed picture of Sri Chabaransha hanging by the door, the same one my parents had, him boss-eyed in the nappy, and I noticed the calligraphic calendar hanging on the wall as soon as we walked through the dining room into the kitchen, which was large and cosy, homely and extra-ordinarily normal. I flinched inside at the sight of the school logo on timetables and various letters pinned to the noticeboard. Over on the dresser, there it was, the telltale crockery. The Organization probably had a bloody catalogue these days where you could order all their spooky shit.

Megan and I kissed; she was chopping up some tomatoes.

'Something smells good,' I said. 'Don't tell me we're going to be having *cooked* food!'

'Oh, Caroline!' she reprimanded me, laughingly. Although why the idea of *not* eating cooked food was suddenly so preposterous, fuck knows.

'That's a nice painting!' I said, the way I occasionally caught myself saying something when in reality I meant the exact opposite, like 'Your hair looks fantastic' when it has in fact only caught my eye because it looks noticeably terrible. The painting was tosh: some serene being hover-ing beside a bush, all flimsy and whimsy with pretensions of holiness. But it was big, and someone obviously liked it, and I must have felt obliged to comment.

'That's by Charles! Remember Charles Grey?' she said cheerily.

Of course I remembered Charles Grey; he was that little drip from the year below, obviously now deemed by the Organization to be a talent. I bet they've all got Charles Greys hanging in their houses. Stick him in the real world, he'd sink without trace.

This was good being here, seeing Steinberg in his home with his insipid Charles Greys and his brainwashed crockery. I felt a million miles away from him. But then he handed me a glass of white wine, and our fingers touched, and the million miles vanished just like that. We caught eyes for a little too long, and I sat down beside Joe on the low sofa. Joe put his hand on my thigh and rubbed my leg, and I noticed Steinberg turn away.

A little while later, Megan and I left the men together under the pretext of showing me the house. I followed her rather snazzy, too-tight skirt upstairs.

'Oh! Look!' I said, stopping. There, framed amongst other pictures, was Megan's painting of the cherry blossom.

'Oh, yes!' she said, uninterestedly. 'My mum framed it.'

Once again, I was transported straight back to that tree. Megan's painting was completely different from Amy's, large and colourful but just as beautiful. I couldn't even remember mine.

Megan was on the landing. She motioned for me to have a look in a dark room. I followed her in. Little Caroline was sound asleep in a miniature bed; her thumb, evidently recently sucked, had slipped out of her little cherubic lips. She looked unbearably sweet, and I felt a pang of envy for the family life and a pang of guilt for encroaching on it.

'Come on!' whispered Megan, tucking Caroline in and ushering me out in one swift movement. I followed her into the room next door, the room where Steinberg and Megan made their babies.

'Lovely bedroom,' I heard myself saying, as Megan shut the bedroom door behind us, but this time I meant it, weird as it was to be shown your lover's bedroom by the cuckolded one. The room was surprisingly messy, as I had noticed was the whole house. I say 'surprisingly so' because Megan's mother, in true fundamentalist style, was obsessive on the cleanliness front. My mother was bad enough, but Megan's mum was scary. She made us take our shoes off and wear house coats the moment we walked in. She once punished me for sitting on Megan's bed and creasing the cover; I had had to spend the whole of Saturday morning scrubbing and waxing her floors. But none of it appeared to have rubbed off on Megan; she was what my mother would have called a 'slut' – obviously not in the sense that Fowler had called me a slut; nothing remotely sexual was ever inferred at our house.

I looked around the room, feeling distinctly odd. Steinberg wore pyjamas. I could see them under the pillow of the unmade bed, really conventional M&S pyjamas. My eyes, ignoring messages from my brain, scanned the sheets looking for evidence of sexual activity, hypocrite that I was.

But what struck me most was the fact that they were parents. I had never been inside the bedroom of a mother

177

and father. I had never been allowed in my own parents' bedroom, not if they were in it. Evidence of children was everywhere: a ragged old elephant toy, a colourful plastic beaker with a rabbit on it, mini clothes, bottles of pink medicine and sticky white plastic spoons. Needless to say, I spotted the giveaway holy books on the bedside tables.

Megan was rummaging in a pair of Steinberg's trousers.

'Look!' she said, handing me a folded piece of paper. I took it.

'Open it!'

At first I didn't recognize it. Park Hotel, it said, £210. Room service, Bollinger champagne £80.

Oh arse. I said the first thing that came into my head: 'Where did you find it?'

She had her arms folded and was leaning on the chest of drawers. She looked cross but resigned. 'Here, in his trousers. The little shit.'

I couldn't quite get used to Organization people swearing; it didn't fit, like the snazzy skirt. I was thinking on my feet. 'Have you confronted him?'

'Can't remember the last time he took *me* to a hotel and bought Bollinger champagne. No, I have not.'

Actually, I had bought the Bollinger champagne, but it was not the time for nit-picking.

'It doesn't look good, does it?' she said.

'No.'

'I think I know who it is.'

'Who?' Oh, Christ.

'That Van Heusen woman from his Greek translation group. I've seen the way she looks at him. And it has to be someone in the Organization; it's so near the building.'

I felt a strange surge of jealousy towards this Van Heusen woman. I almost wanted to help Megan track the bitch down.

'I knew it,' she said, sitting down on the bed, not thinking twice about crinkling the cover. 'I knew something was up. He's just been . . . different.'

'Different?'

I didn't really want to know, but I felt I had to say something. Really, I just wanted to get out of here, out of the house, away from these people, back home with Joe.

'He's distracted, checking his phone all the time.'

'Look, maybe he did have a fling, Megan,' I said, rather bizarrely. 'Maybe he did and maybe it's over!' I decided once and for all that it was.

'Plus . . .' she said, raising an eyebrow. 'He wants sex all the time.'

That shut me up.

'The little shit,' I agreed.

I decided I was going to feign illness downstairs, and Joe and I could go home.

But it didn't happen like that.

When we came back downstairs, Joe and Steinberg had opened another bottle and were getting on like a house on fire. Steinberg had put some music on, Van Morrison. How ghastly, he was trying to show me how groovy he was. In a dated kind of way, of course.

Joe was already sitting at the table, which had been draped with a large blue and white checked tablecloth. Candles flickered, a big casserole dish sat in the middle, and something smelt good. Steinberg had pulled out all the stops. I was hungry and lost my resolve to leave. I had that tightrope-walking feeling again and the same desire to throw myself off.

'Wow! That looks good, thanks, Nate,' said Megan. Organization men normally did diddly squat around the house. I could hear the surprise in her voice.

'Please sit!' Steinberg said to me, pulling out a chair and taking a seat opposite me.

At first I thought it was a mistake. Just after the soup, someone brushed my foot under the table. I pulled my own foot away, like you do, but still the foot found mine again. There was no mistake. I looked up at Steinberg; he was listening to Joe talking about his work with what appeared to be genuine interest. For the briefest moment he caught my eye as if to say, yes, that was me.

I thought how tacky he was, to do that right underneath their noses, in his own home. What a creep! But as he began to massage my calf gently with his toes, my indignation lost its momentum. And after a while, I found myself stretching my legs out slightly to ease his path. Van began singing 'Bright Side of the Road'.

'What does your dad do, Joe?' Megan asked.

'Well, my dad worked on the roads,' he said. The couple of glasses of wine had gone straight to my head, which was unusual for me, and I began to confuse the words I was hearing, I kept thinking Van Morrison was singing about tarmacing.

I don't think Megan had ever come across anyone who worked on the roads; she had only ever met people who worked for the Organization, and there wasn't much road laying there.

'What does that mean, "worked on the roads"?' she

asked. I wanted to say, 'Where've you been all your life?' But I knew exactly where she'd been.

'Laying the tarmac.'

'Oh,' she said, as if she'd thought Joe's father had been a wandering troubadour.

I opened my knees a little wider, and Steinberg's foot went a little higher.

Joe wasn't bothered by Megan, 'Yes, he hated it. The day he retired I remember I said to him, "Will you miss working?" He looked at me as if I was mad. "No," he said. "I've hated every minute of it."'

'How awful to spend your life doing something you hate.'

Welcome to the real world, Megan. We haven't all seen the fucking light.

'Is he alive?' she carried on.

'No, he died years ago.'

'Oh, dear.'

But she didn't say it that sadly, because the afterlife was so guaranteed for her there was really nothing to be sad about.

All the while, Steinberg's foot was slowly working its way up my inner thigh, and I was finding it exceedingly hard to concentrate. I was flushed, hot and aching for him.

'My mum's alive and kicking,' Joe was saying. 'She's a social worker.'

'Really?' said Megan.

At least she knew what a social worker was, not that there was any call for them at the Organization. There you had group leaders whom you went to with your problems; they were fully trained by the Organization, i.e., not at all.

Please, please just a little bit higher, Steinberg. The ache was howling now.

'Can you get the corkscrew, Nate?' Megan asked, and Steinberg's foot stopped. He waited a while and then got up, keeping his eyes on me as if to say 'Patience, Caroline, patience.' He turned away from the others. For good reason. I checked that Joe hadn't seen what I'd seen. Steinberg got the corkscrew and dallied in the kitchen for a moment.

'Caroline,' Megan said. 'Look, I know you'll be cross with me, but I promised her I'd ask and I won't ask again, but, talking of mothers, your mum wants me to give her your number.'

I knew she was going to tell me something about my mum; it was inevitable.

'Well, don't,' I said snappily.

'Oh! Caroline, she really wants to see you.'

'You can tell her it's a bit late for that.'

'She's not well,' she said, sotto voce, and then she looked pleadingly into my eyes. 'She really needs you.'

I felt a kind of sickness well up inside me, sickness and anger churning together. Where the fuck had she been when I needed her?

'Okay, Megan,' I said, sotto voce right back. 'You've asked, and the answer is no.'

Steinberg, who was listening, came back and sat down and topped up our glasses.

'But I see her and she's absolutely desperate to . . .' Megan carried on. She had always been a bit obtuse.

'Megan!' Steinberg raised his voice as he turned to his wife. 'Caroline's given you her answer.'

I was grateful to him for that. I could see Megan looking at Joe, trying to catch his eye as if to say, 'You talk to her, make her see sense.'

Joe changed the subject. I looked up at Steinberg. Come on, come on, come on, where were we? But talk of my mother had spoilt it.

'I've been meaning to ask you two, actually,' I said. 'Is the Whopper still alive?'

And I slipped out of my heels and with my toes lifted the hem of Steinberg's trousers.

'Who's the Whopper?' he asked, glad to have a reason to look me in the eye. He placed one of his hands on my foot and squeezed it.

'Wapinski,' I said, enunciating the syllables carefully, enjoying the brief shock in his eyes before he smiled at my blasphemy. 'You remember: Absolute power and all that,' I added.

I pushed my foot along his inner thigh.

'Yes, he's alive,' Megan answered me. 'But, poor Sir, he's very ill and has been for years.'

'Sir'? They called him 'Sir'. It made me want to vomit.

Megan turned to me, 'No one's allowed to see him any more. He's too ill,' she carried on. She sounded sad, like he was her fucking dad or something. 'It's awful.'

'My heart bleeds,' I said cheerily, tempted to give Steinberg a good kick in the cock. The phone rang loudly in the kitchen.

'That might be Ellie,' Megan said, looking at Steinberg. Eleanor was Megan's sister. Ellie? Ellie? When did they all start using nicknames? The phone stopped ringing abruptly.

'Mum?' came Cameron's voice down the stairs. 'Mum? It's Aunty Ellie!'

'All right! Come down and say hello, Cam! Oh dear, excuse me, guys!' Megan said, getting up. 'Nate, get out the sorbet, can you?'

Megan filled me in on her sister as she left the room, 'Ellie's going through a bad time. I'm going to have to take it.'

Cameron appeared at the door, looking so like Steinberg I almost laughed.

'Hey, Cameron!' I said.

'Hi,' he said, giving me a kiss and giving Joe a cool, black guy, complicated handshake thing that Joe had taught him in Cornwall.

'My man!' Joe said.

Cameron was so mature and polite I found it disconcerting. I'd never met a teenager like him.

'Joe, just the man I need!' he said. Teenagers loved Joe; it was why he was so good at his job. 'I can't fix my guitar strings.'

Guitars? Things had certainly changed. In my day we were only allowed to play pianos and violins and things that Mozart wrote for – I bet when that *Amadeus* film came out the Whopper had to change his tune.

'Leave the guy alone, Cam, he's having his dinner,' Steinberg said.

'No worries,' Joe said getting up, glad for the excuse to get away from the barbed conversation, I expect.

'I'll go get it!' said Cameron.

'I'll come up! Show me your room,' Joe said, following Cameron out of the room.

So, quite suddenly and unexpectedly, Steinberg and I were left alone downstairs. We said nothing, just stared at each other for a little while. Van Morrison sang 'Brown-eyed Girl'. The only brown-eyed girl around here was Megan.

'Are you ever going to tell me why you're so full of rage?' he said kindly, patronizingly.

'No. Are you going to tell me when you're going to start thinking for yourself?'

He got up and on his way to the fridge he pushed to the glass door that divided the kitchen from the hall.

He got out the sorbet and picked up the blue and white bowls and some spoons and brought them all back to the table. He pulled his chair round to the edge so that he was sitting to my right. He sat down and took the lid off the sorbet box and leant on his elbows, head on one hand, and gave me a quizzical look.

I took a sip of wine.

Under the table he took my hand and gently squeezed it. 'I just wish I knew, that's all,' he said.

With his other hand he picked up a spoon and scraped off a layer of the dark pink ice and then sucked it off cleanly. I loved his mouth, I felt jealous of the sorbet.

'Mmmm,' he said, closing his eyes. 'I looove sorbet!'

He dipped the spoon back into the sorbet and scraped some more off and offered it to me. This was a dangerous game, but my body was certainly up for it. I took it, and he fed me another mouthful.

He raised his hand and wiped the edge of my lip with

his thumb and then licked his thumb. Seamlessly, he leant forward and licked the sorbet off my lip. I glanced at the door; it was open. He licked me again. The moment his lips brushed mine, I melted. We kissed as if we depended on each other for the very air we breathed.

The worst thing was, they both must have been watching us for quite some time because, when Steinberg and I parted, after too long, there they were, as clear as day in the reflection of the glass door, which had swung open a little wider, standing at the bottom of the stairs, staring at us, Megan and Joe, faces dropped, frozen in time.

7

School services took place in St Mary's, the church across the road. The vicar, a shiny-headed, pug-faced little man called Father Harris, didn't trust us; he knew we weren't real Christians, but he couldn't quite work us out. Mind you, it was vice versa. Once, when Deborah and I had had to help him out before a service, folding his robes and lighting candles and stuff, he'd said, 'It would be nothing short of a miracle if we got it all ready in time.' I'd said that it was lucky he believed in miracles. And he'd said, 'I don't actually.' I was rather shocked, 'What about the water into wine and loaves into fishes and hem of the garment?' 'Oh, they're just stories,' he'd said dismissively, and carried on counting out the little bits of paper that Catholics think turn into Jesus' body. I kind of liked him for that. I shouldn't have been so surprised though; in most of his sermons it was always his cat that came out tops.

Father Harris stood at the door to St Mary's, watching suspiciously as the school filed past him in absolute silence. His blue-eyed cat made figures of eight around his Hush-Puppied feet.

We all loved going to these services. It was the music. We spent hours and hours every day singing, not just the rubbish songs that the Whopper wrote, but also 'Regina Coeli', 'Laudamus te', 'Domine Deus', and just to hear any one of those could take me out of my unhappiness. Whatever fresh misery there was could be briefly forgotten. The sound of all our voices together, all breathing the same breaths, the boys' and the girls' voices, the basses, the altos and the sopranos, seemed to me to be the whole point of everything. The worst punishment she could give me was not singing in the church; which, of course, she had. But at least I was there, segregated but present.

There were other bonuses to these services. It was rare to have the whole school together, all the girls and boys. Usually those of us girls who had boyfriends would try and sit on the edge seats, as would the boys, and then we could spend the whole service counting how many smiles we exchanged. But the teachers had cottoned on to this and had firmly stationed themselves on the edges.

Fowler was keeping me especially close at hand today, what with the males of the species being present; her purple claw gripped my shoulder as I tried to slide in along the pew with my friends. She held me hard until everyone had taken their seats and she was ready to take hers. Then she prodded me forward down the aisle and poked me into the edge of a pew about halfway down the church. Girls shuffled along to make room for us, and she took a seat next to me. Our thighs were touching.

I noticed she had seated us exactly across the aisle from Mercer, which was handy had I been wanting to smile at Marcus, who was right at his side. But I wasn't smiling so much these days; Marcus might as well get himself a new girlfriend. Megan liked him; he could smile at her if he wanted, and kiss her on the lips at Gloucester Road station.

Mr Steinberg was there, three rows behind Mercer. He caught my eye and then picked up his hymn book. I hadn't told Megan or anyone about what had happened the day before, because I couldn't put my finger on precisely what *had* happened.

I had been in the dungeons on my own; I was late getting changed for gym because I'd been sent on an errand. The rest of the class were rope-climbing in the refectory. I could hear the squeak of plimsoles landing on the stone floor. I was getting changed in a rush – I hate being late for things. I was standing on one leg, completely naked, pulling on my PE knickers, when the dungeon door opened. I looked up. Mr Steinberg was there, a surprised expression on his face.

'I'm so sorry,' he said, blushing profusely. 'Please excuse me.' And he shut the door quickly.

I looked down at myself to see what he had seen. My body was turning into the body of a woman. Almost daily it was changing; childhood was on its way out. My breasts were round now, I had hips and a waist, pubic hair.

He had seen all this. And I didn't mind. I didn't mind at all.

When I came out in my gym kit, ready to join my class, I saw Mr Steinberg in the corridor; he was talking to Mr Baker. He didn't look at me but I noticed him blush again as I passed by.

For the first time in my life, I had understood the power of being a woman.

Behind Mr Steinberg was Baker, and behind him was

the Turkey. The Turkey didn't acknowledge me; he never did on these occasions.

'Stop turning round!' Fowler hissed at me.

I looked at Fowler's hands, her red raw hands, slightly swollen fingers, her nails sensibly filed, ink stain on the side of her thumb. She was clutching a shiny black hand-bag I hadn't seen before. It must be new. As was her dress, a long bottle green, high-necked, ground-brushing thing. I suddenly realized that she looked forward to these occasions as much as we did. She turned her head away from me, and I caught her as she bared her teeth at Mercer. I looked at Mercer and could feel Marcus next to him, trying to catch my eye; it could have been a nice little foursome if it weren't for a million reasons. But Fowler's smile fell on stony ground; Mercer hadn't even noticed it, he was looking at someone else further down in the pew in front of us. I turned my head at the same time Fowler turned hers – Mrs Gentle. He'd obviously never been near her; she had stinky cigarette breath. The corners of Mrs Gentle's straight line mouth curled upwards, returning his smile. Fowler clocked it, and I clocked it, and she clocked that I'd clocked it.

She took her venom out on me; I had been making a boat with the edge of my service sheet. She grabbed it out of my hands, tearing it as she did so.

We all got on our feet to sing that hymn that ends 'To be a Pilgrim'. Deborah and Amy were singing solos, so everyone looked over our way for a while. I caught eyes with Marcus briefly, but it was humiliating to always be attached to Fowler's hip. Steinberg, a few rows back, caught Marcus and me exchanging looks. Fowler noticed as well because she flicked me a frown. Then she gave me a peculiar blink. Her eyes were pink-rimmed and her skin was yellow. Her lips tightened, and she returned to the hymn. 'He'll with a lion fight!' she sang in a voice that was mouse-like, thin and reedy.

She blinked again. Several slow blinks, as if she had something in her eye. And then she opened her eyes wide and looked up towards the wooden bits at the top of the church and stared strangely. I followed her gaze but couldn't tell what she was so transfixed by. Her mouth drooped open and she blinked again as if she were trying to see clearly. She then rummaged in her cardigan pocket for something that she didn't find. She opened her bag and took out a scraggy bit of ink-stained tissue.

I had an uneasy but excited feeling in the pit of my stomach.

Fowler sat down before the last two lines of the hymn had finished. It was disconcerting having her at eye level. Then, in that shuffling quiet at the end of the hymn, I heard her stomach give a loud ominous rumble.

Charles Grey and Ben Sadler made their way to the pulpit and announced in piping, clear voices that they were going to read a prayer from the Upanishads. I glanced across at Father Harris, who was looking a bit bemused. I felt a shudder of the usual embarrassment when a non-Organization person had to witness these things. Ben Sadler said the prayer in Sanskrit, and Charles Grey translated. 'That is perfect. This is perfect,' he said in his high voice; he was a perfect pupil. 'Perfect comes from perfect, Take perfect from perfect and the remainder is perfect. Om shanti shanti shanti.'

Despite it all, I always rather liked that prayer; I found it consoling, that somewhere everything was perfect. I heard Fowler's stomach make another strange noise, so did the girls in the row in front. They giggled and turned around, but stopped giggling pretty sharpish when they realized where it was coming from.

The end of the prayer was our class's cue to shuffle out towards the front with the equivalent class in the boys' school. I had been banned a long time ago from this event, so I had to stay in the pew with Fowler as they all went to the front. I heard her, most uncharacteristically, suppress a belch.

I watched Mr Crane, the music teacher, come out of his pew. He was a tall, skinny man who picked his nose a lot and wore those glasses that make your eyes go big, like a bug. I had once asked him about his glasses; I was very into eyesight. Crane had called me 'impudent'. I'd asked what 'impudent' meant and he had sent me out of the classroom, and Fowler had said I couldn't sing in the service. He knew it was in his best interests to punish me, sheep that he was. Despite the fact that he got us singing so beautifully, he had absolutely no control in a classroom, often sending more girls outside the room than he kept in. We once counted nineteen of us. He had probably never had any intention of teaching music to children, but had been roped in by the Organization because he could play the piano.

Crane made his way to the front of the church, where my class were getting into their places. Today he was in control; everybody was hanging on his every move.

When it all settled down and the singers had stopped

their coughing and shuffling, he raised his hands, and you could have heard a pin drop. Then suddenly everyone started singing 'Regina Coeli', and I was amazed at the sound of the eighty or so voices. It sounded so beautiful, so uplifting; the whole world should listen to 'Regina Coeli'. How I wished I were a part of it. I wished I wasn't so hated. I wished none of this had happened. I wished I could be happy. I wished I could be grown up. I wished the train had hit me.

After a while, I noticed Fowler suppress a cough and put her tissue to her face. She rubbed her other hand along her dress; I could see how sweaty her palms were. There was something wrong; she was wiping her brow. I turned to look at her. Her face was so white it was almost grey, and then slowly it dawned on me exactly what was wrong with her.

She took an audible intake of breath and then tried to get up but she didn't quite make it. She began to vomit violently on to the prayer mat, over her bottle green dress; it splashed on to the aisle. It splashed on to me. I watched in appalled amazement, unable to move, I could only stare as this endless stream of white sick poured out of her.

People around us began to get up and step back with disgust; the singers faltered in their singing. But still she vomited. Mercer stood up. Mrs Gentle got out of her pew and came round to help Fowler. She got her out into the aisle and walked her down towards the doors, but still the splashings of her puke could be heard.

The Turkey was clucking about the church, trying to keep everyone in order. He was looking fierce; anyone who turned around was slapped across the head.

'Please, Mr Stern,' I said after he'd slapped me. I had to call him Mr Stern at school. I preferred it anyway. 'I'm covered in sick.'

I turned to him and showed him all the sick on my dress. For a moment I could tell that he didn't know what to do. He liked to be a little harder on me than on other people, just to prove that his devotion to the Organization was his true priority, but he could not deny that I had white puke all the way down my front. He signalled brusquely for me to go and clean myself up. I followed the stinking trail down the aisle and stood at the big church door.

I looked out and there in the bright sunlight, collapsed on the white steps lying in an ungainly manner in Mrs Gentle's arms, was Fowler, sprawled where all the busy, normal, world could see her. Her red hands were twitching, and her bottle-green body jerked about in public. I stood transfixed, elated to watch her suffer like this, to see her humiliated after all the suffering and humiliation she had caused me. I could have danced a jig. There you go, Fowler, that's for all the misery, all the pain you have inflicted. There you go, that's what it feels like, that's for what you've done to me. For what you've done to others. Yes, it hurts, doesn't it? I looked up into the street. People, normal people, were looking on, their faces shocked and concerned. I heard someone say, 'Call an ambulance!' 'Wait,' I wanted to say, 'Let her suffer! She deserves this. She deserves this pain. Whatever you do, don't pity her!'

Just then she turned her head my way, and I caught her expression. It was one of pure terror. I stood captivated.

I wanted to step out of the shadows, raise my hands and cry, 'Okay, okay! Just a little bit more and then you can stop. That's almost enough now! She's learning her lesson!'

But as I watched her thrashing about, twitching and vomiting, eyes rolling in her head, suddenly it wasn't quite as wonderful as it had been a moment before. 'Okay, stop now! You can stop! Enough!' But no, it went on and on, accompanied by a dreadful wailing which, at first, I hadn't realized was coming from her. Oh my God! It was becoming truly ghastly to behold.

A stranger, a normal person, had run up the steps and turned Fowler on to her side. Her hair had come down. I had never seen her hair loose: long greyish black. It lay splayed out on the white steps of the church. I don't know what I'd thought about her hair – perhaps that when she went to bed she took the whole bun off and the rest stayed on her head in that scraped-back fashion, or she was bald and she took the whole wig off and put it on a dummy's head in the corner of her room. It was certainly never meant to hang loose in locks splayed on the ground covered in vomit.

The full horror of what I'd done was just beginning to sink in.

'Water! Get some water!' Someone shouted, and Mercer turned and saw me in the portal.

'Hurry!' he said. I spun around and rushed through the back of the church, the music crescendoing with me. I ran through to the vestry. I couldn't see anything to put water in, so I grabbed a vase and sped through to the loo. I emptied the flowers on the floor and tried to turn the tap on, but my hands were shaking so badly I couldn't move it. Oh God, Oh God, stop it now! Stop it now! Please, stop it now! That's enough! That's enough!

The stench of her puke was so strong I gagged; I could hear myself making gasping noises, through my chattering teeth. Someone help me! Someone help me! What have I done? I'm going to prison, I'm going to prison.

Far away, I could hear 'Regina Coeli' echoing around the church, its joyfulness at odds with the ghastliness of what was going on.

My legs were shaking so badly I could feel my knees knocking. Who will forgive me? Who will forgive me?

I got the tap on and washed the vase out and filled it with water and ran back through the vestry to the doors of the church. 'Regina Coeli' slipped into a minor key, taking a sinister turn. The Turkey had got the school under control; no one was looking around. The portal doors were now shut, I rushed towards them and pulled one door open, splashing some of the water as I did so.

Fowler was still there, lying on the ground in the puke, but not moving any more. I put the vase down near Mrs Gentle, who splashed water over Fowler's face, in her sick matted hair, but even when splashed with water, still Fowler did not stir. Her eyes had rolled back into her head; she looked like a ghostly version of Old Ginger in the British Museum.

An ambulance wailed down the street and stopped directly outside the church. Three paramedics dressed in the same bottle green as her dress rushed out, one of them opening the back doors, the other two running up the steps.

I swear, God, I swear, God, if you save her life, I'll be good for the rest of my life. I swear. I swear.

The man paramedic put his fingers on Fowler's throat and checked the time. Then he leant over her and started kissing her. Yes, there was a man leaning over Fowler kissing her! Had she been conscious, she would have died of embarrassment. I stood there open-mouthed. But she did not move a muscle; her arms hung limply at her side.

He put his hands together and started pressing down on her chest in jerks. Her arms flapped up, boneless, like a doll's.

More sirens, and I looked up to see a police car pulling in beside the ambulance, fast so that you knew this was a real emergency. A big, bearded policeman got out, slammed the door loudly, gave a quick look up and down the street and then jogged around the vehicle. He looked me directly in the eyes. He could see my guilt.

They're going to arrest me. Oh God, no, they're going to arrest me. I looked up at the church's spire. Please, help me, God. Please, help me.

The sky was blue, and the branches of the tree were full of shimmering, lime-green leaves, and, quite distinctly, I heard a voice from inside me saying, 'Run for it!'

I bolted across the road. In all the confusion, nobody was watching one sick-drenched schoolgirl. I knew I had to go back into the building and get my blazer with my return tube ticket and my house key in the pocket and then I had to get home and change out of this dress and into some normal clothes and then . . . I don't know what. What does a murderer do? Where does a murderer go?

I got back to the school, and, just as I was turning to

go down the basement steps, a line of mothers carrying baskets of bread and fruit came through one door and made their way to the other, their swishing long skirts touching hem to hem. They looked like one of those paper-chain dancing ladies that you cut out in a strip. They were in good spirits, unaware of the scene over the road. There she was, my mother amongst them, her lank greying hair pulled back into a bun, her glasses slipped down her nose, in her shapeless floral-print dress, she was smiling about something. All she needed to do was look up and see me. I willed her to. I wanted to run into her arms, like I'd seen some people do with their mothers. I wanted her to hold me and say, 'Don't worry, Caroline, it'll all be all right. You're coming with me, my darling, away from this awful place. I should have listened to you. That woman asked for it, she drove you to it.' But I knew that would never happen. My mother would never put me before this place, never. And besides, she never called me 'darling'. And had that awful woman really asked for it? Did she really deserve that?

I decided just to flee without ticket or key.

I ran away. I ran past the old smelly woman tramp who lived in one of the grand deserted doorways. Normally she asked me for lightly boiled potatoes with a blob of butter on, which seemed a strange request from a woman who pissed straight into her raggedy clothes without a second thought. But today she watched me run by and called out, 'Godspeed!'

I ran past South Kensington tube station and kept on running into unfamiliar terrain: tall houses, black railings, mews gardens. At one stage I found myself in a cemetery;

I ran through the lucky, safe, dead people. I sprinted past them all; panic spurring me on. I started whispering to myself like a mad person in time with my feet, 'I killed her! I killed her!' like a meditation mantra.

As I approached the river, the panic was turning into a kind of euphoria. It was slowly dawning on me that the impossible had happened. Fowler was out of my life! I was free. A free human being!

'Yes! Yes!' I was shouting as I ran, my body now as light as air.

I turned left at the river, filled with a new energy. I was as fit as an athlete and had stamina and cause, so there was absolutely nothing that could stop me. I ran further and further away from the Organization, further and further away from my life. I didn't once look behind me.

I ran past the houses of Parliament, Big Ben, I kept to the river and eventually found myself at Embankment station.

It struck me as unbearably funny that only a month previously I had nearly died at this station, and here I was alive and kicking, and *she* was the one who was dead. I was overwhelmed by the ecstasy of it all. I put my hands on the brick wall and hung my head and laughed like a mad thing, howling and snatching breath until I realized I was drawing attention to myself. That was no good. I had to calm down. I had to think. Think. Be practical. What to do?

The first thing I had to do was get out of this revolting uniform. I still had Fowler's guts spewed across my front. I followed the human traffic up to the Strand, where I joined the throng and merged with the hundreds of people going about their business. I kept my head down and crossed the road each time I saw a policeman. I darted up a side street and shortly found myself in Covent Garden. A large group of people were watching a street show, two men running in slow motion to the *Chariots of Fire* music. I took this as a good sign, because *Chariots of Fire* was one of the only films I had ever seen. The Organization approved of it, because it was all about putting God first and not running on a Sunday. The crowd were laughing at the men pretending to break through a finishing line. Come on. Come on. Keep moving.

I was a good shoplifter: Megan and I stole sweets all the time. The first thing I needed was a decent-sized, thick, plastic bag. I rummaged in a bin and found one easily. I passed Covent Garden tube and stood on Long Acre, wondering where to go. There it was before me, the Holy Grail of all shops. Flip. Another good sign. Sarah Martins had had to scrub floors for a week because she went to Flip; I had no idea why until I went in. It was American. Pop music was playing loudly. It was chock-a-block with fifties dresses and baseball jackets and leather and good-looking people mouthing lyrics. Fowler would have hated it.

Get out of this uniform.

I saw a fair-haired, middle-aged woman go downstairs and I followed her, hoping that I might look like her daughter. I quite audaciously held up some Osh Kosh jeans. Some jeans! I had never been allowed to wear a pair of trousers in my life! I smelt and caressed them for a bit before finding a couple of jumpers, a baseball jacket and some gym shoes. Not smelly old Green Flash gym shoes, but red ones with criss-crossy laces and the word 'Converse' on the side. I kept my head low and went to the fitting room and briskly drew the curtain. I stuffed the jeans, the jumper and the jacket into my bag and put the shoes on, leaving my own in the corner. On second thoughts, I took them with me; they might be able to trace me from them. The police have got Alsatian dogs that take one sniff and can hunt you down through rivers and over mountains.

I came out of the cubicle and put one of the jumpers back to look as though I hadn't found anything that fitted and then hung out for a moment with 'my mother', waiting for her to go back upstairs. Once up, I casually strolled out of the shop.

I sped up and started jogging, just in case anyone came after me. I needed to find some public toilets to get changed in. I ran back down through Covent Garden and found myself back on the Strand. The station, Charing Cross station, would have public toilets. I could change there.

A cleaner stared at me as I went by, I suppose the dried sick was attracting attention, that and my purple uniform, of course. Once in the public loos, in the safety of a locked cubicle, I opened my bag of delights and started getting undressed. Though I say so myself, once dressed, I could not wipe the grin off my face, I looked so good. Just like a normal person. The jeans fitted me perfectly. If only Megan and Amy could have seen me now! I loved the shoes, especially knowing that my mother would have thrown them in the bin. The grey jumper was tight and soft and outlined my breasts. I was really becoming a woman – not like Deborah, though, Deborah had enormous bosoms with big, red nipples, and she started the curse at eleven. I smoothed down the jumper and shoved the stinky uniform back into the bag. The dogs would love that.

Looking in the mirror, I appeared unrecognizable; they'd never find me now, not disguised as a normal person. I came out of the loos in my new green baseball jacket and looked about me. What should I do now? The logical thing was to take a train. And at that very moment, I heard a whistle and an announcement and made my way over to platform 4.

I passed a bunch of loud American tourists, all looking up at the departure board in their identical beige raincoats and gleaming white trainers. It was too good to be true, it was almost as if God was looking out for me; one of them, a young blonde woman with train-track braces on her teeth, was staring blankly up at the board and had left her handbag invitingly open at her feet.

I swiped it in one smooth, flowing movement. It was almost too easy; I seemed cut out to be a thief. I slid through the crowd, stuffing the stolen handbag into my sick-smelling bag, which I would dispose of later. There was a commotion behind me; goofy tooth must have noticed. But I was smaller than everyone else and felt virtually invisible now that I was normal. I got to the platform where the whistleblower stood and, most extraordinarily, I walked straight past the guard on to the platform and on to the train. Nobody stopped me.

I made my way through the carriage and took a seat at

the back by the luggage rack, where no one would look at me, shoving the pukey bag under my seat – I would have to get rid of that. Then I pressed my head against the window pane as the train began to pull out of the station.

As London slipped by I listened to the thump-thump-thumping of my heart. 'Just keep going, just keep going, just keep going,' I chanted in time with the cha-cha-cha noise the train was making. I had no idea where the train was going, but decided to stay on it until the last stop, the furthest away from London.

It took for ever to get out of the city, maybe half an hour. I had never been out of London before, except to go on retreat. Before long the ticket officer appeared at the far end of the carriage, so I grabbed my new handbag and made a beeline for the little toilet, locking myself in.

I sat on the loo, took some heavy breaths and gazed at the bulky dark brown leather bag on my lap. I unzipped it. The first thing I pulled out was a wallet. 'Lorraine Fischer' it said underneath a picture of the girl with the braces. Only she didn't have braces in the photograph, just buck teeth.

'Lorraine Fischer,' I said out loud to myself. 'Lorraine Fischer. Lorrie Fischer.' Yes, Lorrie Fischer sounded much better. I had always wanted a nickname. 'That's me,' I said. 'Lorrie Fischer.'

I didn't look a million miles away from the girl in the photograph, except for the teeth. The next thing I found in the wallet just proved to me that my luck was in. Two ten-pound notes and ten one-pound notes! I had never seen so much money in my life. And then, to my amazement, in the side of the bag I found four hundred and fifty dollars. I had no idea how much that was in English money, for we had never been abroad and didn't read newspapers, but four hundred and fifty anything had to be a lot. Unless it was like rupees; I knew they were rubbish. She also had a load of credit cards, but I didn't have a clue what to do with them, so I shoved them back in the wallet.

The next thing I pulled out was a passport. God was truly smiling on me. Lorraine Fischer was six years older than me. She was born in Michigan, in the United States of America. I'd always wanted to be American. And older.

I found a little patterned bag and opened it up. Oh! Wonderful, wonderful and out of all whooping! Make-up! Colourful tubes and sticks and pouches and sachets and rouges. I got up and spread them out on the loo seat. Thank you, Lorraine Fischer.

Then I set to work on my face. I drew dark circles around my eyes in a grey liner and shaded the lids a purply blue, like the ladies on magazine covers. I put pink lipstick on and rubbed some on to my cheeks. Lo and behold, Lorrie Fischer began to emerge. She had big dark blue eyes and cheekbones and full lips. I found a pair of nail scissors in the bag and set to work on the final touches. I chopped off my hair and flushed great handfuls of Caroline Stern down the toilet. I gave myself a bob. A bob! I could have danced a dance in praise of Normality.

By the time I came out of the cubicle, it was the end of the road for old Caroline Stern and 'Hello, world!' for glamorous Lorrie Fischer.

*

I rested my forehead on the window pane and watched the world go by, still exhilarated by events. From now on my whole life would be different. I had killed Fowler, I had actually done it. And I wasn't sorry. Even if they caught me, prison had to be better than my life. However, I had no intention of getting caught. I had to start making plans.

The trolley guard was coming my way down the aisle, selling sandwiches and things. He had a ruddy, laughing face, and I watched him share a joke with someone further down. I liked the way he held his head back to laugh. I wondered whether he had children of his own or whether he might want to adopt someone.

It wasn't as bad as you might expect, being a murderer. If you stopped thinking about what you'd actually done, you just had to get on with it. Besides, I wasn't going to be Caroline Stern any more. I was going to be someone else who was quite different from Caroline. For a start, I thought, as I watched the sandwich trolley get nearer, Lorrie Fischer was going to be a meat eater. Yes, she absolutely loved meat; it was her favourite thing. I had, as Caroline Stern, only ever eaten meat once. I had tasted a sausage. Which is dead pig.

It was my mum's fault. She had promised to leave the key under the flowerpot, but she had forgotten, so I had had to sit on the doorstep for hours before they got home.

Carol Watson had come out from her house next door to lean on her wall. She always did this: she spent most of her time leaning on the wall having chats with people as she smoked fag after fag and scrunched them under her pink fluffy-slippered foot. Everyone stopped and talked to Carol, except my parents, of course; they tried their hardest not to talk to her. My mum used to take a peek from behind the curtains when she was leaving the house, just to check whether Carol was out there. But I loved Carol, even though my dad said I wasn't allowed to talk to her. She was enormous and had false teeth that she hardly ever put in – when she did have them in they were always flopping down when she spoke. She wore flowery housecoats with her pink fluffy slippers. Sometimes she just went out in her pink nylon dressing gown, talking to people. She didn't care. She was nice to everyone, *everybody*, even the loony man from the loony bin at the end of our road. He went past our house every single day with a great big map of London held out in front of him, even though he was only going to the bottom shop and back. But Carol always helped him with the directions, 'Straight down here, love, then turn around and come straight back. I'll look out for you.' She said it every day, as if she'd never told him before. And she'd give him a fag if he wanted one. I thought she had more of the Absolute in her than the whole Organization put together.

But on this particular day, Carol found me on the doorstep and said, 'What are you doing there, love?' And I said I'd been locked out and she said, 'You must be wanting your tea. Come in, my petal.'

I had never been inside a normal family's house before. For one thing, they had a telly, which was on all the time. I knew that already because sometimes I'd press my ear to the wall in my bedroom and I'd hear it. They didn't have any bookshelves and they had no holy pictures at all. Instead, they had lovely posters up of kittens tangled up in wool and puppies stuck in buckets. Carol told me she had lots of spare tea because Big Terry, her husband (as opposed to Small Terry, who was her son), hadn't eaten much. She told me to take a seat on the settee, which was a sofa. So I went into the sitting room, but there was no room on the settee because Big Terry was lying on it, taking up the whole thing. He had the biggest belly in the world, and his trousers always fell down so you could see the top of his bum. It looked like he was watching the telly, but suddenly he gave the loudest snorty noise, and I realized he was asleep, even though he was managing to balance a can of beer on his chest and had a fag going. Big Terry was a lorry driver. He travelled round the whole country and he brought Carol ornaments and sticks of rock from everywhere he went; they were all over the mantelpiece.

I sat on the big armchair and Carol brought me in a plate of food. It was the best and most beautiful meal of my life; a mountain of mashed potato with masses of baked beans all around the edge like the moat of a castle and four enormous sausages that stuck up out of the mash like a space ship. It was enough food for about six people. I ate it all apart from the sausages. I took a nibble of one but I just couldn't swallow it. I kept thinking of the pig. It tasted of the smell of a pig. So when Carol went back into the kitchen I pulled out the sausages and hid them in my school bag. 'Where do you put it?' Carol said. 'You're skin and bones.'

I told my friends at school the next day that I had eaten four sausages. I didn't lie often, but I felt kind of responsible that I would have been letting everybody down by not eating them; these opportunities were very rare. Apart from Megan in hospital, none of my friends had ever had any meat, so I was a sort of pioneer.

Then I remembered that they were not my friends any more; that I was on my own, and that gave me an achey feeling inside. I couldn't afford to get sad. I asked the trolley guard for a ham sandwich.

'All right, my darling,' he said. 'One ham sandwich; that'll be forty pence, please.'

There was a lot more love in the outside world. Everyone called me 'darling' or 'love' or 'petal'. In the Organization you have to use people's proper names.

To be honest, the ham sandwich was revolting. I wasn't sure what animal ham was, but it tasted of salty rubber. I ate the bread but took out the ham. I would try again later; this meat-eating business was going to take some perseverance.

However hard I tried not to think of them, I couldn't stop wondering about Megan and Amy and the others. Megan would be worried about me. Mr Steinberg wouldn't notice until the Greek class, which was tomorrow. I think Mum and Dad would just be relieved that I had gone; I was always causing them so much distress. This way it was best for us all. I didn't think I'd miss them.

I pressed my nose to the glass. Fields whizzed by, marked by the occasional house or farm, and then the terrain turned wild and barren, not like London at all, not even like Hampstead Heath, and again I had a sudden lurching sense of loneliness, and my eyes began to prick with tears. I knew I had to make a plan. I would get off the train somewhere, pretend to be an orphan and get work on a farm milking cows or something like that; maybe a kindly old couple might take me in. I would knock on doors and ask for lodgings, find a nice little attic room, maybe, like in stories. In the Bhagavad Gita and the Bible and the Upanishads you're much better off having nothing. Jesus and God and everyone love all that. To be a holy man you *have* to have nothing. Not that I wanted to be a holy man, I think it was too late for that, what with the murder and the robbery and everything. Plus being a girl.

My plans changed suddenly. The moment that the sea appeared on my right. A glorious, stormy, green sea with hundreds of white horses galloping across it whilst a golden sun shone down and puffy little clouds sped by. The train had taken me to the seaside.

A P&O ferry was heading out to sea as another one headed in. The shore was lined with white cliffs. Surely I must be in Dover. What a sign! Here I was, running away with a passport and four hundred and fifty dollars and arriving at Dover. Thank you, God.

There was activity in the carriage at the sight of the sea. An old couple started to put lids on their Tupperware, and a young couple stood up and pulled their bags down from the rack. Out of the window the ferries passed each other, bellowing horns in greeting. Everyone and everything seemed to be in couples, but even this didn't dampen my excitement. This was the beginning of the rest of my life! The Alsatians would never follow me over that rough green sea. I could go to France! The only draw-back was that I didn't speak any French – the Whopper disapproved of French. I don't know why. But I would learn it; I would amaze people with the speed with which I learnt it. Or rather, I would just amaze myself.

Maybe I could take a hovercraft. Amy had been on a hovercraft. She said it was like a big Lilo that flew across the sea without touching the water, but not very far off it. Amy's family had more money than us; that's why she went abroad.

I left the sick bag under my seat and got out at Dover Priory and followed a sign that said 'Foot Passengers'. Everyone else doing the same had a rucksack on their backs. I wished I had one. I wanted to fit in. I sort of shadowed this young couple who kept stopping to snog. I thought I could pretend I was with them so that I didn't stand out too much. I thought perhaps later on they might become my friends and we could shop for rucksacks and stuff.

I got my ticket no problem but at the passport kiosk I suddenly began to get nervous and tried to rest my two front teeth on my bottom lip so that I looked more like the real Lorraine Fischer. The woman in the kiosk was chewing gum as she looked at the picture. She tapped her long red nails across the front of Lorraine Fischer's passport and then shut it and handed it back to me.

'Have a good trip,' she said. Americans like things like that, so I smiled goofily and said, 'Thank you,' in my best American accent. The only American I knew was Mr Steinberg, so I was basing it all on him, buying the ticket and everything. 'One ticket to France, please.' I thought my accent was okay. I'm sure if we'd had a television it would have been much better.

I didn't end up going on a hovercraft – it was full, and I'm glad I didn't, because I don't think you can stand outside on a hovercraft. I stood on the deck, watching the cars driving on to the boat, looking out for police cars. I knew that soon they would be after me. My mind wandered back to London, to Fowler's corpse, now, presumably, on a mortuary slab. I knew that when they looked inside her stomach and found the cause of death, they'd go straight to the cupboard and find the foxglove leaves, and then they'd start looking for me.

I quickly made my way straight to the front of the ferry and leant on the railings, waiting eagerly for it to depart. Soon other people came out to join me. Well, not to join me. I was definitely on my own, but they stood near me, and I liked that.

The sun had got lower and was shining coppery red now, turning the sea into a fiery cauldron. The wind felt icy on my face. I hugged my new jacket tightly around myself and watched the sun sink as the ferry pulled out of the dock. The enormity of what I was doing and of what I had done hit me, and a panic welled up inside me. With hindsight I would advise running away with someone else rather than on your own; it's very hard to keep cheerful by yourself. I promised myself a Crunchie.

Half an hour later, the sun had gone, and the stars were starting to arrive. I was at the back of the ferry now, eating my Crunchie, watching a few gulls looking for fish in the wake of the boat. England was disappearing before my eyes. I could just make out a few lights, far, far away. I thought of Megan in her house in her perfect bed with no creases, all warm and safe. I thought of my parents in our cold house, the overhead light on in the kitchen, the Sanskrit prayer flapping on the wall, neither of them mentioning that I wasn't there. My father deciding that my name would never be spoken again, 'We're better off without her.' They'd accept it as the will of the Absolute. They would be meditating right now; in fact the whole lot of them over there in England would be meditating right now; that's when you have to do it, dawn and dusk. I could picture them in homes all over London, mainly in Chiswick. They'd be sitting up straight as boards on hard-backed chairs in darkening rooms, feet firmly planted on the ground, hands up-turned resting on the thighs, eyes flickering in that reptilian manner, mantra repeating inside their heads. Well, that's the idea. Mostly they'd just be rocking and jerking about the place as they nodded off.

I thought of Fowler, cold and dead in a hospital somewhere, her guts lying about the place. 'She's been poisoned!' they'd cry. 'She's been murdered!' 'Find that child! Hunt her down!' they'd yell, and the police were probably there in Dover looking out at the sea, with their dogs barking and straining at the leash.

'Hello,' said a voice behind me. 'You haven't got a light, have you?'

It was the snogging boy without his girlfriend.

'No,' I said looking about the deck. Thinking perhaps he'd dropped something. He was quite old, maybe twenty, and was wearing a big coat and a woolly hat. He'd obviously done this before. He went up to another man further along the railing, and I watched him struggle in the wind to light a cigarette. Oh! A light. He wanted a match.

Not a torch. I had so much growing up to do.

He came back to where I was and offered me a cigarette. I took it casually, like an American might.

'You'll have to light it yourself,' he said and handed me his cigarette. I had no idea what I was meant to do so I held the two cigarettes tip to tip in my hands. He watched me for a moment and then took them off me.

'I'll do it,' he said, and sucked hard on one as he held the other to it, before passing it to me.

'Where are you going? After Boulogne?' he asked.

'Boulogne?' I said. 'I thought we were going to Calais.'

In fact, I thought all ferries went to Calais. I'd never heard anyone mention Boulogne in my life. Then I remembered that I'd forgotten to do my American accent. Never mind. Lorrie Fischer could have been born in America and brought up here.

'No, this ferry is going to Boulogne.'

'Oh. I'm going to Paris,' I said, nonchalantly, maturely. Paris was the only other place I had heard of in France, apart from Calais. We didn't do geography at school – it might put ideas in our head, I suppose.

'Where are you going?' I asked, taking my first ever drag of a cigarette. It was absolutely disgusting, but I tried not to show it. I didn't cough. He was rather handsome, this man. A thought struck me – perhaps he might jilt the girlfriend and take me with him, wherever he was going. We could travel the world.

'We're heading south,' he said. 'We're going to hitch.'

'Hitch?'

'The old thumbs.' He wriggled his thumbs at me. Oh yes, hitch-hiking. How romantic to be heading south with your girlfriend. I wished I had something interesting to say.

He looked out to sea for a bit, finished the fag and chucked it into the sea with a kind of flick. He seemed very glamorous to me.

'See ya round,' he said and headed back inside.

I stayed on deck and smoked my cigarette. It didn't taste so bad. Yes, Lorrie Fischer was definitely a smoker.

I looked out into the vast and inky night; the last lights of England had quite suddenly been turned off, and the churning of the engine roared monstrously in my ears. Briefly, I felt afraid, tiny, as if I had been cut adrift and was tumbling into the great unknown, my cigarette tip glowing like a solitary, molten planet in a black universe.

8

Etched on to my retinas until I die is the reflected expression on Joe's and Megan's faces as they stood at the bottom of the stairs: confusion, disbelief, incomprehension, a picture of human bewilderment.

There we all were, Joe, Megan, Steinberg and me, in a hideous tableau of deception and revelation. I moved first. My chair scraped as I stood up. I had the awkward task of getting back into my heels, which lay splayed under the table, further evidence of my shame. Typical! The one time I wore heels was the one time I needed to run.

I didn't look at Steinberg. I stood up, took my bag off my chair and walked out of the kitchen, past the motionless Joe and Megan, unable even to look them in the eye. I then had the embarrassment of not being able to open the front door properly, and Megan had to come to my aid and open it for me.

'Hope you enjoyed the Bollinger,' she said acidly to my back as I legged it down the path. I could hear the crack of hurt in her voice.

I left the car for Joe and walked down to Chiswick High Street.

At first I wasn't quite sure what was happening to me. I felt a clamming-up in my throat, and my mouth flooded with saliva. A surge of heat filled my eye sockets and seemed to burn through to the air. It felt as if my eyes were bleeding. But no, I remembered this! I was crying! I was crying a hot, salty stream of tears; they poured down my cheeks. I couldn't contain them and I didn't try. They poured and poured. Passers-by stared. Twenty-five years' worth of tears seemed to have been stored up and were now desperate for escape; out they came in a salty exodus.

I turned up Askew Road. There were people rolling out of the Eagle, happy laughing people.

'All right, love?' a young boy asked as I passed, and his girlfriend caught up with me and gave me a tissue, briefly resting her hand on my shoulder. No questions asked. The kindness of strangers is sometimes unbearable.

I felt as if I could have carried on walking to John O'Groats. I don't know what time I got home; the car wasn't there, the lights were off, and it didn't feel like home any more. It was just a house. I let myself in, and Tilly wildly bounced up and down at me. I'd forgotten all about her. I collapsed in the hall on the floor and sobbed and tried to hug her, which she wasn't that keen on.

I sat up all night, waiting for Joe to come home. I pulled the chair to the window and just waited. Every sound of a car engine sent my heart into a flutter. But Joe didn't come home.

I woke up on the sofa, still dressed in my tarty, tight skirt. I pulled off my clothes and stuffed them into the bin. I phoned work and left a message on the answering machine, feigning illness. I went upstairs and bathed, waiting, waiting, listening out for him. Was I just a foolish child who wanted whatever had been taken away from her? I needed to tell him how sorry I was.

Joe didn't come home that night, or the next, or the next, and he didn't respond to any of my calls or texts.

I called in sick at work every day. I wandered around the house, waiting for him, staring out of the window, charging my mobile, sitting by the land line, nervous if I went into the garden that I might miss his call. I tidied the house, I picked flowers from the garden, I tried to write him a letter, but apart from 'sorry' what on earth was there to say? I texted him, I left messages, I cooked meals and put them in the freezer. I sobbed at the kitchen table. I changed my clothes, made up my face, I became quite frantic.

On the third morning as I lay in the bath – I no longer went underwater in case I should miss the phone – I heard the key in the latch. I sat bolt upright and leapt out of the bath, grabbing a towel. Yes, I wasn't mistaken, I could hear the familiar turn of keys in the door. I reached for the nearest dressing gown, which was his, but things not being as they once were, I rummaged for my own. I came out of the bathroom and sat at the top of the stairs, seeing his big frame through the frosted glass panels on the door. He came in. He didn't see me. Tilly jumped up at him, and he caught her in his arms and whispered sweet nothings into her lucky ears.

Then he looked up and saw me, and his face changed. He clearly hadn't expected me to be there. I should have been at work. He said nothing. I came down the stairs. Please, don't ignore me.

'Hi,' I said.

'I've come to pick up my things,' he replied brusquely. 'I'm moving out.'

I nodded, he had said the words I was dreading.

'You look terrible,' he said, which, I suppose, given the circumstances, was a nice thing to say.

I nodded again, and the tears just did their thing. I could tell he was surprised. He had never seen me cry.

'Well,' he remarked crisply. 'It's good to see that I meant *something* to you. Or are you crying for yourself?'

'Oh Joe,' I said, between gasps.

'You idiot,' he replied, though not unkindly.

'I know,' I said.

'How long has it been going on?'

'Since Cornwall.'

'You stupid fucking idiot.' His eyes filled with tears. This was utterly awful.

I nodded again and wiped my face on my dressing gown.

'Where are you going?' I said.

'To my mum's.'

We looked in each other's eyes. To be the cause of such unhappiness was almost obscene.

'I'm so sorry,' I sobbed.

'Yeh,' he said. 'You should be!'

There was nothing left to say. He went past me up to the bedroom to get his stuff.

'I'll pick up the rest of my gear sometime,' he said en route. I wanted to grab him and cling on like a limpet; instead, the tips of my fingers brushed his jacket.

That was it. That was the end of our relationship. How completely fragile everything was.

Tilly sat at the bottom of the stairs, looking up to where Joe had gone and then back at me, ears back, tail wagging nervously, as if there might be some way she could make things better. But there was no making this better.

I lay in bed and cried. I didn't know what I was crying about any more, just a deep feeling of loss: not specific loss, just loss itself. I lay there decomposing, smelly, unbrushed, unwashed, craving sleep, a big sleep really. Inevitably, my thoughts went to suicide; perhaps it was my default setting. It seemed the only proactive choice to make. I yearned for Joe, I missed him with a fervour, but he hadn't called or texted once. I knew I was unworthy of him. I had kept Steinberg at bay. Twice I'd texted him, 'Leave me alone. I mean it.'

I stared for hours at Tilly as she lay on the bed beside me. I had abandoned all kind of domestic rules; we slept nose to nose. I envied her her doggish ways, her brain that didn't analyse things, her cheeriness at the sound of a bird or a bark or even the rain, her sole motivation being the demands of her senses. I determined to live like her. We both got up for pees and the occasional feed. Only when starving did I go downstairs and make some toast out of the mouldy bread. I would let her out of the back door, and we both sniffed about a bit, but otherwise we didn't get out of bed.

All day I stared at the room and pulled the duvet up around me, breaking down into tears sporadically. Night-time was a slight release. I could stand the darkness better than the harsh light of day and eventually I knew that I would fall asleep. The worst by far was the crack of dawn, when I would wake up, and the sinking feeling would creep in that here was another whole day to get through. Without a doubt this must be the suicide hour, when sleep has abandoned you for the day.

One morning, I woke up to the sound of crying. It was a while before it registered that it was me, and longer still before I could trace the root of the sobs. I was crying for Caroline Stern, for the thirteen-year-old me, for that girl who ran away, who caught that train, who left her life, who lost herself. For the first time, Lorrie Fischer, the adult, seemed to be acknowledging Caroline Stern, the child, and my thirty-eight-year-old self felt extremely protective of her. I wanted to tell her how plucky she was.

Thank God for Tilly, she started to lick my face. Maybe she needed a pee or a crap or maybe she was trying to cheer me up or maybe she'd just had enough stagnation, but she jumped off the bed and skitted about the room, her nails click-clicking as she sniffed the floorboards. Poor dog, she hadn't had a walk for a week. My self-indulgence had to end. I kicked the duvet off and pulled on any old clothes and got us in the car, and we went to Wormwood Scrubs.

It was still dark when we got there. Tilly's white bum darted about the place, in and out of the bushes; she badly needed the exercise. She sprinted off into the playing fields like the whippet-whoppet thing that she was. As I turned into the fields, I looked over at the prison just as a light came on. I envied the prisoners their routine. Someone forcing you to get out of bed, making you have breakfast, making you function.

Then, just as the sky began to light up, I saw a familiar

figure running towards me, the one-legged jogger. Oh fuck, I hadn't brought a lead, and the bloody canister had run out of gas ages ago.

'Tilly!' I called, but it was too late, she'd seen him.

He stopped mid-jog and shouted, 'Get that dog on a lead!'

I rushed after her as she barked at his leg. I managed to grab her collar.

He was still jogging, eager not to miss a step.

'For God's sake, woman!' he began.

That was enough; those four words sent me into meltdown. I burst into tears. I sobbed, unashamed. What had become of me? My first interaction with the outside world had caused me to publicly crumble. I was obviously having a breakdown.

'Leave us alone!' I said, to him from the ground, my arms protectively around Tilly. 'Just leave us alone!' I cried.

He stopped jogging.

I could feel him hovering beside me. I could almost hear the penny drop as he realized I was mentally ill.

'It's just . . .' he said in a different tone. 'I'm scared of dogs.'

I nodded and looked up at him, 'Okay,' I said. 'Well, she wouldn't hurt you. She wouldn't hurt anyone.'

'I didn't mean to . . .'

'Don't worry,' I said. 'It wasn't really you. I cry all the time. It's pathetic.'

I could see the grey day had begun in earnest behind the prison. Lots of lights had come on. The jogger was still hovering at my side.

'Um ... look, it's not really my place but ... there are people that can help you ...' he said.

'I know,' I half laughed, half cried. 'I'm one of them!'

'Oh!'

The irony was not lost. He helped me to my feet, and I found myself walking with him. I could see Tilly eyeing his stick leg, but she seemed to be behaving herself.

'Well, sometimes,' he said, 'life is just pretty awful.'

And I knew he knew about that because of his leg.

'Yes,' I said, and briefly life seemed a little bit better. He walked me back to my car.

I began to do this every day, walking with the sunrise, watching the inevitable light progress, sometimes red, pink or purple and sometimes just grey, no great spectacle, as if the sun just couldn't be arsed to put on a show some days. I watched the subtle changes, the sheer determination of the bracken prising the earth open, each day a little further, the bluebells appearing out of nowhere – one morning they were just there – buds opening on the trees, leaves growing bigger and more confident daily, secure in the warmth that the spring brought.

After a week or two, a thought struck me that I think saved me. Life could not possibly be random. Life was not chaotic. That was totally impossible. The sun rose every day. The sun set every day. In spring all this birth went on, in summer the trees were crowded with leaves, in autumn they died and fell off. In winter there appeared to be nothing but bleakness. Everything was in the possibility of nothing. Something will come from nothing.

There was an intrinsic order to this world.

This thought gave me such a rush of hope that I skipped across the meadow, for all the early-morning prisoners to see. I shouted at them, 'There is order! Don't give up hope!'

By the time I got home, however, I had annoyed myself by the easiness with which I had processed this thought, packaged it neatly and then come up with a trite little theorem. Was that it, sane people just full of theorems that kept them sane by justifying their existences?

I decided that I didn't care. The main point was, it didn't matter what we believed in, as long as it helped us survive. And for me, believing in utter chaos sent me spiralling into despair.

I believed in order.

The next day I went back to work.

It was my first session with some teenage brothers, which I thought was going pretty well. Frankly, it was just a huge relief to be thinking of other people's problems rather than my own. I should have come back to work sooner. I was listening to the eldest boy grunting on about how he didn't care about whether he went to prison, when quite suddenly I stood up, grabbed the wastepaper basket and threw up a jet of puke. They stared at me, and I stared right back, just as surprised as they were.

'Okay,' I said, putting the bin down and taking a sip of water from my glass, as if this was how I finished every session. 'I think that's enough for today!'

I grabbed my stuff and got out into the fresh air. I still felt sick. I was never sick. I could count the times on one hand. Immediately I thought of that lazy storytelling device in films: actress suddenly rushes to toilet, chucks up: 'Oh I get it, she must be pregnant.' But that is exactly what just happened to me. Except I didn't make it to the toilet.

Oh. Fuck.

Oh, please no. Not now. I never keep tabs on my periods. Every single month for the last twenty-five years, my bleeding has taken me by surprise, so the fact that I hadn't had a period for a while had gone unnoticed by me. A lot of things had gone unnoticed by me recently, my time of the month being the least obvious.

I walked down Camden High Street, went into Boots, got myself a test and went into the toilets at Caffè Nero, peed on the stick, and my life changed course in two excruciatingly long minutes. I stared at the two pink lines in disbelief.

This could not possibly be happening. There must be some mistake. I went back out, sat by the counter and downed the whole jug of water and waited until I needed another pee. I went back into the loo, opened the second packet and took the test again. Positive. Two pink lines. I was most definitely pregnant.

I sat on the loo and rocked back and forth. I felt as if my head might explode. A baby? A baby? I could barely look after myself! Who was the father? If I had it, there would be no prizes for guessing who was Daddy. If I didn't, I might not get another chance. A month ago suddenly felt like another lifetime; here I was pregnant, single and with a dug-up past.

I walked through smelly old Camden Town in a daze, amazed at so many women pushing prams that I had never even noticed before or, if I had, only subliminally – big, child-rearing women who got in the way with their paraphernalia, big pushchairs and children. Today, there seemed to be an army of them out there, taunting me; double buggies brimming with blankets, small feet sticking out, bottles and dummies, hanging things, bulging bags full of what? What is all that stuff? I looked around me: shops I'd never noticed selling midget-sized clothes, little shoes, cots, chairs, beds. I carried on walking, staring at mothers everywhere. I passed one with a swollen belly that looked like she was smuggling a fully grown man up her jumper. I watched a bus pull over and a woman trying to get a pushchair up the step on to it. I watched her struggle and hurried on. Where had all these women been hiding?

I walked to Regent's Park, round and round until I noticed it was getting dark. I felt as if I was out of my body, as if I'd been turned inside out. My neat little theorem of there being an order to everything had been turned on its head. The thing I was finding the hardest to compute was that *not* doing anything was not an option.

I sat on my bench. This changed everything. The lover elephants came out to canoodle in the evening light. Show-off bastards. I lit a cigarette. I'd have to pack that in if I had it. Already it was making demands of me. What the hell was I going to do about this ... thing in my body?

As I walked home, a bright crisp ivory moon shone down as if all was well with the world when it blatantly wasn't.

There was someone sitting on my doorstep. I could

see the shadow from halfway down the street. My heart leapt at the thought that it might be Joe, he might have forgiven me. Then I remembered the baby and hoped it wasn't him.

As I got closer, the figure stood up. It wasn't Joe. It was way too small.

'Hello?' I said, as I neared.

'Hello,' it said.

It was Megan. I stood at the gate, frozen to the spot. I was most surprised. I could hear Tilly snuffling at the door behind her.

'Can we have a chat?' she said.

I nodded, and she stood to one side and let me open the front door. She followed me in, and I turned on the hall light and took us through into the sitting room, Tilly doing the usual mad-dog routine.

I took off my coat. She kept hers on, which was not a good sign.

'I don't know about you, but I'm having a glass of wine,' I said, going straight through to the kitchen.

'No thanks,' she replied, still not taking off her coat.

I poured myself a glass of Rioja and came back through to the sitting room, turning on a lamp as I sat down on the sofa. I placed my wine on the coffee table. Megan sat down on the eighteenth-century German sofa, near the lard-sick stain.

'Joe's gone, if you're wondering,' I said.

She nodded. She was pale and tired. She looked like shit.

'Megan,' I continued. 'Is saying that I'm sorry going to make you feel any better?'

'Yes, it might,' she said spikily.

'Then I'm sorry.'

She gave an actressy look up at the ceiling in a parody of thought. 'No, actually, I was wrong about that, I don't feel any better.'

I thought she'd probably over-rehearsed it.

'Are you in love with him?' she asked.

'With Steinberg?'

'Yes, of course with "Steinberg",' she said irritably.

I sighed loudly. 'I was, Megan, I was. But then you knew that.'

'What do you mean, I knew that?'

'At school, you knew I was in love with him.'

'Oh, at school,' she said dismissively. 'That doesn't count.'

'Doesn't it? Does nothing count that happened at school?'

She sat back in the chair.

'Don't try and make *me* into the one who's betrayed *you*.'

'But you did betray me, Megan.'

'How? How did I betray you?'

'In every way. You never tried to find me. You married him. You stayed there. You teach there. How could you do that?'

'Why shouldn't I? How could I find you? I was twelve years old. Your mother told my mother that you had gone to live with cousins in Scotland.'

'Well, did you go to Scotland?'

It was a silly, childish thing to say, but I still felt aggrieved that no one had tried to find me.

'No, of course not,' she said. 'You'd gone. And I married him later.'

'How much later?'

'I was nineteen. Are you in love with him now? That's what I want to know.'

'No, I'm not.'

By her expression, that wasn't what she wanted to hear; my words seemed to make her crumple a little. 'Well he's in love with you, Caroline. You've got him in love with you. Is that what you wanted?'

She started to cry. I'm terrible with people crying.

'You could always do that, couldn't you?' she blubbed. 'You could always have whatever you wanted and discard it when you were done with it. It's always been so easy for you to get what you want.'

'Don't talk to me as if you know me. You don't know me.'

She stood up and she looked straight at me. She was furious. I could feel her blood boiling. But then her expression changed, some pleasant and empowering thought passed through her head. She spoke in a low, calm voice.

'I know what you did,' she said.

My own blood ran cold.

'What did I do?' I asked, and in the silence that followed ice seemed to crack through my veins.

'You poisoned Fowler!'

I have never had to deny this because I have never been accused of it. I couldn't hold her gaze, so I stared into my Rioja and swirled it about my glass.

'Your mother told me,' she said, with a note of triumph in her voice.

I looked up at her, I was shocked.

'My mother?'

'She told me last week. And then it all made sense. You disappearing that day. Why, in Cornwall, no one was allowed to mention Fowler. And guess what? No one even bloody did!' she cried, outraged. Then I could tell that she was about to say something else, but she stopped herself, thinking better of it.

She stood up and tightened the belt of her coat. 'You have it all your own way, don't you? So I've just come here to tell you to leave my husband alone or I'm going to let the world know what you did.'

I drained my glass. I had to be careful what I said, but I've always been a quick thinker.

'How very enlightened of you, Megan,' I replied. 'I see all those fucking sheep years you've put in have really paid off with your love and compassion for the human race.'

I was on a roll now. I was fired up. I raised my voice as I stood up. 'You're going to "let the world know", are you? Tell me exactly, what in God's name do you even know about the world? You've never even stepped out of your own fucking front door! Don't you come here and threaten me! Get the fuck out of my house!'

She did just that.

I had decided to keep the baby. I had bought a book that had pictures of its development in the womb and I had begun to feel powerful and miraculous that I could do this, that I could grow another human being in my belly. In some ways I had never felt this good. Just being a cog in the great machine; insignificant yet vital. Doing what I had been programmed to do – be a vehicle for life. Now I understood what those tedious conversations with mothers-to-be were about. I couldn't help myself, my brain just kept drifting into mothering thoughts. I kept finding myself staring out of the window, mooning in a rapture of embryo, or lying in bed, rubbing my tummy, just growing it.

The book showed the baby getting bigger each month. I would make a point of not turning the page until I had actually got there. I didn't want to jinx it. At the moment, my baby looked like a little pink prawn with stumpy limbs and fishy eyeballs. Every time I ate something, I'd think, 'There you go, little prawn, grow an ear.' I could not think ahead, that in twenty-nine weeks the prawn might become a baby. 'Doctor! Doctor! Is it a boy? Is it a girl?' No, I'd be asking, 'Doctor! Doctor! What colour is it?'

Slapper.

I stopped these thoughts as soon as they started because with them came a surge of sheer terror at the idea of doing this alone.

I was eleven weeks now and had a small neat bump.

I made myself a cup of tea and lay down on the eighteenth-century, silk, sick-stained sofa. Recently, for obvious reasons, I had been thinking about my own mother a lot. And so it had transpired that for all these years she had known what I had done, that I was a murderer. She had put two and two together. I had always wondered whether she might. Who else had she told? Why had she told Megan? She had certainly never reported me to the police. I wondered whether she had told my father. That day I started speaking again, in the garden with the tortoise, the day I had decided to kill Fowler, my mother must have known. She knew what put the idea in my head; she knew that *she* had put it there. Maybe that was why she had not said anything – perhaps she felt in some way responsible. Or perhaps, just perhaps, in her own way, she had protected me.

Had my own mother felt like this with me in her belly? I tried to picture her as a young woman, mooching about the place, patting her rounded tummy, but I just couldn't see it. She would have been too busy scrubbing Organizational steps somewhere. But I couldn't stop wondering: had she felt the same benevolence for me that I was feeling for this little thing inside me? Had she, too, stared out of the window for hours and marvelled at the miracle in her womb? Had she grown me with love?

And then I thought about Thomas. How had that been for her, losing a baby? I was five when he died. They'd taken him to the hospital with a fever, and he had never come back home. I remembered all his little things around the house slowly disappearing. His 'duffy', a piece of fur that he stroked and sniffed as he sucked his thumb, and a dirty old pink rabbit that he slept with, his little blue towelling suits that smelt, not unpleasantly, of sick. Even his dirty nappies had smelt sweet to me, like the bakery on Junction Road. What happened to all his things? The only thing she kept was his duffy. I found it, years later, in her special drawer by her sanitary belt and her dutch cap.

His coffin was so small it looked like a toy. My Sacha doll could have fitted inside.

I remembered hearing her sobbing in their bedroom, low quiet sobs. I had never heard her cry before and I knocked on the bedroom door, worried. My father wouldn't let me in. He came out, keeping the door close to his body, keeping me away from my mother, shutting me out. He told me that Thomas had gone to the Absolute. I asked if he was coming back and he said Thomas would be coming back in his next lifetime when he was ready. It didn't strike me for a long time that Thomas was actually dead.

I stared at the street from the sofa, and my heart felt as if it were bursting for poor little Thomas. I remembered his tiny, hot chubby hands taking mine. He would sniff my fingers as he sucked on his thumb. I would call this baby Thomas or Thomasina. I promised him that.

For the first time in my life it struck me as unbearably sad that I had no relationship with my own mother, the woman who bore me, who gave me life. What if history were to repeat itself? I would never let this baby disappear without trying to find it. I would never let what happened to me happen to my child. Never. Where had she been when I needed her?

I knew then that I wanted to see her. I didn't know what I would say to her or even whether I would say anything at all. But I knew that the time had come.

Besides, I had always wanted my birth certificate. Perhaps she still had that. Who knows, perhaps one day I'd even get myself a passport.

Archway had always been a complete shit-hole. I had never gone back there. If a journey required passing through it, I would always go the long way round. Every step, every paving slab, every shop, every brick is set in my memory; it's probably part of my DNA now. Archway was full of drunks, loonies and perverts. My parents never seemed to notice, though. Probably the shittier the place you lived, the closer to Govinda you were. Maybe that's unfair; we probably lived there because we were poor.

The best thing about Archway was that no other Funny Farmers lived there.

After years of Denial and Avoidance, I had to hand it to myself, I was certainly embracing Confrontation, I thought, as I sat on the familiar old Barnet branch of the Northern Line. Not to say that I was finding it easy: my hands and my armpits were sweating. I looked about me. The fabric on the seats had changed; it used to be a red and green check or sometimes a horrible diarrhoea-coloured check. Everything seemed different to me. Mornington Crescent station had gone. I had fond memories of a derailment there.

I knew precisely how long each tunnel lasted, and a looming sense of doom filled me as the train went past Kentish Town and the countdown began. Tufnell Park, with its ominous orange lettering, and I was nearly home.

Archway tube station had certainly changed. It used to be quite easy to miss altogether: the little yellow lights in the blackness of the tunnel continued on to the dark, dingy platform. But now, Archway was light and bright and modern; it flickered past my eyes as the train pulled in. The people around me, the inhabitants and workers of Archway, had changed too. They looked smart and suited. I stepped off the train on to this new station and I found myself looking out for Caroline Stern in her silly purple uniform. But she was just a ghost now. Like the old station.

I joined the mass of people going up the escalator, a modern one, not the thick-slatted, old, wooden one. Where had all these people come from, who inhabited Archway with such certainty? It was like watching someone driving breezily about in a car they'd nicked off you. What had happened to the old black guy who used to tear the tickets and once chased away a paedo for me?

It gave me some satisfaction that Archway itself was still a shit-hole. They'd tried to trendify it a bit, but not with much success. I retraced my old steps. How many thousands of times had I passed the Nat West and the old Drum and Monkey. They used to collect money in a box for the IRA in there. Carol Watson told me that Big Terry had once 'flattened' a bloke in the Drum and Monkey. Even as I passed it now, with an impending dread, I imagined him rolling around on top of someone like a rolling pin, squishing them flat, with his bum hanging out.

I turned up our street and I felt the punch in the stomach that I knew was coming. By this time, I had assured myself that my mother wouldn't be home; she would be out Organizationalling, but I still wanted to see the house. I wanted to show my prawn-baby where I had been brought up.

I walked up the hill, the sickness rising. The street had poshed up. No more dumped cars and squats; it was now all fresh paint and four-by-fours. As I rounded the corner of the hill, I looked out for Carol Watson, leaning on the wall with her teeth out. But of course she wasn't there; she'd be dead by now. Someone new lived there. I could see a baby-walker thing through the window and I wondered whether my mother had got any friendlier over the years, whether she spoke to those people, whether she smiled at that baby.

I could feel my heart beating in my teeth as I looked out for my house, but the big light-stealing hedge was in the way.

Then there it was, directly in front of me.

My feet stopped and I stared; a tidal wave of memory swept over me, unbalancing me. I steadied myself on the curling black iron gate and gazed at the door. The same old dark green door, two panels of glass that I used to run my finger over, bump bump bump, as I looked into the dark silence beyond.

I pushed open the gate and walked towards the front door. It didn't look as if anyone was in, but then again it never had.

I stood on the coal-hole cover, wondering whether I was going to vomit. Confront. Confront. I knocked on the door. That was my brass knocker. I had dug that up from the back of our garden. I heard some movement in the house. I had an awful feeling that I was going to throw up on the doorstep. I leant on the portal for support. Through the glass, I could see a figure at the top of the stairs, outside the loo. Slowly, one careful step at a time, the figure came down the stairs.

It was a man, a tall but stooped old man. I watched him approach the door. But hadn't they said that my father was dead? I stared through the bumpy glass. The man opened the door.

It had not occurred to me that they might have moved house. My parents were not the sort of people that did that. Material advancement was obviously off the menu for them, and I could think of no reason on earth for them to have moved.

'Yes?' the tall man said, half opening the door, as if I might mug him.

'Hello,' I replied, disappointment and relief battling it out within me. My mouth had gone dry. I cleared my throat but I didn't know what to say. 'Umm . . . is this the Sterns' house?'

'No,' he said. 'My daughter and her husband live here.'

'Oh!'

'They've been here what . . . Janet?' he shouted, turning around. 'How long have you been here?'

I felt tremendously hurt, which I know is ridiculous. How come no one had told me? I felt tears prick my eyes.

'Thank you,' I said, not waiting for an answer, swiftly turning around and opening the gate.

I was the ghost now, I was history. I ran back down the hill towards the station.

Steinberg had lost weight. He looked tired and sad. I saw him first. He was sitting at a corner table, flicking through a newspaper, or pretending to. I saw that he kept looking up; he was expecting me from the other direction. I chose this café on Portobello because it was my turf. I needed to feel safe asking him this. I needed to be able to run home if need be.

Steinberg's face lit up briefly when he saw me come in. He was so comfortingly familiar to me. I wanted to reach out and run my fingers over his cheek and down his jaw but, of course, I didn't. He stood up, and we had an awkward kiss over the table. He tried to hug me just as I had already started pulling away.

I took my jacket off and hung it over the back of my chair. It was either my nerves, being pregnant or just the heating in this café, but whatever, it was boiling in here. Steinberg himself had rolled up his sleeves, and, without thinking, I found myself taking off my cardigan. I sat down quickly. I had no intention of letting him see my bump; I would just have to make sure that I didn't stand up. I wasn't quite sure how obvious my bump was to other people – no one had commented on it at work, but naked in the mirror I looked like the Buddha. I held my cardigan in my lap and stroked it like a duffy.

Steinberg and I held each other's gaze for too long. It was impossible to discourage intimacy with him; there was such a deep connection, sometimes I felt as if he were my lifeline. But I was fully aware of the futility of these feelings, so if this was all the indulgence that they were going to get, then sod it, I would stare into his eyes.

The waitress broke the spell. She was one of those aggressively friendly types, inappropriately confident. Just get the coffee and fuck off.

'Hey guys!' she boomed in a loud, husky, boozy voice, with an Australian twang. 'Just give us a shout when you're ready!' She plonked two oversized menus on the table. It felt as if we were in separate booths.

'Just a filter with hot milk,' I said, handing her back my menu, not taking my eyes off Steinberg.

'Sure, darling,' she replied. 'I see you two have business.'

Jesus, since when did waiting staff get so cocky? I turned to her icily. 'Thank you, that's all.'

Steinberg pushed down his menu and smiled at me.

'You look ... different,' he said, with eyes that loved me. I could tell that he wanted to touch me, but he knew that he shouldn't.

'Yes.'

'Thinner.' He meant my face, of course. He hadn't seen my bump.

'Yes. So are you.'

'But ... still beautiful.'

I wished he hadn't said that. I looked down at my lap and then back at his sad, blue eyes. 'I'm sorry, Steinberg, I'm so sorry.'

He nodded. 'Sometimes I am, sometimes I'm not,' he said, deftly flicking the funky little pepper pot over in his hand. The gesture reminded me of Cameron.

'I didn't mean for it to go like this,' I said stupidly.

'Do you mean you didn't intend for us to get found out?'

'Yes, I suppose. I didn't mean for all this ... trouble.'

I looked out of the window. The waitress brought over the coffee and placed it down in front of me with a lot of unnecessary clatter. She had enough jewellery on to open a shop. I waited for her to go.

'Joe won't see me.'

He nodded in a way that meant he understood Joe's point of view.

'How is he?'

I shrugged. 'Oh, couldn't be better, I imagine. How's Cameron?'

He shook his head as if he didn't want to talk about it. His eyes roamed about the café like a weary general surveying corpses on a battlefield.

'Megan came round to see me,' I said.

He looked surprised. 'Did she? What did she want?'

'She wanted me to promise not to see you again, Steinberg.'

'I see. She's in a bad way.'

'I'm not here to cause more trouble. I'm not here to break up your family.'

He sighed.

'But,' I carried on, 'I need you to tell me something and I didn't know who else to ask.'

'What is it?'

'My mother has moved house.'

'From North London, you mean?'

I nodded.

'That's right, they moved a while ago.' He said it as if everybody knew that.

'You didn't tell me that.'

'You didn't want to know.'

It was true. The waitress was coming over again. 'Can I get you dudes something to eat?'

No. Bugger off.

'Can I have a croissant?' Steinberg looked up at her sweetly.

'Sure,' she said, grinning at him, swivelling round in her trendy attire, clinking back to the bar.

'Well, where does she live now?' I asked.

'You want to see her?'

'Yes. I want to see my mother.'

He looked very surprised, but tried to hide it.

'She lives at St Augustine's.'

I was certainly not expecting that.

'What?' I said flabbergasted.

'She lives at the school.'

'She lives in the school building?' I echoed, like a moron. It shouldn't have been that much of a surprise – it was quite common for the farmers to live at the farm – but it still made me feel sick.

In fact, this time I really was going to be sick. Right now. I got up and rushed off to the loo. Damn this sickness. I puked, rinsed out my mouth, wiped my face and came back and sat down as if nothing had happened.

Steinberg looked stunned. He was gawping at me. 'Are you all right, Caroline?' he said.

'I'm fine, I'm fine,' I replied, not catching his eye. I fiddled with a napkin.

'Has this happened before?'

'What are you, a fucking doctor?'

'Look at me, Caroline,' he said, and then I knew that he'd seen my bump. I should have kept the cardigan on.

I briefly looked up from the salt and pepper pots that I had begun rhythmically banging together.

'Are you pregnant?'

I missed a beat in my banging.

'Caroline?' he was whispering now, as if he already knew the answer. 'Are you pregnant?'

I didn't say a thing; I just raised my eyes to meet his. I could see the blood drain from his cheeks.

'You said you couldn't . . .' He could barely form the words. I put a protective hand on my belly.

'Well, I was wrong, Steinberg, because it turns out that I could.'

He had turned quite white with shock. He shook his head, bit his lip and looked out of the window, beseechingly, as if the cavalry might turn up and rescue him.

'Don't worry, it might not be yours,' I said, cuttingly.

That thought had not occurred to him.

'*Is* it mine?'

'One croissant!' the waitress boomed, leaning her open bosom between us. 'Oops!' she said, loudly, as the knife clattered off the plate. 'I'm so hung-over!'

Steinberg didn't even notice her. He was staring at me open-mouthed.

'I don't know whose it is. Yours or Joe's. There's no one else, if that's what you're wondering,' I said, when she'd gone.

He looked small and frightened.

'But my money's on you,' I added.

He wiped his forehead and took off his glasses and began to clean them with a napkin.

'Look, Steinberg, it's not your problem, okay? Don't worry about it. I'm on my own. That's fine, I can do it.'

He stopped rubbing his glasses and his hand sought mine out. He put the glasses back on so that he could see me.

'Oh, Caroline, I wish things were different.'

I did too. I wished everything had gone differently.

'It's okay,' I said. 'I'll be fine. Me and the baby, we'll be fine.'

I hadn't said those words before, 'me and the baby'. We felt like a powerful unit, a little isolated maybe.

'Oh, Caroline,' he said, squeezing my hand. 'I'm so sorry.'

'Well, you know what? I'm not. I'm not sorry at all. I'm going to look after this child. Properly. It's going to be a very lucky child.'

I felt a lump in my throat. He nodded, baffled by all this.

'I'll give you what I can.'

'I don't care about that. I wasn't even going to tell you. Just don't tell Megan.'

He looked sad, really sad. After a while he said, 'How many weeks?'

There was a tenderness in his voice. He knew about babies.

'Thirteen.'

Then he smiled. I suppose he was picturing the little prawn. 'Can I touch it?'

I had not been prepared for this. I wanted to cry.

'Yes.'

He moved to the corner seat, and I took his warm hand and placed it on my belly. We sat there in silence for a while, his hand resting on my baby.

'Does Joe know?' he asked.

I shook my head.

There wasn't anything else to say now, and I stole

myself away from him. It was much harder than I had imagined. I had loved him, after all. When I kissed him goodbye, I saw a tear slide down his cheek, I felt it on my lips. I carried his salty tear home with me in my mouth and hoped it went down to the baby.

9

That first night in Boulogne, I found myself a hotel. There were loads of them along the sea front, but this one stood out: it had a big television on in the reception. I could see it through the window from the outside. Immediately, the telly gave me a warm, comforting feeling, and my fear eased a little. I stared at the screen, mesmerized by the happy faces and clapping hands. An audience was laughing at a man in a suit who kept grinning and raising his eyebrows as a half-naked lady stood in front of Hoovers and soda siphons. I could have watched it for ever.

Eventually I went in. Luckily the woman behind the desk, who seemed totally uncheered by the television, spoke a little bit of English, and I didn't bother with my American accent. I didn't think that she'd notice it and, besides, I had decided that Lorraine Fischer had most definitely been brought up in England.

I had changed a load of dollars into French francs on the ferry and laid them out on the desk, so that the woman could point out the price for the night. It made me nervous when she took my passport and locked it in a box, but she flapped her hand at me reassuringly. I had a dreadful feeling that she might be in league with the police and the Alsatians, so I kept a careful eye on where she put the box and where she kept the key (in her pocket).

I followed her rustling skirt up numerous flights stairs to my room, with her talking all the while in a gr manly voice. The French word for room is *chambre*, like 'chamber'. It could be from the Latin word *camera*, because I know that the first cameras were little dark boxes, i.e. rooms. But it might be from the Greek word *kamara*, which means 'vault'. But where did the 'b' come from? Mr Steinberg would know. Oh, Mr Steinberg, how I missed him. I wished he was here in Boulogne with me, like on a school trip. He would know where the 'b' came from and he'd make me think that I had come up with the answer. He could make you feel clever and special. Sometimes, when I asked him something, his eyes would light up and he'd say, 'Well, no one's ever asked me that before, Caroline. I shall have to think about that,' and my heart would glow. But it wasn't glowing now; it was dim and heavy.

My room was very small and tidy. Megan's mum would have approved. The furniture was dark and gloomy against the yellowing chip wallpaper. When the woman left me alone, I dumped my bag on the bed and went to the window, opening the shutters wide. I leant out, staring into the black emptiness of the sea before me, breathing in the salty petrol-filled air as I listened to the faint mosquito whine of a nearby motorway. England seemed a very long way away, the thought of which should have comforted me, but it didn't. Instead I felt the flooding, panicky feeling begin to take hold again so I quickly grabbed the shutters and closed the window. The bathroom was so small I could barely open the door and get in. The strange thing was, it didn't have a bath in it.

I'd never had a shower in my life. No one I knew had showers. I felt a little heartened at the sight of some wrapped-up things around the basin, almost like welcoming presents: a see-through plastic hat, a bar of soap and a little bottle of shampoo. I opened them all up, took my clothes off and tried to operate the shower. At first it was pretty miserable, freezing cold and a bit trickly, but once it began to warm up I didn't want to get out. I stood beneath the downpour, lifting up my face to feel the force of it, letting the water drench me as it blasted away all the dirt and the madness of the day. I scrubbed my face, my hair, my whole body and stood there motionless until my skin went soggy and the water went cold.

Afterwards, I stood naked in front of the mirror for a moment; the young woman in the reflection was strange and unfamiliar. I wrapped a towel around my hair and another one around my breasts, like a lady in an advertisement.

Feeling much better and suddenly very weary, I lay down on the hard bed and pulled the blanket up over my face.

The next thing I knew, it was morning. I waited for the crash of my bedroom door and my dad's thumping footsteps as he crossed the room and ripped open the curtains. Soon I would stick my arm out and reach for my school clothes. But the crash never came. Instead, my ears honed in on the distant sound of cars. Something else was different: the view from my closed eyelids felt lighter. I pulled down the cover.

Oh God. It was real. Everything was real. I was in

France. I was on the run. I was a murderer. I had killed Fowler. I had to flee. I must keep moving. I must make plans. But God, how my tummy hurt: a strange, unfamiliar, ripping ache.

I swung my legs out of the bed and stood up. To my utter horror I saw that the towel I had been lying on was drenched in thick dark clots of blood. At first I thought I must have cut myself, but when I felt the warm rivulets running down from in between my legs, I knew what it was. I had started the Curse. Oh, please God, no, no. I held the bloody towel to my body to stem the flow and tugged the sheets off the bed. The blood had soaked through the mattress. I ran the corner of the clean towel under the tap and desperately tried to rub the blood off the mattress, but I was only making it worse.

Hunched in the shower, trying to scrub the blood out of the sheet and towel: it all suddenly felt too much. I rested my forehead on the white-tiled wall and began to sob. Of course, killing Fowler was not the end of it, as if she would give up so easily. Oh no. She was watching me, haunting me, cursing me. She had ripped my stomach and made me bleed today as vengeance.

Gently at first, I began to bang my head against the tiles. I hated her. I hated her.

Stop it! That was Lorrie talking. Think. Think. Stop crying, you stupid child. Get yourself together. Eat something. Get yourself out of here.

I geared myself into action, got dried, took the nail scissors out of my bag, cut the clean towel up into rags and laid them like a nappy in my pants, and in the space of a few minutes packed all my things together, covered the blood up on the mattress with the hotel manual and calmly went downstairs to breakfast.

I smiled politely at the woman when she brought me a croissant and some hot chocolate, but thought she looked at me strangely. Perhaps she'd been upstairs and seen the mess in my room. Please God she wouldn't report me to the police. The dogs would track me easily now that I was bleeding.

I wolfed down my croissant, paid her husband at the desk, zipped up my passport and got out of there as quickly as I could.

It was a bright, windy day, and it felt good to be on the move again. I stepped out into the road and nearly got run over by a car that looked like a wheelbarrow. The driver hooted at me and shouted out of the window. Not a good start.

As I followed the road, a little nervously, letting my ears lead me towards the sound of whizzing cars, I began to hatch a plan. First thing, I had to get to Paris. Once there I would rent a little room near Notre Dame and find work in a restaurant with a black and white floor; I might learn to dance like those women with frilly knickerbockers on, and I could sit in bars looking moodily out of windows with a glass of wine in front of me. Every now and then, after a good soak in a tin tub, I might take a trip to the ballet or the horse races. Everything I knew about Paris came out of a book at Kate's house by the Impressionists. Mr Wapinski didn't approve of the Impressionists – he thought them sentimental and superficial. He only liked the Renaissance. But Mr Wapinski could shove the Renaissance up his bum; he was nothing to do with me any more. Oh yes, Lorrie Fischer thought Mr Wapinski was a hateful man.

By now, I had found myself on a slip road, and the roar of cars was just on the other side of the trees. I stopped, put down my bag and stuck out my thumb, pulling what I hoped was a suitable hitch-hiking expression – friendly yet experienced. A lorry driver slowed down and hooted, but didn't stop.

I rather hoped that I might bump into the snogging couple and we could all travel happily together. One day, maybe, I would be in love like they were, stopping to kiss, being so free with each other's bodies. Steinberg had a girlfriend; presumably they snogged. Maybe they did *it*. The Organization were very strict on *it*: you had to wait until you were married. I hoped and prayed that Steinberg wouldn't marry her. In a few years' time, I could send him cryptic postcards from places I'd hitch-hiked to and he could decode them and come and find me. I knew that this wasn't really going to happen. I knew that my old life was over.

A shiny black car flashed its lights at me, and its silver-spoked wheels crunched to a halt at my side. I couldn't see the driver through the tinted window, just my new reflection. Briefly I admired my baseball jacket. The window wound down a little, and a waft of cigarettes, after-shave and leather hit me. Through the smoke I saw a smart looking middle-aged man leaning towards me, a cigarette dangling from his lip. He said something in utter gobbledygook, which momentarily took me by surprise – it was only just really sinking in that people in France actually didn't speak English.

I nodded keenly at whatever it was that he had said and replied, 'Paris.'

'Paris?' he laughed and gobbledygooked again, wagging his finger. I shrugged. I didn't really care where I was going, just as long as it was away from the police and the dogs.

He leant over and pushed open the passenger door, and I climbed into his immaculate car, placing my bag down on the floor under the creamy leather seat. Then he pulled away and started gobbledygooking again. I nodded a bit, but soon became distracted by his hand on the gear stick. His skin was a silky, milky white, and his fingernails so perfect, so filed and polished that it looked like he had a woman's hand. Whenever he stopped talking, I looked up at his face and said, 'Oui.'

'English,' I said, after a particularly long pause and then, corrected myself, 'originally American.'

'American?'

He seemed greatly pleased by this and smiled at me, revealing some less-than-perfect teeth. I thought he was leaning over to pat my leg, but he reached for the glove compartment and picked out a cassette that said 'Judy Garland' on the front with a picture of a sad-eyed woman on it. I nodded and smiled like she was an old favourite of mine and he put the tape on.

I loved the Judy Garland. She made me feel much better; she made it sound like there was some dignity in loneliness.

We drove past endless flat countryside, interrupted by small villages full of ugly bungalows. Every now and then a cathedral spire spiked the horizon, offering a promise of something else. France really wasn't as romantic as I had imagined, and the people in the cars looked just as gloomy as English people. And it certainly wasn't hot, like I'd been led to believe.

On the outskirts of a small town, my driver turned to me and mimed eating a sandwich. He pulled in and stopped outside a café, checking his reflection in the mirror, dabbing at his coiffed hair before we both got out of the car.

He saw it first, the carnage on the seat, the corpseless massacre over his creamy white leather. I had bled everywhere.

I gasped, horrified and caught his eye across the car roof. He looked as if he was about to throw up.

'I'm so sorry!' I cried, my shame amplified by his evident disgust. I fumbled for my bag and sprinted towards the restaurant, tears of shame running down my face.

I burst through the doors to be met by a solemn, spotty young man.

'Lavatory?' I sobbed.

He pulled a face of incomprehension.

'Toilet?' I tried, and he flicked me a gesture towards a door on his left. I wanted to crawl into a hole and die, which was exactly what I was confronted with when I pushed open the toilet door: a dark stinking hole in the ground instead of a loo, like you'd imagine in the trenches.

I leant against the door, covered my mouth and tried to suffocate my sobs, catching sight of my blotchy face in a scabby old mirror on the wall. I ripped down my jeans, did what I could to clean myself up in the basin. I re-nappified my knickers, but my jeans were pretty much ruined, so I wrapped my jumper around my waist to cover up the mess. How much blood is there in a curse? How long does it go on for?

I wiped my face and stared at my reflection in the mirror. The police wouldn't be able to recognize me as Caroline Stern; Lorrie Fischer looked quite different. She was harder.

'Fuck you, Fowler! Fuck you!' I spat into the mirror.

Oh yes, Lorrie was a swearer.

I wasn't going to let Fowler win. She could rot in hell. I didn't care that I was going to be reborn as a maggot or a scorpion. I'd carry on the fight right until the end, until I was nothing more than bacteria.

I cautiously opened the toilet door and looked out for the Judy Garland man. His car was still outside, but there was no sign of him. I snuck out and ran for it. I'd get a bus or a train to Paris.

I stopped running once I was out of the café's vicinity and headed towards the town centre, keeping my eyes peeled for a chemist, where hopefully I'd find some sanitary towels. But there was nothing that looked like a chemist around.

As I walked, I couldn't help myself, I kept turning around. I was beginning to get an uncomfortable feeling that I was being followed.

After what seemed like an eternity, I found a sign to a station. When I got there, it was a very minor affair, nothing like any station in London. At first I didn't see him, the man behind the counter. He was huge and hairy-faced, squeezed into the minuscule ticket booth, like a gorilla in a basket. But it was he who was staring at me as if I were the freak. I checked that the blood hadn't gone through my jumper before pretending to read a poster.

Then I boldly went up to the booth.

'Ticket to Paris,' I said, clearly in a Frenchy-sounding voice.

He shook his head and said quite a lot and showed me a timetable and circled some numbers which were very hard to work out, as you had to subtract twelve from everything to find out the real time. To be honest, I didn't really care, I would have gone anywhere. So I bought whatever ticket it was he was selling, and he held up ten fingers, which presumably meant that the train was leaving in ten minutes.

I wandered on to the platform and watched a couple of trains whiz by. The French trains went like rockets; you'd die immediately if you jumped in front of one of them. A few people began to materialize, and after ten minutes exactly a green light turned red, and a train slowed down as it pulled into the station. I played my old game of standing as close to the train as possible as the near-empty carriages flicked by my face. France seemed very empty compared to London.

Before I got on, I glanced down the platform, just in case someone really was following me. I sat myself as far away as I could from an old couple at the front of an otherwise empty carriage and put my bag underneath my seat, jiggling my legs impatiently. Hurry up and pull out. A man in a beige overcoat just like my father's boarded the carriage, glancing at me before taking a seat in the row behind. He looked exactly how you'd imagine a plain-clothed policeman to look.

I got up and moved to the other side, parallel to him, but he showed no interest in my seat swapping. Once the train pulled out, in fact, as long as I was on the move, I began to feel okay again. I leant my head on the pane and tried to build on my plans, but the smooth, lulling rhythm of the train must have made me doze off, although it was hard to tell because I dreamt that I was doing exactly what I was really doing – sitting on a train looking out of the window. But in my dream there was no noise; it was completely silent. And the scenery was different: rocky and dangerous. The train slowed right down as it went through a market town full of people in a busy square, but they were moving in slow motion, just like Megan's impression of the Six Million Dollar Man. One by one, the people in the town stopped what they were doing and turned towards the train, their eyes seeking someone out, and when they saw me they stopped searching. The train was barely moving now. I held the gaze of a girl of about my age. She gave me a sad smile and waved before slowly bringing her hands to her face. She clutched the top of her forehead, glancing at me through her fingers, making sure that I was watching her, and then she peeled the skin right off her face. But there was no blood and guts. Underneath her skin, her face was made of metal and wires, like the insides of a television.

Appalled, I looked around at the other inhabitants of the market stall. They were all doing it, every single one, peeling the skin off their faces to reveal mechanical heads. Just at that moment, I felt a firm and familiar grip on my shoulder. I snapped my head round to my left and there she was, sitting right next to me, Fowler, her face inches away from mine, her hair hanging long and loose, her eyeballs spinning back into her skull and her teeth framed by that rictus grin.

I jerked awake with a cry. And the awful thing was, even though I understood that it was only a dream, I could smell the Dettol. The whole carriage reeked of it.

I looked around. Everything was exactly how it had been. I was sitting in the same seat and we were still speeding past the French countryside. There was no market town full of face-peeling people. The seat next to me was empty. The man in my dad's raincoat was asleep.

I put my hand out and touched the fabric where Fowler had been sitting, just to check. Now I know this sounds crazy, but when I looked into the fabric of the seat where she had been, I could quite clearly see the word 'DEVIL' in the pattern of the fabric.

It wasn't until the train stopped at a station that I noticed that my bag had gone. I looked under the seat, I scrabbled around on the floor, but it had, without a doubt, vanished.

'My bag!' I shouted, getting up. 'My bag! Someone's stolen my bag!'

The man in the raincoat opened his eyes and stared at me, shrugging his shoulders. The old couple didn't understand what I was going on about as I ran through the carriage, looking high and low, calling out, 'My bag!'

The train began to pull out of the station. I had to get off; the thief would have jumped ship here.

'My bag!' I shouted, leaping from the train. 'Help me, someone!'

I began to really panic. This was disastrous. God help

me, please, help me. But there was no one. Not a soul on the platform, just a small child watching me through the glass of a carriage. I wasn't sure what to do: get back on or stay here? The decision was made for me as the train slowly pulled out, leaving me bagless and desperate, flapping about on the platform. What could I do? I couldn't report it stolen, not me, a murderer and a thief myself.

I began turning circles at the station entrance, almost dancing, going one way and then another. I had to listen very hard to Lorrie Fischer telling me to calm down. Stop. Stop, she was saying.

So here I was, God knows where, no ticket, no money, no passport, no nothing. I looked about me. No people, no cars. Think. Think. To both my left and right was a long, straight grey tarmac road, lined with tall, thin French trees, their leaves rustling high up in the sky somewhere.

I turned left. I'm always drawn to things on the left. After a mile or so, I arrived in a small grey-stone town, unremarkable in any way except for its absence of people. What did French people do with themselves?

I wandered through the streets and into an empty square; all the shops were closed despite it being early afternoon. I sat on a bench and prayed to God for help, especially to stop my curse.

I walked the streets for a while before I realized that I was starving. My stomach rumbled as I drooled into the window of a bakery. This wasn't like an English bakery with jammy doughnuts and cream éclairs; this one had exquisite-looking little fruit tarts, all varnished and perfect. I gazed at the shining sliced strawberries of a tartlet until something in the reflection of the glass caught my eye. And this time, it wasn't a dream. It was completely real. I swear on the Upanishads. I saw her hands, her mottled red raw hands clutched together, her familiar ink-stained fingers. She was standing right at my side.

I screamed and jumped away from the window, looking around sharply. Nothing. She had gone. The street was empty. But there it was, that reek of Dettol.

I staggered backwards. 'Leave me alone!' I whispered, breathless and tearful. I turned, sprinting to the end of the street, taking refuge against a wall. I slid down and sat on my haunches.

I had to calm down. I had to stop these imaginings.

Somewhere near by I could hear running water and I got up and followed the sound. At the end of an alley and across a street I looked over a low wall to see the brackish churning water of a river. I wanted to be by it, to lose myself in its swirling noise. There were two identical stone bridges crossing the river, one on my right and one on my left. Laughter behind me startled me, but it was just a small boy being chased by his father, playing tag. I watched them go past me, their togetherness making me feel more isolated than ever.

I climbed down the grassy bank on the other side of the left bridge and sat on the grass at the water's edge. Everything seemed to be making me nervous: the banging of an old tethered rowing boat against the stone of the bridge, the noise from the crows in the trees behind, the thin smothering coat of cloud drawing across the sky.

Come on, Lorrie Fischer. Stop the nerves. What are you going to do?

I had to get practical. I would have to steal another bag. Hadn't I put the change from this morning's hotel bill in my jeans?

Sure enough, after rummaging around in my pocket I came up with a hundred and ten francs. I'd spend it on provisions rather than waste it on a hotel. I could sleep anywhere. France was a hot country, everyone knew that; I expected lots of people slept outside here.

I took some deep breaths to calm myself, lay back on the grass, listened to the sound of the water and watched the now-hazy sun slowly drift across the sky.

A while later, I returned to the square and was amazed to see that it had sprung to life. As if at some invisible signal, people had come out of the woodwork. Old men were throwing silver balls along the ground, like they do on Hampstead Heath, only they weren't wearing white and they didn't bother with grass, they just chucked them along the ground.

The tables in the square were packed: families sitting around eating ice creams, children in smart clothes with shiny hair and shoes. All the shops were now open, bustling with life. I wondered whether they did things differently in France. Maybe people got up in the evening and slept in the day. I went into a shop and asked for, or rather pointed at, some bread and some cheese and a cake and, most importantly, I found some sanitary towels. Then I saw to my problem in the public toilets which were in the middle of a patch of green behind the square. They were proper loos, not trench holes.

I spent the next few hours just following families around, pretending I belonged, drinking Oranginas, feeling almost calm and free, as the sky turned red, then purple, then green. I didn't feel like pinching a bag quite yet; I wanted to stick around a while, delay being alone again.

I was one of the last people to leave the square and I couldn't help feeling a little sorry for myself as I walked towards the bridge, looking up at drawn curtains, lights in houses, other people's cosy lives, when it was the old rowing boat for me tonight. I made my way back along the bridge, hands in pockets, head down. The wind had picked up and was blowing dust into my eyes. It was very dark now, away from the square. The only light came from the dim yellow street lamp on the bridge; spits of rain shone like golden threads in its glow.

As I made my way down the bank, I slipped and cursed myself for not spending the money on a hotel. I trudged towards the rowing boat and climbed in, but there was a good five inches of water in the bottom, so I dragged it a little way up the bank and the water sploshed down to the other end. I found a dryish bit, got myself as comfortable as was possible and curled up using my plastic bag full of sanitary towels as a pillow.

I must have fallen asleep because I was woken by a crack of thunder and a flash of lightning, and in the yellow lamplight I could see the rain lashing down furiously. I was completely soaked. I climbed out of the boat and skidded up the bank and sat under the weep of a willow tree, clutching my knees into my body as I watched the elements thrashing around. Thunder growled across the black sky.

I sat back as close to the willow as possible, but still

the rain got me. I put my head on my knees and prayed that things would get better. God knows how long I was like that for, but something made me sit up fast. It was the smell. Antiseptic disinfectant.

'Look at me!'

I heard it distinctly. It sounded like a bark. I opened my eyes and looked around me. But there was nothing, just the rain slashing by the lamplight.

Then in the darkness of the shallows, I saw it. Something was crawling out of the water. I felt my spine go rigid.

'Look at me!' it barked again, and I recognized that voice. It was Fowler.

I stared into the blackness, and then the yellow lamp light caught her head. She was on her hands and knees, and her hair was down, drenched, hanging round her hollow face. She was naked. Her eyes were rolled back into her head, I could see the whites. She moved swiftly, like a dog.

'Look at me!'

This time it came from somewhere to the left of me; I flinched so suddenly my head bashed against the trunk of the tree. My eyes darted about in the darkness. And then I saw the other one. There were two of her; this one was bigger, nearer, and her hair was moving, wriggling.

'Over here!' came another bark from the other side. God help me. There were three of her, crawling towards me. This one had the yellow street light full on her face. Black blood dripped down her cheeks from her eyeballs, her hair a mass of writhing snakes. My whole body was petrified with fear; a scream choked in my throat.

I knew exactly who they were. They had come to avenge the murder. The Furies were going to get me, and I knew that they would not rest until they had.

'Look, what you have done!' they all whispered in unison, spitting at me.

I was too scared to breathe. I watched them crawl up the grass bank towards me, their nails almost a foot long. I tried to close my eyes and tell myself that I was imagining it, but it was too late for that; they were as real as I was.

'Don't shut your eyes!' one of them barked. 'Look at us! You murderess!'

The one on the left flicked her head back violently, and the snakes hissed, 'You'll never escape!' She was just under the willow now, the leaves on the edge branches were touching her hair.

Something in me clicked into action. I got up and scrabbled up the bank towards the bridge. I could hear them behind me, whispering at me. I ran for my life. I knew they were scampering after me. I could hear their nails scratching on the road. I dared not turn around. Faster, faster I ran. As I got to the park I scooped up a branch, freshly fallen from a tree, and turned, armed with my weapon, ready to fight.

Nothing there. They were gone; they were hiding. I gasped for breath, my eyes scanning every alley, every parked car, every tree, waiting, just waiting for their attack. I knew what they would do, how they would claw me, their razor-sharp nails scratching the skin off my flesh, peeling me like an apple.

I staggered on, gripping the branch, alert and ready, soaking wet.

As soon as I saw the public toilets I knew that would be the place to hide. It was a small hut with only one door. I ran inside, closed the door and pressed my back against it, listening to the sound of my panting breath. It was pitch black in here. I kicked open each cubicle and thrashed the branch against the toilets in the darkness just in case they had got ahead of me. But it was empty.

I had fallen when climbing up the slope of the bank. I was caked in mud. I could feel it, wet and clammy all over me. I stood by the door for a long time, clutching the branch in my arms, ready to swipe. And then, just as the street lights were turned off but before the sky had got light, they came. I heard their claws clicking on the municipal flooring. I heard the hissing of their hair. They were outside the toilets. Click click, hiss hiss. I got up. I stood behind the door, and when the first one came in I brought the branch smack down on her head. Blood burst from the crack in her skull, splashing up the walls. I could feel it on my face, warm and thick.

I struck again.

I didn't know where I was, nothing seemed familiar. I was wearing some sort of ill-fitting pale green gown. It barely covered my nakedness. It kept falling off my shoulder, but I didn't seem to care. I let it hang there. I didn't have anything on underneath. I wasn't even wearing shoes, just this gown.

I was walking down some stairs, really slowly, as if I had just learnt how to walk. Although the floor appeared to be grey, I could see flecks of red and blue in it, like little jewels in volcanic sand. My head felt thick and heavy, and I focused my eyes on the calloused heels shuffling on the grey sand ahead of me. With difficulty, I raised my eyes to see the pimply neck of a man in front of me. There were people in front of him as well; we were all wearing the same pale green gowns, descending stairs at the same slow pace.

The air smelt of chlorine and bleach like the changing rooms at Park Road swimming pool, but it wasn't Park Road swimming pool, I knew that. Perhaps I had been sent back to the Organization, but I didn't think so. I didn't recognize anyone, or the building, but it could have been: it was that silent, just our shuffling feet.

A fat woman wearing a white apron stood at the bottom of the stairs, holding a clipboard. She looked familiar, but I couldn't remember whether I liked her or not, and it seemed like a great effort to think about it. I could hear a gentle crying and with a monumental effort I turned around. The sobs were coming from the woman directly behind me. One of her bosoms was hanging out. It was not much higher than her tummy button and was right at my eye level.

I slowly turned back to the front and carried on following the line of people. We went round a corner. It was very quiet in this corridor, silent almost except for the sobs. There were windows very high up and beyond them grey sky. There was no colour anywhere.

We filed down another flight of stairs and along another corridor. It seemed to take for ever. We were all moving so very slowly, waddling almost, like a row of ducklings. Then we went down again to what must have been the bowels of the building. There were no windows down here.

Our leader was the fat woman in the white apron, and she made us stop. She didn't have to say anything; we just stopped and bumped into each other like dominoes. I bumped into the pimply neck and the low bosom woman bumped into me. None of us cared, though.

I noticed the ceiling, which was not very far up; it was covered in pipes and fans. If you were tall, you could have just reached up and touched it, if you had the energy.

Along the corridor there was nothing except for a line of torn vinyl chairs. The blue plastic had come off, and the orange stuffing poked out of some of them. I stared at the colours. It smelt of mould and piss. It felt as if we were way down below the surface of the earth.

Perhaps I had been sent to Hell.

Suddenly we all started moving again; people began to sit, and I followed suit and sat down on one of the chairs. A few more people started crying. No one was looking at anybody else; everyone was staring at the ground. I too hung my head. Every movement seemed to require so much effort; speaking was unimaginable. Not that I had anything to say.

I felt a bead of sweat drop down from my armpit along my naked body down over the bone of my hip and on to the chair. I waited for it to land on the concrete floor, but it didn't make it that far. I felt a cramping feeling in my stomach.

The woman with the white apron called something out, and a tiny man slowly stood up, eyes still fixed on the ground. He looked like a mad person, and I wondered if I looked the same. I put my hand up to my face and felt my mouth. My lips were cracked and dry. I felt my cheeks; they were hollow. I felt my hair, but it had gone; there was just stubble. Someone had shaved my head. I could hear myself making a noise, a whining sound. I'd always had beautiful hair.

The tiny man was following the woman in the white apron, and she took him into a room on the right and, after a while, a horrible noise came from the room, a whizzing and a crackling and a banging and a moan, not a scream exactly, more of a howl like a dying animal. It chilled me to the bone, and my legs began to shake uncontrollably. The crying woman with the low bosoms was swaying back and forth on her chair. What was this place? What was I doing here? How long had I been here? I wanted to get up and run away, but that was impossible; my body seemed to be weighted down.

I watched, shaking, as the tiny man came out of the room on a trolley. At first I didn't see him; he was being pushed by two men in white coats. He wasn't moving any more; he looked like he was dead. I thought that perhaps they'd killed him.

The bones in my knees began knocking together so hard I could feel that they were making bruises. My elbows were shaking. There had been a terrible mistake. Surely, *surely*, someone was going to come and take me away from this? My mother? Where was my mother? I should not be here. Someone was going to save me. Steinberg? Somebody.

My head was shaking now, and sweat was trickling

down the sides of my body. I became mesmerized by my knees: they were knocking together at an incredible speed. I knew that my turn was coming up. Where was my mum? When would she get here? I looked down the corridor, but there was no sign of her. Maybe she was running around upstairs looking for me, frantically trying to find me to get me out of here.

The fat woman called out another name, and a black man started wailing. He gripped his chair and refused to get up. I saw him dig his heels into the ground. He frightened me. The fat woman blew a whistle, and two men came out of the room on the right. They had white masks on, and one of them had a needle in his hand. The black man had folded his arms into the back of his chair. I could see his willy hanging out. The needle man stuck the needle into the black man's leg, and after a moment or two the black man lost all his strength, and they just picked him up and dragged him into the room. I heard the whirring and the crackling, but I didn't hear the moaning, and I didn't watch when they carried him out on the trolley.

'La fille anglaise,' she said. Nobody moved.

'La fille anglaise.'

She started coming this way and stopped in front of me and said it again. 'La fille anglaise.'

I realized she meant me, but I couldn't stand up; my legs would not do it, but I didn't want those men coming out with the needle. I tried to push myself up with my arms, but my hands were so clammy they slipped on the vinyl.

She pulled me up. Somehow, I managed to stay up

and walk. I followed her into the room where the others had gone.

It was a small room with a table in the middle and a big black box to the side of it with a dial on it. I looked at the letters. 'Hoffman,' it said. Nothing made any sense; it was as if my very thoughts were heavy, weighted down.

There were about five people in there, all of them wearing white masks and white clothes. Two of them were talking, and the other three were looking at me, not with any curiosity or friendliness or even hostility; they were just waiting for me to do something. I knew what it was that I was meant to do. I climbed on to the table with my head near the big black box, and the three of them approached me. I was shaking so much they started to hold me down, but they were holding me too hard. They were hurting me. They were pushing my limbs down and strapping me to the table.

The person by my head was a woman. She had make-up on: blue eyelids and red cheeks. I tried to catch her eye so that she could see that this was all a terrible mistake, but she wasn't looking at me as if I were a person. She was looking at me as if I were a piece of fabric she was about to do some mending on.

I tried to speak but she stuck something in my mouth, something rubbery that tasted of tyres. I thought I was going to be sick. I tried to scream, but no one took any notice. She was putting something over my forehead and she rubbed something wet and cold on my temples.

I couldn't move my head at all and I started to panic. I could see the man with the mask coming towards me. I knew he had the needle in his hand. Then I saw it, such a big needle full to the brim with a clear liquid, and I knew he was going to stick it in me. I tried to free myself. I tried to thrash about, but I couldn't; my arms and legs were strapped to the table. I was beside myself with fear. Where was my mother? Where was my mum? Where was my mummy?

The man with the needle jabbed it into my hand. I could not believe he was doing it, such a big needle in my small hand. He started counting and I thought I must be learning something, because I could understand, 'Un ... deux ... trois ...'

The relief; suddenly I felt calm and removed. Not for long, because then came the most enormous jolt of electricity. It ripped through my body and jerked me about like a rag doll. I felt my pelvis fly to the ceiling. How I stayed strapped to the table, I do not know. My eyes filled with a blue flash of light, and then I was out.

Time had lost its meaning. Days and nights were punctuated by pills. It was repetitive to the point of distraction and it seemed inconceivable that anything would ever change. I didn't think I would ever get out. It was not that dissimilar to the Organization; they were trying to get to your brain one way or another.

As all hope dwindled, I gradually retreated into myself, until I was no bigger than a dot, until there were miles of numbness between me and my skin, until I was just a shuffling husk.

There is only so much to say about bleakness.

The shocks never got any less frightening just because I knew what was coming. Afterwards was the worst bit: it was as if I'd been shaken upside down until everything had fallen out, until all the 'me' bit had gone. Even the dot had fallen out and all that was left was my worthless old body. Aside from the terrible headaches and the muscle aches everywhere, it was as if my brain had been scrambled, like when you open up a torch and all the bits fall out on to the floor and you think, how will I ever get it back together in the right order? Immediately after a shock, I wouldn't even be able to get my face to do what I wanted it to do; the messages from my brain just couldn't reach it. Blinking was a feat.

I knew exactly what happened to me, because I saw it happen to the others. Take Jordi, who was chatty and friendly normally (especially after he'd been sniffing glue), but he would come back from the fryer like a zombie. He'd sit in his wheelchair, slumped like a limp marionette, dribbling, looking out of the window for days. And there was nothing out there to look at, just a row of tall French trees lining the big, long, empty drive and a little fountain in the middle which was only about an inch deep in case we tried to drown ourselves, I suppose. I knew I looked like he did; I always had a wet patch on the chest of my T-shirts.

After a few days I could start remembering things like my name, Lorrie Fischer, which I told them, and then I'd start remembering things that I wouldn't have minded forgetting, like Caroline Stern and killing Fowler and my parents and the Organization and all the badness. But I couldn't remember the small things, like how I brushed my teeth and how I dried myself after a bath, and, I tell you what, when you strip it all away, life boils down to the small things. I'd try to brush my teeth, but I just couldn't get the hang of it. Everyone has their own special way of doing it; it's like a fingerprint: it's your identity, and somehow I'd lost mine. Top left, bottom left, bottom right, top right, front teeth, whatever. I'd stand on the rubber bath mat after a bath and I wouldn't know how to dry myself. Where did I start? With my back? With my feet? Did I wrap the towel around my whole body or just below my arms?

It would hit me then that I was truly lost.

It took me a long time to find a little pleasure, and there were two things that afforded me that. If I stored up my medication – hid it underneath my tongue right at the back so that when they checked my mouth they couldn't see it – for a week, say, if I then took all the pills at once, I had a nice feeling take over me, really nice, like dying maybe. My only other pleasure was television, which became my main activity. They used to line us up in wheelchairs in the lounge area, up to twenty of us, all pretty much vegetables because of the medication. We'd sit there, staring at the television. We'd watch anything; I liked the adverts best. Once, somebody turned it off, but no one seemed to mind much; we all just carried on staring at the little silver dot in the black screen.

Most people had visitors. I'd always look out when people were arriving, just in case my mum would come, or Steinberg, or Megan. Maybe one day somebody might come for me. But I knew they wouldn't, and not just because they didn't know my name ... So, instead, I'd pretend that I had a visitor. I'd hang around someone else's. I took to one woman who used to come in and see her son. She was beautiful and cosy like a mother should be. Sometimes I'd run up and hug her when she arrived. She didn't seem to mind. She even gave me a Christmas present – some soft, fleecy, pink socks. She let me call her 'Maman'.

But one day, as I was hugging Maman around the waist, tightly as I liked to do, the nurse told me to let go of her, that 'Madame wanted to see her son on his own.'

'No!' I cried and clung on tighter.

Maman stroked my hair and said to the nurse that it was all right, she didn't mind, I could stay. But the nurse tried to pull me off, so I grabbed Maman tighter around her huge waist. Then the nurse started to get cross and called me a 'bad girl' in English.

'Let go, you wicked girl!' she said.

I lost it. I went crazy. I started kicking her. I bit her hand. I could taste her rusty, French blood.

'I'm not wicked,' I shouted. 'I'm not wicked. I'm not the Devil. I'm good. I'm a good girl. Maman, tell her I'm a good girl. Tell her that you love me!'

But Maman started crying, and I started crying, and then I saw the man come out with the big, big needle, and even Maman started trying to undo my hands.

I quizzed Gemma inordinately in our next session. She had sat there opposite me looking better than I had ever seen her. She had put on a stone in weight and had colour in her cheeks. She was looking pretty and cheerful. It was hard for me to take her in, such a transformation in such a short period of time. I was, of course, deeply suspicious.

'Do you feel that you have to be positive about St Augustine's for your parents' sake?' I asked her, and watched as she crossed her legs with such sophistication that I was taken aback.

'No.'

'Are you finding the discipline too much?'

'No,' she said.

'You can tell me, Gemma. You must tell me.'

'No, it's fine. I like the discipline. I hated my other school.'

'Are they forcing you to do things against your will? For example, meditation?'

'No, no one's forced.'

'Is the headmistress bullying you?'

'No. I don't really see much of her.'

I was getting absolutely nowhere. I didn't believe her.

'Do you have to wear a long dress when you get to sixteen?'

She looked at me as if I was deranged.

'You can confide in me, Gemma.'

Eventually she sighed and folded her arms. 'Can't you just be pleased that I'm well? What is it with you people, always looking for problems?'

That shut me up. I sighed too. 'Sorry. I am pleased, Gemma, I am really pleased. You look ... so well, beautiful even.'

She was embarrassed by that; she rolled her eyes, but I could tell she was chuffed. 'Thank you for everything, Lorrie,' she said when she got up to leave, and it sounded ominously like goodbye.

'I'll see you next week!'

'I think I want to stop for a while,' she said. 'I just want to have a go at things on my own, sort out my own issues.' I had known she was going to say that, but I desperately didn't want her to go, to leave her in their hands. I'd come on too strong.

I pushed back my chair and walked around the table and stood in front of her. How brave she was. I gave her a hug.

'Well done you, Gemma. You've done so well. I can't tell you how pleased I am to see you looking so well.'

She smiled.

'Now listen to me,' I added. 'You can ring my mobile any time. Okay? Any time, day or night. You promise me. If there's anything you ever need to talk to me about, you just ring me. I will always be there for you. Do you understand?'

She nodded.

When she left the room, I felt hollow and abandoned.

*

That night I lay awake most of the night, despite the fact that I was tired. My head was whirring and by the time the morning came I knew what I had to do. I would have to find out for myself whether Gemma really was okay; I needed to see it with my own two eyes. I would go back to St Augustine's and watch her. I wasn't quite sure whether it was Gemma or my mother I was going to see. I just knew that I would face that bloody building if it killed me.

I make that sound so easy. It wasn't, and I couldn't do it. In fact, it took me a week to build up my courage, but with a baby in my belly I was living with a ticking clock and I realized that I just had to get on with things.

I dressed carefully. I pulled on my black jeans. I had to wear trousers as a matter of principle. The jeans no longer did up around my waist; I had to wear them low, underneath my bump. I put on a big black cover-all cardigan, black seeming an appropriately sombre colour for the task ahead. I realized halfway through dressing that I was disguising myself. I wore more make-up than I usually did; initially I tied my hair back and then thought better of it – the Organization did not approve of loose hair, so I shook it down. Before I left the house I put on my big-framed, black sunglasses.

I could not face the tube. In all my adult life, I had not gone back to South Kensington or Gloucester Road. It would have been foolish, an unnecessary flirtation with unhappiness. Also, I doubted whether I could have physically done it.

So today, I walked up Portobello and took the bus

from Notting Hill. I would approach it from the north, a route I rarely took.

But even this was surprisingly difficult. As the bus turned into High Street Ken, my stomach lassoed itself into a knot, and I had to get off quickly before heaving into the gutter. I walked east and, when I hit Hyde Park, I turned right into Organization Street. I had to force my feet to keep going. A familiar feeling of dread rushed through me, only now I was going there of my own volition.

I watched my trainers walk as if an entirely alien being inhabited them. I thought I would have found number 50 even if I had gone blind in the intervening years. I knew exactly how many paces it took to get there. However, I was incorrect – either the street had got shorter or my legs had got longer.

I kept looking out for funny farmers in the street. They were easy to spot. I'd seen one already. They had indeed changed, but they were immediately identifiable to me: the skirts were minimally shorter, no longer sweeping the ground, now daringly revealing a bit of ankle. The 'comfortable' footwear was still going strong, only Dr Scholls were now in fashion. I was not fooled by a trendy necklace or a denim jacket. I could sniff them out from a hundred paces, like a trained dog. The men were slightly harder to identify, but they tended towards blazers and cords. They were clean-looking and upright. However, one thing they couldn't get rid of was that practised expression, somewhere between godly and smug.

At first, I couldn't do it – my trainers just stopped walking at the first glimpse of a longish dress. I kept anticipating being recognized, I didn't want to be known. I decided that it would be easier to cross the street, get a view of the building from afar.

To my left was St Mary's, with the white stone steps and the big plane tree. It was a grey day today, not like that last day when Fowler had lain on the steps dying in the sunshine. They say a murderer always returns to the scene of the crime; well, I'd certainly taken my time.

I didn't walk as far as the church; I stood outside the portal where the smelly old woman tramp used to live and pee. It was now a smart hotel with squeaky clean people coming in and out.

I leant against the railings and allowed myself to look across the road. There it was, unchanged, as familiar as the back of my own hand. The huge plane tree outside with its blotchy trunk, the calligraphic lettering of the numbers 50 and 51 on the white pillars, the pale stone steps, the black railings, the black iron gate that led down to the dungeons, the balcony outside Room 4, Room 8, Room 10. These buildings were huge. They were so high that, when you looked out of the top window, the tree-tops waved beneath you.

I looked up. High up on the sixth floor was a little ledge beneath the window that ran the length of the whole street. Pigeons perched and shat on it. It was about two foot wide and sloped downwards towards the road beneath. Sarah Martin had once been dared to do a cartwheel along it and she had done so, nimbly, accurately, like a circus performer. She had topped her cartwheel by bringing out a chair and placing it on the ledge; she had sat on it and pretended to read a book. I had admired her sense of comedy. We had all laughed our heads off. Now when I looked at it, I could see how lucky we were that she hadn't fallen. Whatever had happened to the Sarah Martinses of this world? I hoped she had survived. I wished her well wherever she was.

I stood there against the squeaky clean hotel for a long time, breathing deeply. I believe buildings are living beings. Everyone knows that walls have ears. They have eyes and noses as well. They absorb it all, everything that happens; every layer of paint has a tale to tell; every roll of peeling wallpaper has seen, heard and smelt the intricacies of our human lives. And that building over there, across the street, number 50, had born witness to all my private early life. The building alone knew the truth. Those bricks and mortar harboured somewhere within them my intimate secrets, my happinesses, my unhappinesses, my victories, my defeats, my laughter and my lickings. The stone steps had felt the grudging tread of my feet. The doors within had been pushed, slammed, peered round, hung on, leant on, kicked, licked and wept on by me. How could they fail to bear my traces? This building owned a part of me. And for that I felt a fondness. The building wasn't to blame. I wondered whether it would remember me.

I noticed what must definitely be a funny farmer coming out of number 49; she had a low, floppy bun and the new, radical, three-quarter-length dress. She was definitely one of them. So they were buying up the street, were they? Somewhere over there, my mother lived. In number 50? Or 51?

Then the children started coming out, and my heart

began to beat in my teeth, and, to my surprise, they ran out, still wearing those bloody awful uniforms, but they were skipping and jumping and laughing and chatting like normal school children. We always had had to exit and enter the building in a stony silence. My eyes scanned the children for Gemma. I waited as form after form came out and then I saw her, her red hair marking her out. She was with two other girls, and they stopped beside the big plane tree and swapped some books in their bags. Gemma and one girl waved goodbye to the third and left together, laughing and talking animatedly.

I watched her until she turned the corner and only then did I realize that I had been holding my breath. I don't know what I had expected – a solitary, white-faced lost soul? But she wasn't me. I had to let her go. There was nothing more I could do for her except be there if she needed me.

I stayed there at the hotel, watching the children leave. When they had all left and the school door shut, I sat down on the step and rested my head on my knees. Inside I wept for Caroline Stern and Helen Winters and any other child who had been broken and was now misplaced by time.

I returned to the building the next day, and the one after. I sat outside the hotel and watched. By the third day I was ready. I wanted, at last, to see my mother. I wanted to confront her. I wanted to resolve something. I wanted my birth certificate. I wanted to reclaim myself. I wanted to carry this baby with a clean sheet. This time I wasn't sick. This time I went straight there.

I climbed the front steps one at a time. They had warped and been made shiny by time. I stopped at the door; it was not too late. I could turn around now. But I didn't.

On my right I could see the dungeons – how small they were! I held my breath and pressed the buzzer. There had never been a buzzer in my day, merely a knocker as if this building were just an everyday home.

'St Augustine's,' fuzzed a woman's voice through the brass monitor. I knew those voices, those soft, gentle, fleecy, butter-wouldn't-melt-in-my-mouth voices. They didn't wash with me.

I cleared my throat.

'I've come to see Judith Stern,' I said.

The door buzzed open.

The first thing I saw was that black, brown and white mosaic floor; it felt as real as a slap in the face. I stepped in and closed the door behind me. I was in the proverbial lion's mouth now, and with a click of the latch, a lick of the lips, there was no going back. The place was deserted, which was what I had hoped, it being a Saturday afternoon.

Already there was something different, aside from the fact that it had shrunk. What was it? I walked through the glass double doors. I knew what it was: aside from the red carpet now being green, and the walls no longer being papered with green and gold relief material, this building now looked like a school. The austerity had gone. There was evidence of children all over the place. There was colour! The classroom on my left now truly resembled a classroom, rather than a meeting room; it had a half-glass door like you see at a normal school. Inside the classroom there were no longer calligraphy boards on trestle tables with quills and ink – no! They had tables like a normal school. On the walls were childish pictures and poems, just like you would find in the outside world.

But it didn't smell like a school should; it smelt of baked bread and Brasso and coffee grounds. They couldn't make it smell like a normal school. When the time comes for me to choose this child of mine a school, I will not underestimate the importance of the smell of the place. I want old cabbage and sawdust.

The chandelier was the same, as was the mirrored wall up at the top of the first flight. But I didn't go up. I took a few apprehensive steps past the classroom. I knew what was coming next. I paused just before I got there, around the tiny corner. I took a deep breath and turned. There it was, the door I knew more intimately than any other in the world, every fraying splinter: the door to her study. I looked from the ground upwards with a burning sensation in my chest.

They had lowered the handle and its brass mounting. I wondered why. It took me a moment to realize that it was I who had changed height. My fingers reached out tentatively to touch the handle, as if it might be booby-trapped. I traced the shape of it with my fingertips. With both hands, I felt the mount. How often had I gazed into its shining reflection and seen my puffy, distorted face? To my left was the pipe, my warm friend the pipe, painted now with unknown paint. I gently rubbed my forehead on it.

'Hello!' came the voice, the soft Organizational voice.

I jumped and turned to see a woman, presumably the one who had answered the buzzer, peering round the door at the end of the corridor. She must have been the school secretary doing overtime out of the goodness of her spiritually advanced heart. She was smiling. I knew those smiles. I didn't return it.

'Please come through!' she said, and I followed her sweeping skirt into the office, or what had once been the office. It still was.

It had not changed much, except that it had shrunk. I had often sat in this room waiting for Fowler. Botticelli's *Primavera* hung on the wall. How could I have forgotten that? Five stupid nymphs skipping about in a garden. It had been joined by one or two insipid watercolours and what looked like an A-level-standard sculpture of a bronze head on a plinth of a round-cheeked fellow with a flabby nose, no doubt made by some funny farmer risen to the dizzy heights of Organizational success.

There was not a lot in there to show that two decades had passed, except for a huge, grey, old-fashioned computer, probably bought reluctantly. I bet the Whopper had fought against computers; I would have enjoyed seeing that, the admission of fallibility.

The woman picked up the telephone and dialled an in-house number.

'Judith!' she said. 'There's someone here to see you.' Her smile remained intact. 'Yes,' she continued, and then covered the mouthpiece. 'Who shall I say is calling?'

I should have known it would be like this. I thought of leaving there and then, but I had come this far. I could not chicken out now.

'Tell her it's Caroline,' I said, pushing my shades further up my nose.

'It's Caroline,' said the woman and then, 'Hello? Judith? Hello? . . .' I could picture the surprise on my mother's face. 'Will do!' and she replaced the receiver.

'She says please come up.'

'Thank you. Which room?'

'Right up to the top. Shall I take you up there?'

'Oh no,' I said. 'That won't be necessary.'

'Have you been here before?' she asked, subtly looking me up and down. I was still in my disguise outfit. The trousers, the make-up, the hair, the shades all made my non-Organizational state very clear, just as I had intended.

'Yes,' I replied. 'Once or twice.'

But I didn't make it to the top of the building.

I was finding it extremely difficult to physically climb the stairs. The thick, green carpet bulged over itself on the edge of each step, revealing the stone beneath. I watched my feet go up one step at a time. I gripped the banister, the smooth dark wood that coiled back on itself at each landing, as sleekly as a snake. I remembered it all, every join in the wood. The sweat on my hands made a squelching noise each time they left the banister.

I looked in the mirrored wall on the first flight, fully expecting to see my old self in my horrid uniform with my scraped-back hair, my face pale and gaunt. But no, there I was, a grown woman, a survivor. I removed my shades, taking courage from my appearance, and climbed the next flight.

I remembered the speed with which I used to ascend and descend these stairs when sent on errands, jumping a full one hundred and eighty degrees on each penultimate step. Here I was outside Room 4.

I had been sent outside this room more times than I had chanted Vedic sutras. The building seemed empty, but I still checked the staircase, looking up and down. There was no one around, so I carefully pushed open the door to Room 4. The moment the door opened, it was as if I were opening the lid on a music box, but instead of *Swan Lake*, a flood of memories poured into my mind: assemblies, Vedic dancing, exams, singing lessons, speech days, punishments, standing in corners, humiliations, starvations, being whacked with rulers, trying hard to contain laughter, face pressed to the corner over there.

I shut the door again firmly.

Instinctively my hands reached for my belly, more for my own comfort than the prawn's. I walked up the next flight, silently: something about the carpet and the stone ensured a lack of noise.

Opposite me was the punishment room, a small cell of a room, enough space for one child and a calligraphy board on which to draw straight lines with a Sanskrit nib, a wobble in them clearly indicating a lying child. I opened the door and walked in. These days this room appeared to be a stationery cupboard. Ah ha! I pulled out drawers. Ink pens, nibs, yes, Sanskrit nibs. Thank God for that. I'd found a chink.

I was drawn to the window, the only real focal point. The view, of course, was unchanged, the waving plane tree and the top of the church. I remembered that day, and pictured someone looking out of here, seeing

Fowler's corpse on the vomit-soaked steps, her hair splayed out. The ambulance, police cars.

I left the room. Next door to the punishment room, they had certainly made some developments: they had built a science lab. It looked disconcertingly like any other school: through the half-glass door was a laboratory room exactly as you might see on a television show or in brochures selling normal schools, pupils wearing plastic eye masks congregated around a Bunsen burner. Except there were no pupils. The room was empty. I was intrigued and I went in.

I wandered about the room, soaking in the details. So they did proper classes, did they? There were charts on the walls, periodic tables and even a white board, all hugely impressive for the likes of the Jamesons. Presumably Gemma sat in here. I looked for a list or a row of pegs to see her name.

As I scanned the shelves, I became aware of a distant coughing. It was louder at the back of the lab. It wasn't just any old cough; it was one of those old smoker's hacks that made you think the person was going to choke and die. I wandered through to the back, following the sound. Surely there was nothing here. Then I remembered the back stairs. It was coming from the back stairs.

Winding the height and depth of the building right at the rear was a stone spiral staircase that was completely out of bounds to us children, although that drew some of us to it like moths to a flame. It became a very handy hiding place. The stairs led to private rooms at the top where devotees had meditation checks. In times of distress, the Organization housed people in those rooms.

Hannah and her mum lived up there for a time when her dad left. It was a haven for the bereft, so I presumed that was where my mother was living. I wondered whether that was her coughing.

At first I thought that the door had been blocked off – you always used to be able to get through from back here, before this was a lab. Then I saw it, the brass handle behind a pile of equipment. I moved the lab coats and boxes full of test tubes and I tried turning the handle. It was unlocked, and the moment I opened the door a blast of cigarette fumes hit me. Gauloises. The coughing sounded much nearer now, it was liquid and phlegmy.

I went through the door and found myself on the little landing halfway up the stone spiral staircase. The hacking cough echoed about the walls, and it was hard to tell immediately from which level it was coming. I presumed upwards and followed my nose.

It sounded like a death rattle: watery gasps, and then a runny intake of breath, multi-noted like the sound of a mouth organ. It was both disgusting and intriguing. I stopped outside a door at the next level. This was new; this had been converted. This was definitely where the cougher lived. The door was slightly ajar.

I gave it a little push, and it swung open to reveal an apartment, a truly Organizational affair: two large, green, uncomfortable-looking sofas, Renaissance paintings on the wall and some fucking Charles Greys, by the look of them, and another one of those minging sculptures. I noted that there was slightly more opulence than in a traditional Organizational home: a costly looking vase, a golden Buddha, a jade paperweight, an ornate trunk.

It reeked of fags. I did not get the sense that my mother lived here. Unless she had taken up smoking with a vengeance, she must be on the flight above. I walked through the sitting room, heading for the cough over on the other side. I passed some fading roses in a vase, a gleaming silver ashtray, a bookshelf full of the predictable spiritual reading and the obligatory piano. The coughing came from a little room on the side.

'Hello?' I said, as I opened the door to a surprisingly grand room. The door swung heavily shut behind me.

I didn't see him at first; the room was rather dim. There was a huge, luxurious four-poster bed covered in an army of pillows. The wallpaper and the curtains were made of blue silk. On the other side of the bed was a large oxygen tank with a Darth-Vader-like mask attached to it, and neatly placed beside the tank was an ashtray with a cigarette still going in it. Various empty chairs circled the bed, as if a meeting had just taken place; only the bedded chairperson and all the staff were absent.

Then I saw him. On the floor lay a fat, little old man in blue paisley pyjamas. He was at the end of an impossibly long cough and had just started a ghastly, eternal in-breath, his face quite puce, his eyes bloodshot and bulging.

I went to help him. I tried to get his trollish body upright, but he was surprisingly heavy. I pulled him up, and the cough subsided somewhat. I noticed that his pyjamas were made of silk. I patted him on the back and passed him a glass of water, which he drank greedily. I somehow managed to haul him up on to the bed, noting his fingers, which were stained a brownish black. He stank of cigarettes and sweat. I propped him up on several of the pillows, and gradually he stopped coughing and started taking small gasps of air.

He pointed towards the oxygen tank, so I leant over the bed and handed him the mask. He pressed it to his face and took long, deep breaths until he calmed down. Then he removed it and, to my surprise, immediately picked up his burning cigarette and took a long, deep drag before stubbing it out and reaching for the packet to light a new one.

I was rather impressed. That took some commitment.

The room was not warm, so I pulled up the covers as he struggled to light his new cigarette. Behind me, I heard the door squeak open, and I turned around.

I actually jumped in surprise, maybe six inches off the floor. I knocked over the bedside table and the lamp clattered to the ground and went out. The jug of water fell to the floor. The hairs on my head all stood up, and I felt my body go cold.

She was standing silhouetted in the doorway, holding a tray, her upright, unmistakable posture, her hair pulled back tightly in the bun, the long dark sweeping dress. She had the same fierce expression on her face.

It was the ghost of Fowler.

She didn't move, and neither could I. I had frozen internally, and my heart had stopped altogether. I could feel my legs and my hands beginning to tremble. I had never seen a ghost before.

'Who are you?' she said crossly. 'What are you doing here?'

Her voice was as familiar to me as my own. Did ghosts speak?

She took a step towards me, and I thought she was going to leap on me. I jumped right back away from her and made my way to the other side of the bed, as if the old man might protect me! I couldn't form any words. I waited for her to walk through the bed and fly towards me. But she didn't, she bent down and placed the tray she was holding on the carpet. She picked up the bedside table and started collecting the fag butts and the jug of water. She put the tray on the table and then she tried turning on the bedside lamp. After a couple of clicks it went on. Oh my God! It was Fowler all right, virtually untouched by time.

'Who are you?' she asked again. 'Answer me! Who are you?'

I could not believe that she needed to ask me this.

'Who am I?' I said. 'Do you not recognize me?'

She took a step towards me and eyed me suspiciously. I watched her as she studied my face. I swallowed hard. I needed that water by the old man, but I didn't dare take my eyes off her.

Fowler was searching my face as if it were a page of poor homework. And then I saw it, a flicker of recognition.

'Good Lord!' she said. 'Carolyn!' And she flashed her teeth at me.

She could not have said anything more crushing if she had tried. Carolyn? Carolyn? She had mispronounced my name. This woman who had sent me to the brink of despair and beyond, this woman who had broken me in every way, whom I had hated with every last drop of passion in my being, whom I had murdered and paid my dues for, this woman, my nemesis, did not even know my name.

I felt knocked down, as if I had been hit by a truck. I shook my head slowly with sheer disbelief.

'No!' I cried, my voice sounding unintentionally weak. 'My name is not Carolyn.' Then I choked as I said it. My voice cracked. 'My name is Caro*line*.'

Futile tears of anger sprang to my eyes. My chest felt as if the life was being squeezed out of me.

'Caroline,' she corrected herself, as if it were a trivial matter.

'Yes,' I said, through gritted teeth. 'Caro*line*.'

She gave me another flash of a smile.

'You're dead,' I said.

'Dead?' she laughed that horrible, flirty laugh she used to give Mercer, and she looked towards the old man in the bed. I could hear him wheezing, but I wasn't going to take my eyes off her, the ghost.

'Are you dead?' I whispered.

'What are you talking about?'

'I killed you.'

'I'm sorry?'

'I saw you die!'

'I assure you I am alive.' She thought she was being witty.

'I hated you.'

'Being a headmistress is not a very popular business!'

She laughed again. The flirting was for the old man in the bed. How could she laugh? It just wasn't funny. She was laughing at my life.

'Are you real?' I said, moving cautiously across the

room towards her, wary lest she should disappear. I needed to reach out and touch her just to check.

She had begun to look a little afraid of me as I approached. Was it possible that they had revived her that day? She looked almost exactly the same, her hair a little greyer maybe, but not much. She had always been an old woman. But something was different. It was me. I was taller than her now; I was seeing her from a different angle. I was an adult.

I raised one hand and gingerly touched her bony shoulder. She was solid, she was real all right. I felt her flinch a little. She raised a hand to protect herself, as if I were going to hit her, and then I could smell it, her perfume, eau de Dettol. She was most definitely not a ghost. She was alive. I could not help myself. I placed my other hand on her other shoulder and I hardened my grip upon her. I started to shake her. And I could not stop. I shook her hard.

'You! You! You!' I cried.

'Stop!' she said. 'You're hurting me! Stop!'

'You! You! You!'

It was all I could say.

'Help, Sir! Help!' she cried, looking at the man in the bed.

I stopped shaking her. Did she say 'Sir'? I released my grip.

'What did you say?' I asked her. She slumped against the wall by a mahogany chest of drawers, looking at me as if I were a lunatic. I turned to the pathetic, little figure on the bed.

So this was him, this wheezing, pitiful, tar-sucking

thing. He put his shaking, yellowed fingers to his mouth and sucked on his cigarette, looking at me through curious pale blue eyes. So this was what all the fuss was about; this was the Whopper. I recognized his face from the statue downstairs. I'm surprised there wasn't a fucking hologram on the front door. But statues can never quite capture eyes. His were pale and icy, full of haughtiness despite the state of him; they were the eyes of a man accustomed to being worshipped. His skin was red, blotchy and large-pored; purple veins darted about his nose, giving the impression of a life lived to excess, a goutish demeanour. I had never met the Whopper before, and he seemed to me to be a bit of a let-down. He certainly did not look like a leader of men. He certainly did not look like the reason I was so low down in my parents' priorities.

'I don't think we've met, Mr Wapinski,' I said. 'My name was Caroline Stern.'

He remained expressionless, just watching me. Then his eyes flicked to Fowler. I thought I saw fear there. Where were his minions when he needed them?

I sat down on the edge of his bed and crossed my legs. I wanted to say something to the old man, something pertinent and cruel, something scathing and hurtful, something that in some small way could counter-balance the damage that he was responsible for. But I could think of nothing.

'Well, isn't this nice?' I said instead.

I saw Fowler wince at my audacity, sitting on her guru's bed as if I owned the place, making sarcastic comments.

I think Wapinski tried to say something to me. I saw his mouth twitch, but instead he commenced a marathon cough and leant over towards the bedside table in an effort to get the oxygen mask.

It was just out of his reach. I didn't help him. I watched him struggle.

'How the mighty are fallen, eh?' I said to him, his fingers straining for the elastic just an inch or so away.

Fowler moved forward as if to help, but I stopped her by standing up. I swear she was afraid of me, almost leaping out of my way.

'You, Fowler,' I said, emboldened by her fear. 'You're going nowhere until you give me an apology.'

She looked confused and twitchy.

'You owe me an apology!' I spat the words at her. The coughing had started again.

'What for?' she replied. She was scared of me. Her voice was high and thin. I thought I must have misheard her.

'What for?' I laughed.

She was totally bewildered by me. She blinked her old woman watery eyes, pleadingly.

What for? Suddenly, I understood the whole thing. This was my Eureka moment. The heavens might as well have opened up and shone a beam of sunlight over me. At last, I grasped it! Twenty-five years later! It was as clear as day: Fowler truly had no idea what I was talking about.

I was nothing to her.

Nothing.

Absolutely nothing.

She had never given me a second thought in her life. I was just an ex-pupil, nothing more, nothing less.

I let out a sound, half sob, half laugh. It was the sound of a great thing being released. And in that one moment I gave it up. I gave it *all* up, all my hate, all my anger, all my bitterness. I let it all go. She was not worth it.

I had nothing more to do here in this room with these people. I took a last look at the pathetic sight on the bed and I turned around and walked towards the door.

Fowler's voice stopped me, my fingers on the handle.

'Tell me!' she said. 'What should I be sorry for?'

I turned back, my voice low and quiet, all my energy dissipated now.

'For getting my name wrong,' I said, and closed the door behind me.

My name is Caroline Stern. I use Lorrie Fischer at work, but my name is Caroline Stern. I am proud of my name. I am proud of who I am. I am not a murderer.

I'd been practising saying these sentences to Tilly. They didn't exactly roll off the tongue. She didn't seem too impressed; she put her head down for a nap.

It was a peculiar sensation, the discovery that so much of one's life had been based on a misconception. My biggest secret did not exist, after all. I had a sneaking feeling that behind the relief lay a little disappointment. I was not a murderer, I was a failed murderer. Previously I carried a modicum of success about me, albeit in a twisted kind of a way, but now I was someone who had attempted to do something and had failed. Personally, I saw no reason why the perpetrator of an attempted murder should get less time than a successful one. If anything, it should be the other way round. Should we be rewarded for our failures? But there we go, we have the big book telling us what is right and what is wrong; we mustn't question that.

My mother was upset that I never made it up to see her. She had decided that she would come round and visit me instead, and, even though I was expecting her, when I opened the door I was not prepared for it. Although she was old now, there was something still girlish about her. She had never been vain or conscious of her looks, which just went to show what a bad idea that was. No make-up, no hair dyeing, no attempt to beautify. God help us all! They have programmes on telly for women like her, not that she would know that. She looked older than Fowler, who had somehow been frozen in time.

My mother's hair had gone white, and she had those puffing eye bags that make the bearer look toadish. She smiled at me and brushed the hair off her face, the gesture of a child. I had never noticed her innocence before, but then why would I have done? I had been a child myself. She looked like someone who had never said 'No' to anything or anyone in her life. She had a shat-on demeanour. She was the type of woman who had borne her lot unquestioningly. I suppose that was the deal, what with devoting herself to the glory of God or whatever the fuck she thought she'd done. I had the very strange feeling that it was she who needed the mothering.

We stared at each other on the doorstep, just to check that we were who we thought we were. We didn't fall into each other's arms as we might have done if we were from another household – no, that was not the Stern way. The Stern way was to nod and say, 'Hello' and 'Would you like to come in for a cup of tea?' as if we'd seen each other last week.

That was when I noticed that she couldn't walk properly. She had crutches and she shook as if she had MS or something. I wondered how she had got here, because the journey could not have been easy.

I saw the house through her eyes: modern and strange. She didn't know where to look, certainly not at any of the post-Renaissance artwork. With some difficulty she took off her sensible two-tone jacket, the sort that old men wear at bus stops, a garment that probably bore the words 'windproof' on the label. I hung it up for her.

She sat down on the edge of the eighteenth-century, sick-stained, silk-upholstered sofa, and I sat on the other one, a healthy distance between us. We stared at each other again. Bloody funny farmers were all too comfortable with silence.

'I brought the birth certificate,' she said.

'Thank you,' I replied, and watched her fumble about in her handbag like an old biddy. Yet I could not get away from the fact that she seemed like a child. She passed me the paper. 'Caroline Ruth Stern, London Borough of Islington.'

I put it on the coffee table.

'What's wrong with you?' I asked her.

'MS,' she said.

'Oh.'

'Yes, well,' she replied, as if it were a minor inconvenience. She didn't want to talk about it, I could tell. Now

I remembered that we didn't talk about real things in our family. Just the Absolute and the Truth and all that shit.

'I'm having a baby,' I said.

I saw the surprise in her eyes as she pushed her glasses higher up her nose with one shaking hand. I didn't know whether it was me or the disease making her so nervous. She looked genuinely pleased. I remembered that smile of hers, her large, rather horsey teeth, the eyes wide and open like a child's.

'By myself,' I added. I didn't want her getting carried away with joy.

'I see,' she said, the wind slightly taken out of her sails. She blinked as she processed the information and looked down at her shaking hands.

'I'm going to call him Thomas,' I added.

I heard her little intake of breath. I felt like I had slapped her. Her cheeks flushed, she looked out of the window, and I could hear her quietly exhaling through her pursed mouth. I thought she was trying not to cry.

'Milk? Sugar?' I asked, getting up.

'Um ...' She was far away. 'Just milk, thank you, Caroline.'

She watched me go; I could feel her eyes on my back. From the kitchen, as I busied myself with the tea making, I saw her bend down to stroke Tilly, who made the most of the attention and jumped up into her lap. How indiscriminate dogs are with their affections. My mother made a fuss over her. I'd forgotten how much she loved animals.

When I came back through, Tilly was asleep across

her lap, and my mother was still stroking her. We sat in silence and sipped from our cups.

She put her tea down on the low coffee table and said, 'Your father died this year.'

'I heard.'

'Heart attack.'

'Yes.'

'In the night.'

We both took a sip at the same time.

'Do you miss him?'

She gave me a look of surprise. 'Of course.'

'Out of curiosity, did he ever mention me?'

She shook her head. 'No.'

I knew I would have been right about that.

'Not until he was dying,' she said. 'He wasn't conscious, but I heard him say your name.'

'That's it, he said my name?'

'Yes.'

The fucker. The old fucker.

'He did love you, you know, in his way. We always did what we thought was for the best.'

How utterly predictable this conversation was. I sat back on the sofa and cradled my tea.

'Answer me this: do you still think it was all for the best?' I asked her.

I could see her struggling. She had, after all, dedicated her whole life to the Organization. It would have been impossible for her to admit that her whole life had been in vain.

'I don't know any more, Caroline. I don't know.'

I could also see that this was a momentous admission

for her. Her shaking hands were folded in her lap, her thumbs brushing each other. I vaguely remembered this gesture.

'Well, that's a good start,' I said.

She didn't look convinced. Her head was wobbling a bit, presumably the MS.

'Where did you go, Caroline? That day.'

I knew what she was talking about. I leant back in the sofa and sighed. I suppose she deserved to know.

'France.'

'France? You didn't have a passport.'

'I got one.'

'How?'

'I stole one.'

She looked shocked. For God's sake, she was so naive.

'I had no choice. I had to survive. I stole a handbag, and it happened to have a passport in it.'

'What did you do in France?'

'Oh, this and that, you know, saw the sights.'

She appeared so disappointed that I was going to be like this that I couldn't carry on with it.

It was my turn to look out of the window. I felt a lump form in my throat. I wasn't sure that I could tell her all this.

'I had a breakdown,' I said, as matter-of-factly as I could. She was hanging on my every word. 'You know . . . cracked up, went mad, off the rails, call it whatever you want.'

'No, no,' she said, and I could hear from her tone that she had already imagined this, maybe in the night whilst he was asleep next to her, after they'd slipped calligraphic bookmarks into their spiritual night reading and turned the bedside lights off. I suppose she must have imagined all sorts.

'Yes. They locked me up . . .'

Obviously, I have lived with this knowledge for years, but there is something about the actual saying of it that makes it more true, more concrete, more real and, most poignantly, new again. I had not anticipated the powerful effect of sharing the information. My voice wobbled, '. . . in a psychiatric institution.'

I looked back at her. She was holding one shaking hand up to her mouth, tears spilling out of her eyes like an overflowing basin. I averted my gaze. I didn't want her pity.

'For how long?' she whispered.

I had to release the back of my throat to make sure the words came out, 'Over a year.'

She just sat there, shaking her head, dropping tears on to Tilly, on her lap. She made a move to comfort me, but I raised my hand to stop her.

'Don't!' I whispered. 'I have to ask you this, Mum . . . Why did you never come for me?' I sounded like a little child.

'I didn't know where you were.'

'Did you look?'

'Your father thought it was better.'

'I bet he did. My father, my father . . . You are my mother. Why did you never look?' I couldn't stop the anger.

'I'm sorry, Carry, I'm so sorry. I knew what you thought you'd done. I knew you thought you'd killed her and I knew you didn't want to be found. But I did look, Carry, I did look. I looked every day of my life. At every blonde-haired child, at every school girl, every teenager, every drug addict in the street, every young woman ...'

'Did you go to the police? Did you report me missing?'

'No. I went to Mr Wapinski.'

'You what?' I kind of laughed, but mainly to stop myself from crying.

'He said to let you go.'

I didn't even feel angry any more. I rolled my eyes. I could have smothered the fat little fucker yesterday. I sighed a long sigh and shook my head, running my hands through my hair.

'Will you ever, ever think for yourself, Mum?'

She was crying now.

'I don't think I can, Carry, I don't even think I can. I'm not strong like you, I'm ...'

She would never have spoken like this if my father were alive, never. She found a tissue in her bag and blew her nose. Hard, like a man – I remembered that.

'Can you ever forgive me?' she asked.

I shrugged.

'I can't bear to think of you there. All alone,' she cried. 'Did anyone look after you?'

I looked out of the window again and then after a while I said, 'Do you really want to know?'

She nodded.

'People checked my room every fifteen minutes, but there was nothing in there except me and the bed that was bolted to the ground. Someone else gave me different-coloured pills four times a day and asked me if I had suicidal thoughts, and someone else regularly gave me electric shock treatments. If that's looking after then, yes, I was looked after.'

Her head was really wobbling now, but she'd asked for this.

'Was anyone kind to you?'

The question took me by surprise and carried me right back.

'Yes,' I said, eventually. 'Someone was.'

All these things I'd never spoken of, they all seemed brand spanking new again.

'Who? What was their name?'

'Why does it matter?'

'It matters.'

'Albert. Albert Gens.'

I had not uttered his name for over twenty years.

'Albert? Tell me about him.'

'He was just a man, Mum, a psychiatrist who came to work there.'

'Please!'

I drew a deep breath.

'Why?'

'Because I owe him,' she said simply.

I could see him as clear as daylight, his twinkling blue eyes, his white beard, his shaggy, wild hair. He had looked exactly how a psychiatrist should look, unconcerned with the external appearance. There was nothing judgemental about Albert Gens. He had never treated me like a mad person, never.

'Please!' she prompted, when I paused.

'He believed in the power of the human spirit, Mother. Not God. Not Krishna. Not the fucking Absolute.'

How strange to be talking to her like this.

I could remember everything. That bright windy day as I sat watching *The Six Million Dollar Man* dubbed into French, wondering why Steve Austin was running six million times slower than the baddies, slumped in my chair in the day-room, and Albert standing by the window in a beam of sunlight. Why not tell her? Why not tell her about the very moment that I was saved?

I took a deep breath.

'Okay,' I said. 'Albert had been seeing this drug addict called Jordi, who'd take anything he could get. Anything at all. Bleach if he could get his hands on it. Everyone knew he nicked glue from the office whenever he could. I was always hoping Albert would see me some time, because I noticed that the people he did see were slowly leaving the hospital. But his English wasn't good. Anyway, this one day, I was watching telly – one of the bonuses of a loony bin . . .'

I couldn't resist these little digs, but my mother didn't rise to them; she just carried on stroking Tilly.

'. . . And I saw him standing alone by the window, looking out on to the drive. First of all I thought he was crying, because I was used to that, people crying, but then I realized that he was laughing. He kept dabbing his eyes with a handkerchief and walking up and down, trying to get his act together, but he'd keep turning to the window, and his laughter would spill out.'

It was more of a chuckle than a laugh, I could hear it now . . .

'I badly needed some fun. There sure as hell wasn't much in there, so I got out of my chair and made my way across the disinfected lino to the window to see what it was that he was laughing at. Only there was nothing there, except a huge, great juggernaut lorry parked in the drive. Albert nodded "Hello" to me and tried to stop laughing. But he couldn't. In fact, my presence seemed to make whatever it was even funnier. I asked him what was so funny, and he pointed at the lorry and said, "Jordi! Jordi!"'

I could see Albert there, as if it were yesterday, standing by the window, his short, sturdy body rocking with joy as the tears poured down his face, his fat, little fingers clutching his sides lest he should burst.

'Well, he could see that I didn't get the joke and he turned me round and pointed at the payphone in the corner of the day-room and said, "Jordi" again and pointed back at the lorry. My brain, not being quite what it was, took a while to get it, but then I saw that the juggernaut outside had a huge logo on the side: "UHU GLUE".'

My mother didn't get it.

'Was he doing arts and crafts?'

'No, Mum, he was a glue-sniffer who had ordered twenty tons of glue to turn up at a loony bin.'

My mother laughed. We both laughed.

Albert and I had slid down the wall, our legs collapsing under the weight of so much funniness. Every time we tried to stand up we wouldn't make it. We'd have to do another impression of the lorry driver turning up at reception, trying to get someone to sign for the glue before realizing he was surrounded by fruitcakes.

That had been my turning point. That was when I realized that things might get better. That was when Albert knew for certain that he could put me together again.

Then I noticed that my mother wasn't laughing any more. She was crying. Not with any sound, just a terrible rocking and a grimace on her face. I sat back in my seat and felt okay about it.

I looked out of the window as she sobbed.

Oh, Albert. Oh, my saviour. He'd known that I was lying, that Lorrie Fischer wasn't my real name. There had been no 'Lorrie Fischer' reported missing. Mind you, now I knew that there had been no 'Caroline Stern' reported either. Albert just didn't know *why* I was lying, but he never pressed me for answers. In fact, one time he put his arm around me and said, 'You keep your secrets, *ma chérie*.' I think he realized that they were all I had.

'Why did you come back to England, Carry?' my mother asked in a small voice from the sofa. She was dabbing at her nose with the crumbling tissue.

She looked so forlorn that I told her.

'I was fourteen and, believe it or not, was missing home. I don't mean you and Dad, by the way – I'd given up on you long ago. I missed England. I missed London. I missed the tube. I missed jokes. Making them and getting them. But I couldn't risk London itself.'

Albert had promised he'd help me. And he did. Quite illegally, of course – he was not a by-the-book kind of person. He persuaded an English friend of his to come over and get me. I can't remember her name – Annie? Annette? Something like that. But I owe her one. She had a daughter my age on her passport, and no questions were asked. It was easy.

'So where did you go?'

She sounded hurt that I hadn't gone to her. I sighed.

'Please, Caroline. Please tell me!' She moved forward, a little closer to me, her face one big question mark.

'Initially I lived with a friend of Albert's in Norwich, Marc, a social worker. After a while I moved out and started finding work. Then three years later I went down to London to start my training.'

She was looking confused, blinking a lot and shaking a little.

'But how did you work? You weren't legal . . .'

'More tea, Sherlock?' I said, getting up, holding out my hand for her cup. She was struggling to take it all in.

'Mum,' I said, picking up my birth certificate. 'Being a fake is easy, you have no idea. Especially when you're a child. Children can get away with murder.

'Or almost,' I added, briefly catching her eye as I went into the kitchen to make some more tea. She followed me through, and we both stood there watching the kettle boil.

'Will you forgive me, Carry?' she whispered.

What could I say? She was just a lemming. My father was a lemming. What is a lemming to do but be a lemming?

'Yes,' I said, turning to her. 'I will.'

Her eyes seemed to light up. She was almost radiant. 'Thank you. I shouldn't have listened to everyone.'

'No, you shouldn't have.'

'I should have listened to myself and I might not have lost my other child.' I felt for her, I truly did.

'Yes,' I said. 'Shame on you, Mother. Shame on you.'

She smiled at me, and I smiled back: smiles of recognition.

If we'd been a different sort of family, I might have put my arm around her. But for us, it was good enough that I wanted to.

It was my thirty-ninth birthday, and I was fat now, absolutely huge, and ready to burst. I was a week overdue; three more days and they were going to induce me. Hat off to Mother Nature, who had managed to reprogramme me and make me actually *want* to give birth, to get this alien thing out of me.

Despite being the size of a bus, I was in total denial that I was about to have a baby, that this bump was in fact a child. I had desperately been trying to get myself into the whole business. I'd been rolling around on a floor doing pregnancy yoga in a church at the end of Ladbroke Grove. I'd had to change classes because of the bendy little teacher who at the end of the sessions had sat cross-legged on her mat, palms upwards, eyelids quivering in that pseudo-spiritual manner as she chanted Sanskrit like it was groovy. One or two of the other hippos joined in with the chant, slightly competitively, I thought. I looked around with weary disgust.

At the end of my new classes, we'd all sit around drinking camomile tea, wondering who would be next to burst. Most weeks someone reappeared with a strange little creature in their arms, full of tales of miracles and wonder. We all cooed about how gorgeous the baby was and how the mother was glowing, but, to be honest, they all looked completely fucked and the babies were hideous, tiny, furless, blinking moles. They terrified me.

All the other mothers had a man around. I could tell from their expressions that they pitied me and quite often they all stopped talking when I approached. I hadn't even told them that I didn't actually know who the father was.

I pitied me, too. I had moments of sheer terror at what the future was to bring. I sobbed in the bath when I couldn't get out. I sobbed in Sainsbury's when my trolley wobbled out of control. I sobbed in a bus queue when a girl told me to get in line.

Already I couldn't sleep properly. I was out of breath after everything. I couldn't climb stairs. I couldn't reach top shelves. I was useless. I really and truly didn't think I was going to be able to cope, especially after I'd been ripped and mauled by the birth. How could I have got myself into this mess? Not even to know who the father was.

I was waddling down the canal tow path as the Canada geese exercised Tilly. She chased them along the canal, barking at them madly under the delusion that they might stop and let her eat them. The expensive citronella canister was long gone; Tilly had seen to that when she'd jumped into the canal to chase a plastic bag. Besides, I'd just surrendered to her by then. Thank the Lord people were a bit nicer to you when you were pregnant: little courtesies, smiles and offerings of seats and slightly more leniency on the mad-dog front.

I sighed inwardly as I saw a bicycle coming towards me. 'Tilly!' I called, but she wasn't listening, she was in goose-mode. She didn't see the bike until she was virtually on top of it, nearly knocking the owner sideways. At first I thought he'd fallen off, but he was propping it up. He was a big black guy in a hoodie.

I watched Tilly jump up at him, into his arms.

Oh my God, it was Joe.

For a pathetic moment I thought of hiding in the bushes, but that was never going to work. There was absolutely no disguising my bump now. I watched his expression change as he made out my new shape, pushing the bike towards me. I knew the moment he saw the bump, because he stopped. We met at the smelly bit with all the litter, where the tramps drink.

We had talked a couple of times over the last six months – curt, brief conversations about where I should leave the key for him; he'd rather symbolically lost his and wanted to pick up the rest of his stuff. During the first conversation I'd tried asking him how he was, but I got a crisp 'Fine' and didn't bother asking the next time. I'd made sure I was out when he came round. I didn't want him to see me pregnant. I wanted to wait and see before I hurt him any further. However, looking at his face now, perhaps that had not been the best tactic.

'Hi,' I said.

His jaw was virtually hanging on the ground. He was staring at my bump.

'Happy Christmas!' I said.

He looked up at my face.

'You're pregnant.'

I flirted with a sarcastic response, but there is a time and a place for everything.

'Yes. That's right.'

'When . . .?'

'Um, any day, really. Should have had it last week.'

I could see him making internal calculations.

'So . . . who . . . who's the father?'

'Um . . .' I sighed. 'Either you or him.'

He winced at the word 'him'.

'I see. And were you ever going to tell me?'

'I was waiting to see what colour it came out.' I was being glib, because that's just what I do when things are shit.

He gave a mirthless smile, 'You're cruel, Lorrie.'

'I miss you, Joe.'

I really did. I really, really missed him, and seeing him made me miss him even more.

He looked as if I'd just dug a knife into his heart. It was horrible, loving and hating someone all at once. I could see it in his eyes. He glanced up at the sky. The days were short; dusk was already falling.

'I'm not asking for anything, Joe,' I said. 'I'm just telling you that I miss you.'

He bit his lip and begrudgingly nodded, accepting my bleat.

'Don't fuck with me, Lorrie.'

'Well, there we go. See you, then.' I turned on my heels. I'd had enough. How dare he say that? There's another matter, another life that's a bit more pressing at the moment, in case he hadn't noticed. Besides, I'm the one who's fucked.

'Come on, Tilly!' I called, walking on past him, tears filling my eyes as soon as I had done so.

'Wait!'

'What?' I said irritably, wiping my face. Why should he have the monopoly on misery?

'Happy birthday!' he said.

'Oh, yes.'

That just made me cry a bit more. Jesus, these hormones really screwed you up.

'Thanks,' I said. I meant it. I'd been on my own all day. My mother had sent me a card, not a holy one either, nice safe flowers in a vase, and not Organizational flowers either, really loud garish ones. I think she must have put a lot of thought into it, and I appreciated that.

'Are you still seeing him?' he asked.

'Who?' I hadn't seen Steinberg since the café. 'Oh, no. Not at all.'

Joe bent down and stroked Tilly's head, as if he wasn't really bothered one way or the other.

'Joe, if you want to hold it against me for ever, fine. Just right now is not a good time to give me grief.' I could feel my face puckering up again.

He nodded. 'I'll give you a call sometime. Maybe go for a drink,' he said.

'Well, better make it soon, 'cos things are going to get a bit hectic after that.'

So we did. He took me for a celebratory drink in Portobello there and then. We took Tilly with us. I put on some lipstick in a car's wing mirror, and it almost felt like old times. Except that he hated me and I was the size of a rhinoceros, probably with someone else's baby inside me. I kept having to stop to get my breath back.

He offered me his arm. It felt nice to be pregnant holding someone's arm.

We went to the same bar where he'd asked me to marry him, not deliberately. I'd tried to steer him away from it, but the guy came out just as we were going past and said, 'Wow! Haven't seen you two for a while!' and 'Congratulations!' Which didn't help.

'Joe?' I said as we sat down, me with a glass of Sauvignon, him with a lager. 'I know it's a bit late, but I want to tell you something. No, I want to tell you more than something. I want to tell you everything. Just so that, when you think of me, you can maybe understand things a bit better and not hate me too much.'

He looked at me cautiously. 'What? What are you going to tell me?'

'Just listen.'

I can't bear this fad for honesty, when you watch those awful women on reality TV shows endlessly bragging about how honest they are: 'I am what I am; I tell it like it is; that's just the way I am! You get what you get with me. I say it straight to your face.' Well, I don't want to hear it like you think it is: edit yourselves, you stupid little bitches. Civilization has progressed.

So I told Joe most of everything. In essence, I told Joe it all. Obviously I left out certain Steinberg intimacies, but I told him all about the Organization, about Fowler, about my parents, about the builder, about Embankment station, about the foxglove, and then I told him about the murder. I told him it in a dramatic way that made him think I really had killed her, just how it happened to me.

I wanted to know what he would think of me when he thought that I had killed someone, because that was how I'd lived my life. His expression didn't change. Slowly he shook his head. When I got to the bit with Fowler writhing around on the ground outside the church, he reached over the table as if he were going to take my hand, but stopped just short and said, rather angrily, 'You poor little thing.'

I stopped mid-flow. I think I needed someone to say that, someone to be angry for me, to justify my own anger. No one had ever said to me, 'You poor little thing,' and it meant more than I can say. I found that, once again, I had a lump in my throat. He was looking at me, waiting for me to tell him more.

I told him about France and hitching, the blood on the seat, the Furies coming to get me, the institution and the shocks and the pills. I just wanted to get to the end in a factual fashion, without self-pity, although I realized how grim and unrelenting it sounded. When I stopped talking, he didn't say anything. He kept his head bowed.

'So you've been living with a psycho,' I said, trying to lighten the tone. But it sounded all wrong.

He put his elbows on the table and covered his mouth and nose with his hands, almost in a praying position. He looked at me with big, watery, brown eyes.

'Anyway,' I said quietly. 'It was a long time ago.'

As if that made it all okay. But something *did* feel better in me. I felt a kind of release, as if the wardrobe had just slipped off my back.

'Oh, Caroline!' he replied sadly. 'You silly girl, you could have told me these things.'

Caroline – he had never called me Caroline before.

'Is it too late?' I asked, in a whisper.

He nodded, looking me in the eye. 'I think so,' he said and stared out of the window.

I moved my great bulk round and joined him on the bench. Tilly jumped up between us and quivered, unsure whether life was good or bad.

I covered his hand with mine, and he squeezed my fingers hard. Too hard.

'Ahh!' I cried.

'You deserve it!' he said, not unkindly.

But it wasn't my hand that hurt. I could feel something breaking softly inside me, followed by a splashing sound on the floor beneath. I shifted in my seat and stared with horror at the wooden planks. A pool of water was forming, and it was coming from me.

'Oh my God! Joe!' I said, panicking, grabbing his arm. 'Oh my God! Help me! It's happening!'

He just wanted a decent book to read ...

Not too much to ask, is it? It was in 1935 when Allen Lane, Managing Director of Bodley Head Publishers, stood on a platform at Exeter railway station looking for something good to read on his journey back to London. His choice was limited to popular magazines and poor-quality paperbacks – the same choice faced every day by the vast majority of readers, few of whom could afford hardbacks. Lane's disappointment and subsequent anger at the range of books generally available led him to found a company – and change the world.

'We believed in the existence in this country of a vast reading public for intelligent books at a low price, and staked everything on it'
Sir Allen Lane, 1902–1970, founder of Penguin Books

The quality paperback had arrived – and not just in bookshops. Lane was adamant that his Penguins should appear in chain stores and tobacconists, and should cost no more than a packet of cigarettes.

Reading habits (and cigarette prices) have changed since 1935, but Penguin still believes in publishing the best books for everybody to enjoy. We still believe that good design costs no more than bad design, and we still believe that quality books published passionately and responsibly make the world a better place.

So wherever you see the little bird – whether it's on a piece of prize-winning literary fiction or a celebrity autobiography, political tour de force or historical masterpiece, a serial-killer thriller, reference book, world classic or a piece of pure escapism – you can bet that it represents the very best that the genre has to offer.

Whatever you like to read – trust Penguin.